Goodbye, Hessle Road

DAPHNE GLAZER, born in Sheffield, has lived in Hull for many years, where she gives creative writing workshops and is Quaker Visiting Minister to several prisons. *Goodbye, Hessle Road* is her third novel. In addition, she has written four collections of short stories, and many of these stories have been broadcast on BBC Radio 4.

Praise for *Goodbye, Hessle Road*

'A bold and compassionate novel. Hull is intimately evoked as a place haunted by its proud, seafaring history and almost eerie with menace in those areas blighted by drugs and crime. Daphne Glazer has an unerring ear for dialogue and a talent for astute observation. The immediacy and vigour of her expression make for a compelling read. But it is the subject matter which makes this novel so important, putting me in mind of Pat Barker. Daphne Glazer deals with the nature of human evil, its causes and consequences, with unflinching candour and without lapsing into sentimentality or facile solutions. Authentic, gripping and beautifully realised'

Linda Anderson

'*Goodbye, Hessle Road* is a closely observed novel with universal themes, a serious work with lots of laughs'

Zoë Fairbairns

'Daphne Glazer has captured the struggling and disenfranchised underbelly of a hard-working city in all its shabby grace and faded colours; in its past glories, and in the evaporating dreams and unravelling hopes of its present occupants; and in all its vibrant, determined, blowsy, spirited splendour'

Robert Edric

'Strength, sadness, love and joy in abundance, yet without a trace of sentimentality. An enriching read'

Valerie Wood

'A tough and tender story about three generations of women in a tough and tender city. Daphne Glazer sees straight and writes the same way – and like our neighbourhood poet said: what survives is love'

Alan Plater

Goodbye, Hessle Road

Daphne Glazer

**Tindal
Street
Press**

First published in March 2005 by
Tindal Street Press Ltd
217 The Custard Factory, Gibb Street, Birmingham, B9 4AA
www.tindalstreet.co.uk

A CIP catalogue reference for this book is available
from the British Library

ISBN: 0 9547913 1 2

Typeset by Country Setting, Kingsdown, Kent

Printed and bound in Great Britain by Clays Ltd, St Ives PLC

For Peter

I

Reggae thumped away on the radio. Donna tapped out the beat on the steering wheel and her six earrings jiggled in time. Traffic light on red. She took the opportunity to examine her face in the rear-view mirror. Her nose jewel glinted back. Bags under her eyes from last night's bevvy. The beginnings of a sore throat. She opened her mouth and gaped to make sure she hadn't daubed scarlet lippy on her front teeth. No.

Somebody peered at her. She felt the eyes and turned. A chap in the next lane grinned. He had evidently been watching her. Embarrassed, she grinned back.

Green; the cars shot up the dual carriageway and then over the bridge and Donna glimpsed beige silt and anchored barges. Traffic lights. Facing was a disused funeral parlour, the front boarded up and covered with fly-posters announcing DJ somebody or other. It would be a freaky venue for a club night, she thought, and pictured dancers swathed in revealing white shrouds.

The car zoomed on past woodyards, fences scrawled with razor wire. Another roundabout and now lorries pelted forward bouncing and accelerating up the road towards the BP oil terminal and the docks. On the right, crane arms poked monster heads above a high fence. Somewhere over there lay a dock. On the left, derelict buildings: women got assaulted and murdered down here at night. A second-hand tyre mart, a garage and a newsagent's were jammed together. The lorries bucked and snorted, the cars sped round them. Donna kept well back, waiting for the left turn. She saw the perimeter wall of the prison and indicated to turn into the car park. It was full already but she managed to squeeze into a place on the driveway.

The wind slammed in off the estuary and froze her cheeks. She crossed by lines of smart, officers' cars.

Gulls screamed past. She glanced up at the clock tower. Eight thirty. Not bad. Work started at nine. The prison officers behind the bulletproof glass screen nodded at her and released the electronic catch on the cast-iron door for her to enter.

She fumbled the tally from her key chain and dropped it down the metal chute. An officer went to the keyboard to fetch her keys. She grinned under his appraisal. Ever since day one, the officers had made her feel uneasy. On her first day someone was delegated to take her on a tour of the prison. They progressed across a yard pocked with crumpled paper bags, rotten fruit, orange peel and all manner of flotsam: things you wouldn't want to investigate.

Don't get too close to the windows, the officer instructed. They can throw stuff out and they might pee on you . . . And indeed a jet of yellow piss did fountain out.

Passing one set of windows, the officer paused. In there's a feller who murdered a lass with the same name as you.

How do you mean?

Donna.

Oh, nice one.

They visited the hospital ward where a chap with strange manic eyes stared at her and she asked herself whether or not she really wanted to do this job. The officers eyed her up. She didn't look the regulation Christmas tree fairy nor the grim-suited brigade. Drugs worker – they were suspicious right from the off. Well, of course they were up for drug work too, and she was competition. It was about then that she'd begun to feel claustrophobic. You'd be locked in there, doing time along with the inmates, on a day stretching from nine in the morning until evening. Nowadays she was too busy to dwell on such thoughts.

Donna crossed the draughty yard behind the gatehouse. The wind whined. On her right were huge metal gates and a massive electrified-mesh enclosure topped with razor wire. She unlocked the final gate to the inner compound and locked and unlocked and locked her way up narrow stone steps into the inner sanctum. Pictures of the prison in former times; an old-style prison officer's hat; a length of what looked like a hawser as thick as a child's arm with a knot in the end prinked under glass. Royals inclined their heads graciously as they bestowed awards on smiling prison officers.

Donna checked her pigeonhole, found some referrals and wished she'd drunk less the previous evening. A headache throbbed over her left eye. She unlocked and locked two further doors and emerged onto D wing. The familiar harsh intimate smell crawled into her nostrils – it could be sweaty flesh, stale food, something necrotic and putrefying. After a long while you didn't notice it, didn't even smell it any more, and that too was scary.

D wing YP lads in maroon track suits swept the landings. They stared at her – the same every day. Their hungry eyes fastened on her as though they'd never seen her before. She strode out in her tartan Docs and gave no sign of being aware of their scrutiny. Some called out to her, trying to think up any sort of pretext to see her alone.

She passed along the threes by closed cell doors. Someone yelled out. In there everybody bellowed. A big lad brushing the landing didn't stand back to let her through as she reached him. She knew he would try to rub against her.

'Morning, excuse me!' she said in a brisk, bright, no-nonsense voice. He had to give way. He surveyed her with burning eyes, taking in her name badge.

'Drugs. I'd like to see you, Miss.'

'I'm sure you would,' she said, gave a little laugh and strode on.

Once in her office, she made herself black coffee in her cat mug. She knew caffeine would increase her hyper mood but she needed it. A quick drag on a fag and she began to feel marginally better.

She switched on her computer and logged onto the local inmate database system. She looked down the names and checked who she could see. Three interviews in the morning and three in the afternoon – an hour per interview if possible.

First C wing to see a chap called White – Ian, thirty-five, heroin addict. She stubbed out her ciggy, brushed down her combats and her T-shirt. In there she had to moderate her dress, but she wouldn't let the institution force her into a uniform. Currently her hair was in a rather striking pink spiky style. Everybody stared and commented. Her aim was to stir them up. She couldn't bear traditional nunty stuff. Most people looked dead. It was four months since she'd moved into her own house and she was busy painting the walls jade green, scarlet, sunflower yellow – great bursts of colour. Charity shops and cut-price places provided all manner of objects, like duvet covers that she could transform into curtains. She stopped herself concentrating on her bedroom colour scheme as she negotiated the barred metal doors and made her way round the dizzy drop in the centre to the barred door which led to the passage into C wing.

Men clattered down the open-tread stairs from the fours – the VPs off to work before the others moved. The two groups must never meet or the other C wingers would tear the VPs apart. The slightest glimpse of a VP would set the C wingers howling *nonce*, *sex case* and worse. The VPs were a strange collection of elderly men, younger ones with eyes that clawed at you and some who looked to be stranded way back in a childhood they could never leave. Some called out to her. 'Hiya, morning,' she shouted back. They were creepy people she had to admit, not the sort you'd ever want to meet on the other side of the prison gates.

She headed for the officers' room at the foot of the stairs. Several guys pored over an inmate movement board. One was on the phone, another at a computer. They all nodded at her, straightened up for a fraction of a second, flexing their pecs and doing a little preen, and then continued with their tasks, but their antennae quivered and they didn't miss a trick. A fuddy probation officer always seemed to be chatting them up; Donna wondered if she ever did any work.

'You're bright and early,' an officer said, trying to engage her in conversation. She quite liked this chap: he didn't seem as boys' owny as the rest.

'Yer – the early bird catches the worm.'

'Too right.'

She shouldn't have said that bit about 'worm'; she didn't mean anything derogatory – oh shit! 'Well, actually I'm hoping to interview Ian White.'

On day one at the nick, when she'd used an inmate's first name, the officer, a raddled-looking chap, turned on her: They don't have first names – we've nobody of that name here. And he'd launched into a full-scale harangue while she gawped at him in amazement. This only increased her determination to use first names – she was a stubborn git.

'Yes, White's up there.' He made no move to accompany her. As she didn't hold cell keys she was dependent on an officer unlocking the man's cell for her. It was the same every day – they'd stand about pretending not to see her or take their time in reacting. She'd heard mutterings on occasion about 'do gooders'. You're wasting your time, one had told her. Geek, she said in her head.

'Great. I'll go up and see him in the interview room,' she said, refusing to show any irritation. Nobody moved. 'Anybody like to be an angel and open the gent's pad?' She gave a sweet smile laced with poison.

'White's no gent,' somebody guffawed. 'Anything but.'

'Anybody like to assist?'

'All right, love,' the pleasant officer said and started up the steps before her.

'That's it, chat her up. Don't let him try it on, love,' said a grandfatherly officer (no doubt a wolf in sheep's clothing), jollying her along. He lumbered up behind them and stood gazing up the metal staircase as she set off.

All this male pressure could be quite overwhelming if you thought about it – but you didn't. It was just something that dodged along in the background, and the best way was to pretend you didn't notice it and be brisk and jocular. Up now to the threes. This was when you noticed how unfit you were and how you should cut down on the ciggies but – but, always but.

Ian White, threes in cell 21 – along the landing, careful to avoid anything left stranded by the wing cleaners. Everything was metal. The doors were like those you'd expect to see in the hold of ocean-going vessels. The officer whipped out his cell key, opened the door and shot the lock. You shot the locks when you unlocked the cell doors so the doors couldn't be locked behind you. But Donna didn't have to worry about this, as drugs workers weren't allowed cell keys. She stood at the entrance and looked in. They told you about hostage taking at security briefings. If taken hostage, you mustn't scream or resist. You must do nothing, just wait. If you made a fuss, you'd cause people to get killed.

'Hiya – Ian White?'

'Yer.'

The cell smelled fusty and of feet. A chap on a bed in the other corner covered his head with a sheet.

'Drugs?' the man said.

'That's right. Do you want to come with me?'

'Yer, love.'

The guy was skinny and wiry, the sort who'd be quick at sliding into places and escaping. His arms swarmed with traditional tattoos. Donna led him to the interview room, sat down behind a table and smiled at him.

'Do you know why you're here?'

'Yer.' He gave a funny smile. 'I asked, didn't I?'

'That's right. OK, Ian, I'm Donna from the drugs team, and I've got your referral. This will be just an initial assessment. First I need to explain that anything you say to me will be held in confidence – with certain provisos. If I got the idea that you might self-harm or injure somebody else then I'd not be able to remain silent about it. Also if children happened to be at risk or if I heard something about drugs being brought into the prison. And if there was anything that might impinge on prison security. If you've any concerns about using drugs in prison I won't pass them to security, nor will I put you in a compromising situation as to the source.'

'Oh, right, fine.' He didn't seem to know how to respond to that speech. To Donna it always sounded like the sort of incantation that police officers chanted at offenders when they were nicked. She gave him the confidentiality form to sign and watched as he struggled to write his name in big crooked letters.

Next she slid another form out of a folder and the rigmarole of checking the man's name, date of birth, ethnicity, level of numeracy and literacy got underway. Was this his first time in prison? Was he sentenced or on remand? On remand. With what had he been charged? Robberies. She was trying to get an idea whether he was headed for a probation order or a custodial sentence.

The interview progressed onto the drugs Ian White normally used: what had he been using before he came in? For how long? Had there been any breaks when he didn't use? Yes – so what had caused him to get back on? All this led onto why he'd decided that he wanted help now.

'Right – well, like – well, I wanna kick the shit – been goin' on a long while.' He grinned. 'Like since I was this high.' He demonstrated.

'You were a little kid?'

'Yer, about eight – not smack, right, but dope, then phets. Done everything, right.'

'I see.' She waited, watching his face.

'On the out you spend all your time wondering how you're goin' ter score – you have to be robbin' from the moment you open your eyes. Then you're gouching but that dun't last long and you're at it again. It's like depressin'.'

Donna nodded. 'You got a family?'

'Daughter – don't see her no more, like. She'll be ten now. Her mother blocked it, right.'

'What about parents?'

His mother threw him out. He'd not lived at home since he was fifteen. Hated his stepfather.

She asked him if he'd ever worked.

'Oh yer. I'm not one of them who never has . . . worked like, labouring, but I was usin' as well – did for a long while and then I couldn't make enough with it for me habit, see. Needed to be robbin', so I got finished.'

He wanted to go on a rehab and if he didn't get on a rehab as soon as he walked out of the prison gates, he'd never escape. And he might get probation and not prison and then he'd be straight back in it again.

She had to explain to him then that to get on a rehab was tremendously difficult. You needed funding and that was really hard to come by. He might get a DTTO if his sentence turned out not to be custodial. Privately, she didn't know what good such things were: OK, they made sure clients were occupied with courses all day during the week and they were tested for drugs, but there was no 24-hour support. You needed someone there all the time to help when you were slipping . . . For a few seconds she struggled with feelings of frustration. She could understand the man's distress, his need, and she wanted to change things, help him, but she was manacled. He was in a pit struggling up its sides but falling back because nobody would grasp his hand.

'You get while you'll do anything for smack,' he said.

After Ian White she saw two more men.

The third, Dave, little and apricot haired, had no front teeth. 'I've lost two partners and four kids with it, you know. It gets more important to you than anything else – you'd do anything for it.'

She felt she'd been listening to the same story all morning. They wanted to escape a trap, more secure than any prison, only most of them didn't realize it and continually underestimated what they would have to forfeit for freedom.

Addictive personality – interesting stuff at uni. But this, this was something else.

Smack's better 'an any sex you ever had, I'm tellin' you, Ian White said. You never had a go?

Always the same message, the yearning and the revulsion. The men were weighing scales, first one side dipped, then the other, but there'd be moments of equilibrium when it might go either way. If you could only catch them

9

before the scale let either side drop. And even when you'd got everything moving for them and they were trying like mad to give it up, then the authorities let you down; there was no way of supporting them and they slipped back into the pit.

Lunchtime. Her stomach growled. All she'd managed that morning was a coffee and one slice of toast and raspberry jam. Returning to her office, she came across a familiar face, a chap she'd interviewed a couple of months ago.

'Hiya,' he said and gave a sheepish grimace.

'Whatever are you doing? I thought you were on the out?'

'Was . . .' He wove some elaborate tale of being on remand and he never done it; then the crunch: 'They was waitin' on us like at the gate – the mates, like.'

Crazy, stupid geeks, she thought, caught in a wave of irritation. You got caught up in their horrendous stories, wanted to change something, did what you could for them. They said they'd never touch the stuff again and two minutes later it was the same old story, only worse. They wouldn't change. They were so depressing. The whole scene was depressing.

She stomped back down D wing and passed a gaggle of maroon YPs hurtling down the stairs to get their lunch and re-emerging with sad squidgy chips, what looked like a piece of fried batter-coated panscrubber and some mushy peas, all slopped on metal trays.

Someone wolf-whistled. She gave a lippy-luscious grin and shouldered past.

Approaching the final door off the wing, she took a long appraisal of herself in the one-way glass; saw her pink sea-anemone hair, nose jewel, big red lips, and wondered where she was heading . . .

*

After eight years with Rob she was cast adrift. Eight years of acting as go-between for Rob; explaining to people that his rudeness and abruptness were just his way; that he was a really sensitive person who found relating to others difficult. Whereas now she could admit it to herself: he was a total no-hoper, a dweeb, someone with a deeply paranoid side, who ferreted after the worst in everybody and should he fail to find it, invented something. A sad soul whose main interest in life was gawping at a TV screen. She couldn't watch sport on telly now – and certainly not football, too reminiscent of dead Saturday afternoons or evening matches with Rob sprottled immovable on the settee in the front room. He'd tell her that her bum was like the back of a bus and she shouldn't have all her piercings and she knew this had nothing to do with her bum and everything to do with the fact that United lost four nil.

And of course it all turned on her mother marrying Nick and bringing Mark and Helen to live with them and then the birth of Lee, who was always the little prince, got all the attention; Lee, the petted one, the one who was spoiled out of his mind.

By now she'd handed in her keys and was out in the road, making for the canteen. She ought to be having a lettuce leaf and fruit. Five pieces of fruit or veg a day – yuck! She loved unhealthy, fatty things that would clog her arteries. Life as a vegetarian was difficult in that you were supposed to like ghastly nutty things and seeds and that gone-off-tasting ricotta cheese stuff and obscenities like tofu and soya. You could easily find yourself bracketed with the cagoule- and sandal-wearing, water-swilling, yoga-practising mob. Stereotypes lurked to embrace you and rob you of your own individual zing.

Everything was too annoying – why not say to hell with New Year's resolutions and have a large helping of chips?

The smell tantalized: chips, golden brown, crisp on the outside, mouth-wateringly soft within; chips to shoot up your calories, all that fat making another fine array of pink splodges bloom; bum like a shelf, stomach the counterbalance.

'Big decisions, eh!' It was the prison officer from earlier. He had a hefty dollop of chips, beans and two burnt sausages on his plate.

No, she wouldn't pig out on chips. Instead, still lusting after them, she picked up a salad sandwich, sighing.

They sat down opposite each other.

'How you like it here?'

'Don't ask me today,' she said. 'I'm not in a good mood.'

'Tell me about it.'

'I wonder why it is, come January you get to feel you need a change, a challenge?'

'Is that right?' he said.

'Can I just try a chip?' she couldn't help asking.

'Sure, go ahead.'

She nipped up a crisp, golden stick and closed her eyes, smelt it, popped it between her lips and chomped.

'Here, let me get you some.'

'No, no, I mustn't give way to temptation.'

He laughed. He was called Wes and seemed quite friendly. She just hoped he wouldn't start haranguing her about the uselessness of the inmates because she wasn't in the mood for an argument.

They were joined at the table by two other guys, one of whom slung down the *Hull Daily Mail*. Donna glanced at the headline: WOMAN FOUND MURDERED.

'This young lady keeps stealing my chips,' Wes announced. The others made some risqué comments but she wasn't listening. Her skin went cold and goose pimples prickled along her back and forearms; she thought she would scream. The room and their voices receded and she was stranded, struggling to hide her reaction.

The woman's body has been identified as that of Joanne Singleton. The police are following up a number of leads.

She couldn't finish her sandwich but sat quite still and then took a long swallow from the Evian bottle beside her. The men's talk rumbled on about shift patterns and government threats to privatize more prisons, and some inmates, who were an effing nuisance, pardon my French, young lady present. Sly looks and grins, but she simply wasn't there.

Joanne Singleton – best mate from primary school days and into secondary – Joanne murdered. But your friends just didn't get murdered. It didn't happen. Only it could, you knew it could, you saw men who had murdered their children, wives, girlfriends, partners – and those women and girls had left behind mourning friends.

She struggled to pin down when she'd last seen Joanne, but try as she might she couldn't remember. The pressure of the news seemed to block out everything else.

Talk went on around her. Officers piled in with plates of food. Laughter barked. She must be able to think about this, understand what had happened. She couldn't just dismiss it.

She emerged into the street where the lorries continued to bounce along on their way to the dock or the ferry terminal or the oil refinery. She stared at the spiky tropical-looking plants which grew by the prison wall. You would expect the fierce wind to kill them off.

Joanne Singleton. The name rang in her head, repeated over and over. She felt its very repetition would make her ill. She didn't want to believe what had happened; it was too sick. Over the years she'd talked with those men, the murderers, had them sitting opposite her in interview rooms. Sometimes they'd be weird and you could believe that they'd beaten their partners to death, but at other times they seemed just like any other men you might meet in the street. Once you realized that, you entered a nightmare. Mostly she didn't dwell on any of this any longer, but now it all came back, fisting her in the face, stunning her, and she felt again the awful possibilities of what a man might do. Some man, a man like anybody she might see today, had taken Joanne's life. He could have killed her through jealousy, like that bath attendant, a man of forty-seven who had sat before her, unable to stop telling her about the seventeen-year-old girlfriend he'd bludgeoned to death because he thought she was having an affair. He'd been addicted to coke, thought the coke had killed her. He was just an ordinary little chap, a bit scrawny and losing his greasy black hair, only he had taken the life of this girl. He described her: She was that bonny with her long black hair . . . and I can't get over her . . . I never meant . . .

This was awful; it threatened to overwhelm her on this ordinary day with a working afternoon to get through. At the same time the past unlocked itself and assailed her: she saw Joanne, both of them, young girls. They seemed to walk before her and she felt the tears pressing up her throat. Oh my God, the pity of it . . .

They were walking to school together and moaning about their mothers. Joanne said, Oh, I'm fucking fed up – let's twag off! She effed and blinded a bit more and Donna laughed – she loved Joanne's casual cursing, because in her house only her stepfather, Nick, swore. It was domestic science, and Joanne made the pastry too wet and they tipped flour in to soak up the sticky clods while Miss Walters' back was turned. Of course when it came to tasting the jam tarts, the pastry was as tough as ancient spat-out chewy. Miss Walters scowled at Joanne and anybody would have thought World War Three had broken out, which just made Joanne laugh even more.

*

Time to go back to work. Donna strode to the clock tower; entered the building; passed by the bulletproof screen and the smiling wary eyes behind it; turned the metal handle and pushed the steel-reinforced door open; dropped her tally down the metal chute; drew her keys – all in exactly the same way as she'd done that morning. Only now everything had changed just because she happened to glance at that headline.

Three more interviews this afternoon and she must concentrate, but she couldn't. She needed to think about Joanne, who she was, what she looked like – all in the past tense now. Frightful scenarios presented themselves: Joanne might have been cut up and stuffed in a suitcase, or dismembered and thrown into the drain. Last year, she remembered, a 23-year-old woman's legs and arms had been discovered by two boys fishing. The horror of it made your head reel. Then there was the man who carried his partner's body round Europe in a case. Please God, let it not be anything like that . . .

First client, Barry Ridley. He came into the interview room and stood looking at her. She struggled to prevent the tears behind her eyes from cascading down her face.

'Oh, hello, I'm Donna, one of the drugs team,' she heard her voice saying.

'Hiya, love.'

'Do sit down.' She must buy a newspaper and read the details, but could she bear to know? How many times had she sat facing men, looking across a table, while they came out with horrors, all said in a broken, inarticulate way? Well, I gave him a clatter, like . . . Yes, she had listened and translated – he killed someone – and it was a fact and quite naked. It would be a statistic somewhere and she didn't let herself feel the dreadfulness of it.

She opened with the usual guff about confidentiality. This would help her through, it was something she could rattle off. She must concentrate on the man's face, which wasn't weak or crafty; he looked quite sensible – but how did you know? Her eyes fixed on his hands.

'Well, I'm here,' he said, 'because I'm forty-two and this week in visits I'm sitting there and I see this woman I lived with eighteen, twenty years ago and she's visiting this YP – I look at him and I know it's my son. He'll be seventeen, on remand here. She doesn't bat an eyelid. I don't either. The kid has no clue I'm his dad. That's when I knew I've got to kick the H, right.'

She went on trying to listen. He meant what he said, she could see that, and she struggled to focus on how to help him.

After that a chap in his early twenties shambled in. Drowning brown eyes. Rotten teeth. The druggies nearly all seemed to have decaying teeth. He subsided into the chair and bared browning stumps in a smile.

'Hiya, Donna.'

She recognized him vaguely. 'You've been here before, haven't you?'

'Yer, last time. Didn't manage, right – they was waitin' at the gate. Just score once and then you'll give up. Yer, yer, you think, OK – and you do.'

She let him run on. The chap in the morning used almost identical words – 'they was waitin' for us at the gate' – always the same. She quelled the urge to yell at him: Have some self-control! Take charge of your life and stop being so spineless! Addiction wasn't like that, though. You couldn't snap out of it – or could you? Could human will triumph?

The man left and she interviewed her final client of the day.

Dennis Linton's case was slightly different.

'Never done no drugs, right? Well – a bit of dope and speed but nothing serious. Right, I get this sentence and then when I come out, I find me partner's on smack. She says to me: Come on, give it a go, you'll like it – and I do, right, and then I'm hooked and I start robbin' because of me habit.'

At last she was out in the street. The sky shone a strange iced blue and seemed very high up. Above the city the sun tumbled like a peeled blood orange and sank below the buildings, smearing everything with a hectic orange tint. The terracotta glow reflected in shop windows and on car windscreens. The road shrilled with unspoken drama. She struggled with the car park door, tapping in the code, but couldn't make it open. She seemed incapable of focusing on anything except the jumble in her head – all the horrors she'd ever heard came blundering at her to form a collage of severed limbs and headless torsos. Tears splashed down her cheeks. A prison officer following her took over and had the door open in a twinkling. She realized that he was staring at her but she didn't care, just stumbled forward towards her car.

Joanne Singleton – plump, shoulder-length dark brown hair, brown eyes, big mouth – a bit sulky looking but pretty.

It seemed important to visualize Joanne exactly. You needed a picture if you were going to think about someone, understand. The past unscrolled, it flowed from her in her tears – two giggling girls slipping through the school gates and away . . .

They were meant to be in PE, out on the field playing hockey after lunch – or it might have been double maths – but instead they slipped out at twelve thirty when everyone was in the canteen, and didn't return. They sat on the top deck of the bus, laughing their heads off, and Joanne pretended she was Miss Kaye, the French teacher, who sprayed the front row when she did her best French accent. Her mouth twisted and pulled like an elastic band. Donna howled as spit ran down Joanne's chin.

Now gels . . .

Her best take-off was Miss Clements, English, whose bust was two enormous shopping bags, crammed to capacity, which banged and bumped before her as she sailed down the corridor.

A lot of the time Joanne was hyper and her little girly voice squeaked. The voice could annoy Donna – but then it was Joanne.

They branched to Boots and the perfume counter where rust-faced ladies wafted about batting their sky-blue eyelids at you and, when they addressed you, reducing you to the status of dog shit flattened on the sole of a boot.

How may I help? Were you looking for something?

Joanne and Donna in a huddle pressing perfume testers and sniffing, crying with the effort of controlling hysteria. If only they could have ditched their navy shirts and blazers and their stupid striped ties.

Donna sat in her car and for a few moments she could almost smell the sneeziness of those French perfume sprays and hear their laughter.

Eh, Joanne said, as they sloped out of the store, I nearly wet meself in there. Eh, look what I got.

She'd stolen a cheap bottle of perfume. Donna relived the shock and admiration she felt, heard her own voice saying: You didn't! And then Joanne passed it off as nothing and boasted she could do better than that.

The pictures wouldn't stop coming. Donna turned on the ignition and backed the car down the drive by the huge perimeter wall, narrowly missing a flying buttress. She'd staved in a tail-lamp unit with that a few months ago when she was staring at her lips in the driving mirror instead of looking where she was heading.

The drama of the road sucked her in. Lorries thundered down on her, all pelting onwards, lights flaring; the road humped and brakes screamed at traffic lights; the sky bled.

She strained to concentrate on her driving, but all the time her thoughts tugged away, tugged back to Joanne. Women got murdered by drunken men all the time, or by men demented with crack or speed or a cocktail of drugs – she knew it, had heard it all before; but this was different. This was the murder of a part of herself, her childhood and young womanhood. Shame on her that she'd been so involved in her own life that she hadn't bothered to try to find Joanne when she came back to Hull. You could lose people in this city quite easily, lose them for years on end. It had been university for her and that excluding relationship with Rob – he didn't want her to see anyone else. But she was making excuses.

Memories rushed at her in an endless stream. That time they went to the fair and Joanne wanted to have her palm read. From the first moment when they stood by the gold horses on the merry-go-round and Donna just wanted to stare in wonder, Joanne chivvied to find Madam Clara or whatever she was called.

Don't you want to?

No way.

Why not?

I don't know.

It would be awful to find out what might be coming to you, because you wouldn't be able to avoid it anyway – like in RI when Mrs Braithwaite got on about Jesus knowing he was up for crucifixion and there was no escape. Or in Greek myths where Oedipus is bound to murder his father and marry his mother. Horrible, disgusting things . . .

Joanne seemed to have a built-in radar system. They were pushed and elbowed by the crowd but she eeled her way through, dragging Donna after her. The loop-the-loop spun up into the navy blue sky and as it churned round you could hear girls screaming and objects showered from people's pockets and the machines groaned, engine fumes reeked and made you cough, and the music yowled. But Joanne kept on and Donna hoped they wouldn't be able to find Madam Clara, the fortune-teller. Of course they did.

Madam Clara lived in a big cream caravan with maroon tassels dangling round its door and a board by the steps proclaiming: TRUE FORTUNES TOLD BY GENUINE ROMANY. The caravan's windows had maroon blinds and you could see plastic flowers pinned everywhere. An orange lamp glowed. All spooky and tacky – a place to make the goose pimples rise and your hair stand on end.

Joanne clonked up the steps in her white stilettos and knocked. A figure draped in several cardigans and a long skirt opened the door and indicated she should enter.

Donna remained outside, feeling anxious pricklings up and down her spine. She didn't like it at all. A couple stumbled over some Calor Gas canisters as they snogged near the caravan. Voices, distorted by amplification, boomed through the grinding of machines. Underfoot the black mud squelched.

Joanne seemed to be in the caravan for an age and then she lurched down the steps and out.

You were in there for ages, Donna said.

Wasn't. Only about ten minutes.

Donna couldn't ask what Madam Clara had predicted. Now she was struck by the fact that she'd been unable to ask. Here must have been something significant, meaningful. Nor did Joanne volunteer any information; in fact for a short time she seemed to clam up and only a few minutes later, as they let themselves move with the jostling crowd, Joanne allowed herself to be picked up by a lad – and of course he had a friend. Joanne always managed to persuade lads to buy her things, and by wheedling and rubbing her tits on this geek's arm, she got him to buy them some chips. The grease shone on her lippy as she gobbled – though it wasn't gobbling: no, she dangled the stalk of a chip quite precisely before her pouted lips and then bit the golden wedge.

Want one? she said, showing the pink insides of her mouth as she presented the lad with a chip and smiled into his eyes.

Donna remembered feeling hot and embarrassed at Joanne's behaviour – it hadn't been so much what she did, as the aura that she spread about herself. She suggested things and Donna was afraid it all might bound out of control. While wanting to experiment, see where things might lead, and being hooked on scary books and films and stuff about ghosts, she still had gut feelings that prevented her adventuring too far.

The fair night ended up with her leaving Joanne and the two lads and pelting down Walton Street, dodging by the stalls, into Springbank West and onto the Avenues, home. Mum had set a curfew and if she breached it she would be grounded for ages.

Mum always seemed ambivalent about Joanne: on the one hand she occasionally let drop that she felt Joanne was a bad influence on Donna but on the other, being a supporter of the Underprivileged with a capital U, Mum would see it as her duty to be hospitable to Joanne. The Singletons lived in the middle of a terrace facing Chanterlands Avenue, five minutes away from Donna's home – though that short distance was crucial. The houses by the main road were smaller and occupied by a different type of people altogether.

At Joanne's the telly was never off. Her mother was 'Mam' and at that time she looked vaguely attractive, though her clothes were too young for her and she was weighed down by four small children. Joanne didn't like her mam's present boyfriend, John. He wore a thick gold earring and chain and cowboy boots and his black sideburns were as sharp as scimitars, but he was always matey in a heavy way, which embarrassed Donna. She tried to avoid calling at Joanne's if there was any chance of running into him. Joanne came in for a lot of babysitting while her mother and John went out to the pub.

Donna was still retracing past threads as she parked her car in the road and fastened the steering lock to the wheel. Hers was a neighbourhood of tall Victorian terrace houses, a bit seedy and mostly occupied by students and struggling families. Cars jammed both sides of the road and some parked on what was once a grass verge but was now flattened to bare earth. The council had turned the road into a one-way system. The street had been lined with mature trees but now, owing to rumours that they might cause subsidence, many had been replaced by scrawny saplings, which got vandalized by kids.

Cursing to herself at all the locking business, Donna made off down a little paved alleyway between two blocks of houses. Her terrace faced a square of gardens and was hidden away in an enchanted nook.

Rupert, her ginger tom, greeted her at the door and miaowed, showing his spiny white teeth and his coral-pink tongue.

'OK, OK, Rups, let me get in first.'

He wanted food, must have his chicken or rabbit, but it had to be the expensive varieties with thin foil lids. He turned his back on anything else. He continued to fluff and pad about her Docs, making her stumble. She flung her rucksack onto the couch, flicked on all the lights and stomped through into the minuscule kitchen, with Rupert trotting alongside, his miaowing now changing to a rumbling, velvety purr. She forked out chunks of a pinkish substance in jelly and dropped them into the blue-and-white flowered cat dish.

'That's you sorted. Now give me a break!'

She filled the kettle and plugged it in. She wanted to tell someone. The horror of that newspaper headline was unbearable. Lisa used to be in the same class as Joanne so Donna tried her number. But she got Lisa's answerphone voice and a burst of Northern Soul.

'Lisa, Donna here. Can you give me a call later, please?'

She felt totally spooked. She couldn't stop returning to Joanne's face. The lips smiled, but behind the eyes was a deadness. Joanne in a white top, black hair dripping to her shoulders. Who took that picture? She shivered, thinking she could hear feet tramping along the pavers outside the window. She banged into the living room and snapped on the telly in an attempt to make everything safe and normal.

After she'd made a mug of pale sweet tea, she phoned her mother, Maggie. 'It's me,' she said in her forlorn, little-girl voice.

'What's the matter, love?' her mother said. 'What's happened?'

'Do you remember Joanne Singleton?' And she told her about seeing the newspaper headline.

'Goodness! But that's appalling – how on earth did it happen?'

Somehow the evening's threatening quality was toned down and she felt her shoulders relaxing as she talked. Her mother made sympathetic interjections. Then she launched into a tale about how the dividing wall between her garden and her prattish neighbour's had been blown down in the night.

'Come round tomorrow, love, and have a look,' Maggie said.

But after that phone call, Donna didn't know what to do. The evening had closed in on her. Even the telly voices couldn't drive out the air of menace. Somewhere Joanne's murderer was at large. She hadn't been able to buy an evening paper because they were sold out, so she still didn't know any details. Joanne would be lying in some mortuary drawer somewhere. In cases where women had been very badly disfigured the relatives didn't get to see them. How could you look at a hand found in a drain and say, *Yes, this is my daughter*? Would Joanne's family have had to identify her? But who was there? She'd had an Auntie Sylvie, only she'd died in a road accident when they were still at school. Her mother disappeared from the area, so the link had snapped. Donna tried to think of any other person who might have known her but couldn't call any to mind. There had only ever been Joanne's mother and her boyfriends. Her brothers and sister must be somewhere – they were all younger and the mother took them with her when she left.

Somehow she had to get her thoughts away from this obsessive churning and onto another track. Right, she would phone her grandma, who she hadn't seen for a while. She had a curious relationship with Gran, she thought. When she was little, Gran often looked after her if Mum had to work. When Donna visited her high rise on the estate it seemed as if Gran lived on the top of the world. She'd buy Donna treats like Mars bars and there'd be teas with jam doughnuts and Battenberg cakes; Donna would pull off the yellow marzipan before spending ages dissecting the yellow and pink inner squares. Chips were on the menu too – at home they never ate such things because Mum's menu was governed by healthy living principles, though she'd have relapses with pizza and stuff, but she conveniently forgot those when she reeled off what eating chips would do to your coronary arteries. In robust moods Donna would think, Oh, what the hell; in more fragile moments she'd imagine the purply tubes coated with a sly white substance like plaque and shudder.

But nowadays things with Gran could be a bit strained.

For instance, when Gran caught sight of the dragonfly tat-too – Donna's first tattooing adventure – she was horrified.

Lasses don't get tattooed, she said. Whatever have you done that for? It'll not come off, you know. Tattoos are what men have – fishermen. Billy had tattoos on both arms. A heart on one with an arrow going through it and my name, Ruby, Ruby on a little scroll.

Only Gran wouldn't say who Billy was. Remembering Billy's tattoos made Gran forget about the dragonfly for a while. Now Donna knew she must keep all her body decorations hidden. The day Gran caught sight of her belly ring Donna would be in the black books for ever. The sub-ject cropped up from time to time and Gran would huff and puff and say she didn't know what kids were coming to – no standards, they didn't know how to behave.

'Hiya, Gran,' she said.

'Hello, Donna, how are you? And how's that brother of yours?' Gran's voice had a grainy texture. It sounded formal but was splattered with Squawker's watery trills. The sounds made Donna smile. Here were known, safe things, far removed from battered bodies and severed limbs. Squawker had been around as long as she could remember. Squawker laughing in a deep male voice, banging to and fro on his perch and holding slices of orange in his starfish claws.

Donna ran on, confining herself mostly to bits about Lee and not saying anything about Joanne, because she dared not, and promised to drop round for tea. Then she hung up, relieved. Gran was always so reassuringly the same: gritty, out of step, stubborn, warm hearted and something of a termagant.

Late on Lisa phoned.

'Hiya, Don. Oh God, I am so fed up with that Andy – he just gets on my tits. First we were going out, then he says we can't, he'd promised the boys – well, I mean to say. And of course he thinks I'll sit here twiddling my thumbs. Well, I didn't, did I? Nearly rang you up but I was in a right old mood – anyway, went to pub, feel more cheerful now.'

'Good, you'll need to when I tell you this,' and she explained about Joanne.

'Fucking hell!' Lisa gulped on the other end. 'Fucking hell!'

'Yer, too right.'

'I don't believe it.'

'Where did she live, Lisa, do you know?'

'Her mother moved back onto the estate – that's where they came from – but you know Jo – she left school at sixteen, didn't she? Never ran into her or anything. I mean she wasn't daft, she just twagged off though and mucked about and the teachers didn't like her, did they? Thought she was common, I expect. Christ, I mean to say, you don't expect people you know to get murdered, do you?'

'No, you don't. Any idea where she worked after she left school?'

'Don't know, Don, though I did once see her working at a burger joint, but I don't think she stayed there that long. She told me it was crap wages and she hated it.'

They talked on for an hour. Donna loved long phone calls but tonight she really needed this one. Her telephone bills were enormous. She tried not to use her mobile too frequently both because of the cost and also because Mum said she'd read somewhere mobile phones might cause brain tumours. Mum knew the causes of all manner of ailments. You had to keep your ears flapping nowadays, she said, or you could succumb to some dire disease. Gran didn't believe any of it.

By the end of the phone call, they had agreed to meet for a drink. Soon. They both felt a certain urgency.

After that Donna toured the house, checking locks and bolts. Working in a prison made you wary. She was ex-directory for one thing and only gave her phone number to selected people. Although the prison was on the other side of the city, she was aware that if someone really wanted to find her, it wouldn't be hard.

Rups knew it was bedtime. He leapt upstairs on his Dunlopillo pads and after one final leap landed on the bed where he served as an excellent footwarmer. Donna never felt comfortable unless he was there at night.

She looked round her buttercup-yellow room, seeking reassurance. The wind had risen and she could hear it slamming bushes in the gardens. What if someone was trying to force the back door? The neighbours said somebody tried to lever up their downstairs back window but didn't manage it.

Smudges of conversation from work showed up in her head: Well, like, you have to – dun't matter whether you're robbin' off of your mam, you have to get the smack. You get this cravin', this turn on. More 'an sex, I'm tellin' you.

There was this time I'm just gettin' over this fence, like, with a telly an' a video and I sees this woman and she's cryin'. Don't take 'em, she says, please don't take 'em. I felt real gutted like, but I had to.

When it was like this, you knew that there wouldn't be any mercy either. You wouldn't stand a chance. She shivered although the room was pleasantly warm, because during the day it was a suntrap where Rupert would milkbottle at the window peering down over the gardens and lash his tail back and forth whenever he spotted an interloping cat.

She pulled the duvet up to her neck, snapped off the bedside lamp and waited for something deadly to pounce out of the blackness. The saving grace was Rupert, whose warm breathing presence didn't stir. If rapists, murderers or robbers were lurking there, he would be upright, ears twitching, and then she would know.

2

Maggie poured herself a glass of red wine and went to sit in the front room. She wouldn't be disturbed there by Lee's music, which vibrated and rasped through the kitchen ceiling. Donna's news had crashed into her evening like a grenade. She had meant to sit in her study and make sure all her paperwork was in order for the Ofsted inspection but she couldn't concentrate. This was too much; it drove out her preoccupation with the blown-down wall and opened up fissures into which she didn't want to peer. Am I one of those women who won't face up to reality? she wondered. When the abuse case that came to light at school went to court, she'd heard the girl's mother had known what her partner was doing but couldn't bring herself to act. They'd discussed the case in the staff room and Maggie had condemned the mother for being so uncaring and weak. But could she absolve herself from all responsibility when it came to Joanne? When you'd been through a series of failed relationships and several useless affairs you began to think of yourself as a tough character – OK, not as tough as old boots, but perceptive, clear-sighted. Why hadn't she paid more attention to that child? She'd just been Donna's friend who kept on turning up – not Maggie's responsibility. That wasn't the point though . . . If you noticed things, then you ought not to keep quiet about them. The way Joanne used to look at people with those big innocent eyes that weren't innocent. She'd been hyperactive too, wandering about rooms, fiddling with things.

All sorts of clues were there if she thought about it. The bruising on her arms and legs, which you couldn't miss on sports days, when the stringy little kid in shorts and T-shirt pounded down the school field to win the sprint. Of course Mrs Singleton was never there – you didn't see her at parents' evenings either. She'd be pubbing with that dreadful medallion-man boyfriend. On several occasions when Nick was still around she'd seen Mrs Singleton in the Avenues pub with him. He'd prance to the bar in his cowboy boots and lean there chatting up any female within range. He'd looked a good bit younger than Joanne's mother.

It was so tangled and impenetrable and this awful thing had been gradually ripening, like some horrendous seed. All those failures had conspired together and combined to kill her.

Joanne murdered. It could easily have been Donna. Maggie sensed a flush starting in her abdomen and crawling up her throat until her whole body felt hot, tingling unpleasantly. She pulled open the neck of her shirt and fanned herself with an old A4 envelope. She'd always considered that Donna would be a good influence on Joanne and she'd often invited the girl in for tea, but sometimes, looking back, Maggie realized that she'd felt uneasy, that maybe Joanne was influencing Donna. Joanne didn't always attend school and at thirteen she'd be toppling along in stilettos off to some nightspot in town. That was when Donna started saying she wanted to go too and everybody would be there and she'd look idiotic if she had to say her mother wouldn't allow it – and anyway what was wrong with it? The rows must have gone on for a couple of years, with Donna yelling abuse and slamming out of the room. I hate you, hate you, she'd bellow with real venom in her voice. That hurt.

Those were still the Nick times. You're too hard on the kid, he'd said, let her go. That was Nick all over: he couldn't be bothered. It was much easier to let kids do what they wanted. Perhaps that was where she was failing with Lee – no, better not start exploring that too – but it weighed on her constantly, just another worry. It was all about when to let go. She'd always believed that people only learned anything if they'd found it out for themselves.

But Joanne – Joanne dead, dead at twenty-eight. No, that was something she couldn't take in. How could a mother cope with news like that? Your first reaction might be: what's brought this about? There was always a reason. Only this, this went beyond reason – the killing of a young woman. You were dealing with something which went against nature. Your gut instinct was to protect, see the next generation grow up and do better than you did, know the moments of euphoria as well as pain. Rationalizing stopped when you had to deal with the personal like this.

The snapshots kept on coming: the little dark-haired girl walking to school with Donna, her face white and wistful. The kid needed a decent meal and a proper bed-time – more than likely she'd have been up half the night watching telly with nobody to tell her when to go to bed. And no breakfast, of course. A chip butty, she said, if you asked her what she'd had for her dinner. She had a dry cough and her nose was always running. Tell your mum to take you to the doctor – that's a bad cough you've got.

But nothing happened. Nobody seemed to notice and the cough didn't go. You'd hear it, when the child stood on the doorstep: Is Donna playing? You'd tell her Donna was in bed and that was where she ought to be. You watched as she didn't turn round to go home but set off scurrying away down the avenue in the dusk.

The evening of Donna's birthday party – her thirteenth probably – Donna had invited a group of girls round for tea. Joanne turned up in a very tight skirt and skimpy top that forced you to look at her developing breasts. Ruby said later: Did you see the way that child wiggled? For goodness sake, she's too young to be doing that. And her mouth, that pout. Make-up plastered all over her face! You'd said, Lots of young girls nowadays like to pretend they're grown up. Secretly, though, you'd been shocked and felt a coldness in your chest.

She must go upstairs and use the computer – oh, it was the blessed Ofsted! She dreaded it. No matter how many times you went through an inspection, its threatening quality never faded. As a failing school they had lost confidence now after months and months of the inspectors breathing down their necks. You could pull your guts out and the kids' work did improve, but those inner-city children would never be able to compete with the well-heeled middle-class schools in the suburbs.

That dead girl . . . she could have been Donna . . .

Maggie went upstairs and turned on the computer. Her head ached. She could sense a migraine coming on. Tonight's news had taken away both Donna's comfortable feeling of permanence and her own; they had lost their innocence and must face their own guilt. Any certainty they might have clung to was gone for ever. You couldn't reverse the fact of that young woman's death – nothing could ever change it.

For a long time she continued to sit at the computer unable to do anything. She could hear the blackbirds singing in the old pear tree and the music was so unbearably sweet that she found tears falling onto her hands. Here she was, a self-reliant, middle-aged woman who had weathered crises, seen hopeless men off, brought up children largely on her own, worked all her life, only to find herself totally devastated by Donna's telephone call. She had no answer to this. I don't believe in evil, she told herself, I've always known it's a non-word. But what's this, then? Is there any other name you can put on it?

3

'See you, Gran.'

Ruby replaced the receiver, trundled into the kitchenette and plugged in her kettle. Donna must have rung up for some reason, but of course she never said, which made Ruby speculate. She worried about Donna; she wasn't settled, seemed wild – of course she'd had wild times herself, she supposed.

With Ivy's grandbairns it was pregnancies and lads who had scarpered. Lasses these days seemed to switch fellers so many times it got like musical chairs and made you dizzy. Ivy's days got eaten up with babysitting for grandbairns' kiddies. Ivy was her friend from West Dock Avenue school days but she still lived back in the old area. Donna was different from Ivy's grandbairns, though. No lad in the offing, not since that weird Rob who always took offence at everything you said. No great-grandbairns. With Donna it was all prisons and with her mother, Maggie, it was school inspections.

Ruby sat sipping her tea and dunking a digestive biscuit. A wind was blowing up, making the building rock in the buffets. She used to lie awake, in the old days, finding herself out with the trawlers threshing on spuming Icelandic seas, being tossed up on sliding mountains and crashing down into the troughs. You couldn't survive in those waters

33

so it was useless being able to swim. The shining wedges of water slammed along the decks where men clung to the rails all with the fear of death in them but never letting on, garrulous to the end. You might call it bravery.

Over thirty years she'd lived in this tower block on the other side of the city, cut off from the world she grew up in, but she found herself falling back into it, as though it lay just round the corner. Hessle Road contained a host of unresolved stories, like the mystery of Billy, lost at sea when he was twenty-four. She had a browning snap of him in his Waistell's suit with his arm round her waist, and he looked so young, young and untouched by life – yet that wasn't how she remembered him. Now Billy in that photo was the same age as her seventeen-year-old grandson, Lee. Often she searched Lee's face, looking for Billy, and she imagined she traced his full lips and those blue eyes but she knew she was being fanciful because Billy never gave her a baby. He died childless as far as she knew.

In the early summer, the summer before war had broken out, Billy and she took a Sunday tram ride out to Little Switzerland, where they wandered by the chalk pits. Magic down there in the hot afternoon with the white rock cliffs shining and the dark pools throwing back strange craggy images. She remembered picking up a piece of chalk and holding it in her hand. Faerie stones, and she had a feeling of timelessness: the white stone was part of an enduring process, a remote, mystical link, which made Billy and her part of the past and would lead them into the future. She shivered in the heat at the enormity of it. They said that once this land joined Lincolnshire and there was no water here, no estuary slapping away into the distance. Only the tides had gradually worn away the land.

What would we do, she said, if the water rose and rose and we couldn't hold it back?

Billy called her a daft lass and squeezed her to him, telling her she was too fanciful. He didn't daydream nor would he ever admit to fear.

On that afternoon down in the chalk pits with the air filled with the cloying sweetness of May blossom, Billy bit her neck until a bruise flowered and pressed his hard rod against her belly, making her tremble. It was then that they heard the shot. He drew away from her, his breath snarling in his chest. They wouldn't be blasting on Sunday, so what could it be? Looking back now, down all those years, Ruby thought it was an omen of what was to come.

Billy proposed to her on that afternoon and she accepted. Nana, who'd brought Ruby up, had already warned her against getting involved with Billy Wilmot. The Wilmots were a huge, notorious family given to drunken dos, fights in the front gardens, and Mrs Wilmot was forever at the pawnshop with the men's suits as soon as they'd gone to sea.

He'll not make you happy, Nana had said. Don't do it, he'll only make you miserable. Their mam's had to wash their sheets every day because they've weed 'em. Think of that! You can smell that woman coming. You don't want to marry a man on trawlers.

But you did, Nana.

Aye, and look where it's got me.

Of course she did marry Billy Wilmot and every detail of their wedding day is scratched on her memory, but Nana was right, he didn't make her happy. Ruby thought of Maggie. She simply went ahead and married that Trent person, Donna's dad, who cleared off and left her with a baby in arms. What if Donna had got some barm brain of a lad that she didn't want to tell them about? Ruby decided it was time for a drink to calm her down. These thoughts were stirring her up too much. Squawker woke from his doze and shocked her with his rumbling laugh.

35

Returning with a stiff port, Ruby's eye picked up her as yet unread *Hull Daily Mail*. She took in the headline: WOMAN FOUND MURDERED. Then she saw the picture and read the name beneath it. She spluttered with shock and the port shot up into the back of her nose and emerged through her nostrils, stinging her. So that was what Donna wouldn't tell her about. Joanne, that lass who was always hanging about on street corners – but *murdered*. These days nobody was safe. She'd told Maggie that umpteen times but of course Maggie didn't listen because it was always: Mum, you carry on as though we're all under siege – well we aren't. But she was wrong.

The poor girl. Even though she'd dressed like a tart, she didn't deserve to be murdered. She wished Donna didn't work at that prison. The very idea of Donna spending all day long locked up with murderers made her blood run cold. Ruby didn't think she'd ever get to sleep after this – it was going to be one of those nights when she was out on the high seas, remembering Billy and her dad and all the others. And now there was Joanne . . .

4

Donna arrived straight from work at her mother's house. Mum obviously wasn't home yet. The light hadn't yet gone and as she climbed out of her car, she noticed the ice-blue sky, which faded above the black plane-tree branches into a misty luminosity. She had a strong sense of expectation but shrugged it off. She began to feel trembly; that meant she needed food.

In she stomped. The fuggy, spicy smell of the house greeted her. Normally she wasn't aware of it, because this house was home, well, home mark II, but now she seemed at a distance from it and she noticed details that would have previously been merely part of the background.

She snapped on the hall light. Drum and bass thumped upstairs. Lee must be in. Lee could be too annoying.

Through into the kitchen-cum-living room and she didn't have time to put on the light because her eyes had taken in the scene through the bay window on her right. The dividing wall between this house and the adjoining one lay in heaps of bricks in the yards outside the back doors of both houses. But it wasn't the ruined wall that riveted her gaze; her eyes fixed on the man out there. Tall, with a shovel in his hand, he had paused, about to sling earth and rubble into a barrow. She recognized that face and the curious pale eyes, the eyes of a tomcat. In the dying light his face was in deep shadow. Their eyes locked. Shane. Shane what? She must acknowledge him. This was too close to home. This was over the line. Her skin prickled. She walked to the back door, drew the bolt, turned the key and went out.

'Hi,' she said in her briskest, chirpiest voice. 'We know each other, don't we?'

'Yer,' he said.

'How are things? Doing a grand job here by the look of it.' By the look of it nothing much had happened, but she twittered along.

'Yer, yer. Lot to do.'

'That's right.'

She heard the sound of the barrow humping up the passageway between the houses and another man emerged.

'Shall I get you some tea?'

'Ta, love,' the newcomer said.

'Sugar, milk?'

'One sugar, please.'

'Two, love.'

She returned to the kitchen, filled the kettle and plugged it in. The other chap might not know Shane's history and she mustn't give him away. In Mum's cupboard she found a packet of chocolate digestives. The smell of dark chocolate seeped into her nose and mouth and made her want to scrunch down the entire packet. She could taste the chocolate's smooth sweetness and rich creamy texture on her tongue.

She placed four biscuits on a blue and white plate. Two had their rippled surface facing upwards and two down. Two mugs of tea steamed beside them. Out she went. They looked across at her.

Shane didn't speak but his eyes registered something. 'Ta, love,' the other man said and nodded.

Donna hurried back into the kitchen to escape them and shot the bolt in place. She stood for a moment wondering whether to attack the biscuits, succumbed and mid-chomp turned the kettle back on. Placation was the name of the game. She must be friendly because now he knew where she lived – well, where her family lived, which was basically the same. If she wasn't careful, she could bring the vengeance of the estate down on them all: the house could be targeted by druggies. They'd never be safe. Every day someone would be breaking in. What if Mum or Lee or Gran or Mark found them ransacking the house? Mark did sometimes just turn up – he'd spent more time at Mum's than he ever did with his own mother and he didn't seem to like Nick anyway. They'd all be freaked out if they walked in and found somebody stashing away gear.

There'd be no mercy – they'd stop at nothing. The blokes inside told her so many dire stories, like the one about the man who died of an overdose. Oh, yer. He'd ODed right, and they wouldn't call an ambulance. No, they just shoved him out into the road after they'd emptied his wallet, then they cleared off. He was their mate as well, like.

She remembered seeing Shane at the initial assessment interview some months back and then she'd lost sight of him because his case had fallen to another colleague. At the time she thought, What a waste, he wasn't stupid, and he said he was determined to give up his smack habit. But anyone she met in there was tainted; it was a different world from this one – though did she really believe that? On another level she was full of hope: she'd seen men struggling to fight free of drugs and sometimes they managed to make progress. There was the guy who used to carry a gun about the city – OK, he was in prison again, but at least he'd vowed to quit the firearms. That was a certain progress. It must indicate something.

She poured boiling water into a mug, dolloped in one sugar and milk, stirred it and removed the soggy teabag.

They were out there, just beyond the glass – not even over the wall, because there was no dividing line now. They would knock off soon anyway as the light went. Better retrieve the tea things.

They were just packing up.

'Thanks for the tea,' Shane said and smiled.

What had he told her? Stuff about a mate saying try this and injecting him, because he'd had a phobia of needles – but not any more?

'That's all right.' She could hear the mate rumbling the barrow away up the passageway out to the skip. 'How are things then?'

'OK. Well, could be worse.'

'You mean the job?'

'Yer, crap wages. Have you just come from there?'

'Yes,' she said.

'How do you find the work in there?'

They hadn't had this kind of conversation before – this was personal and it threw her.

'It's all right, can be a bit depressing at times.'

'Yer, I suppose.' He hovered as though he were about to say something else, but the other man banged up.

'Right. Off then.'

'Aye. See you.'

They went, boots echoing under the arch between the houses. She looked down at the heaps of rubble. They'd be here a while yet. She shuddered and went back into the safety of the house. Lee's drum and bass seemed unexpectedly reassuring.

Should she tell her mother about Shane? She didn't want to alarm her, but if something happened it was better that she was prepared. It'd be worse if she wasn't. She would have to tell her.

'Gerr!'

Donna jumped. 'Oh, it's you! Don't do that to me.'

'I only spoke. Aren't I allowed to open my mouth now?'

'I didn't expect it.'

'So?'

'I've told you, you gave me a shock.'

'Scaredy cat. Where's Mum? I'm famished.'

'You aren't frigging legless you know – there is a fridge.'

'Don't get arsy with me.'

'I'm not.'

'Yes you are.'

'Aren't.'

'Are.'

She watched as Lee belted open the fridge door, clawed out a tub of hummus, wrenched off the lid, slid a finger across the twirled surface and licked it.

'Hey, you dirty brute, pack it in!'

'What?'

'Don't do that.'

'Scaredy cat, scaredy cat!'

'Cut it out.'

She scowled up at her six-foot-two baby brother who'd been annoying her ever since he first drew breath. He tore pages in her favourite *Milly-Molly-Mandy* books, left splats on Enid Blyton's *Famous Five* and wrenched the door off her dolls' house – things from childhood she'd wanted to keep that he'd found in her bedroom and ruined. And worst of all she had to look after him. Later he always seemed to be barging into furniture as though he'd got a third leg. He'd grown and grown into this lumbering, gawky beanpole, who wore Blue Bolt jeans with enormous flappy legs, and black hooded tops. A sweet smell hung about him: cannabis. His clothes were impregnated with it. She was frightened of that smell attaching itself to her clothing. At the prison there were sometimes spot checks. Three weeks ago when she had just entered the prison compound an officer appeared with a frisky brown and white spaniel – a real sweetie. But if that dog were ever to pull on its lead and strain to sniff her, she'd be in severe trouble – the very thought sent her into a panic.

He moved to grab some biscuits and she attempted to fend him off.

'No you don't.' She tried to hold the packet out of reach. They indulged in a minor wrestling bout and she finally capitulated and handed him a biscuit.

'Phew, you do pong, Lee. I hope that's not rubbed off on me. I don't want to end up in court.'

He gave a slow smile. She noticed his big-eyed, glazed look. She made an elaborate show of dusting herself down but the sight of him had her grinning.

The front door banged and Donna found herself flinching again.

'What is it with you?' Lee asked. 'You're dead jumpy.'

'Nothing. Is that you, Mum?'

The door thumped open again and Maggie lugged her bags in, bringing with her a scoop of cold air.

'Hello, love,' she said, smiling at Donna. 'What a day. Sorry I'm late. It's just the blessed inspection – everybody's going spare.' She dropped the evening paper on the table.

Donna picked it up, compelled to read it. 'No leads in prostitute murder case.' Another picture of Joanne; the same smiling face, a thinner Joanne than the schooldays' one.

'Joanne Singleton, a known prostitute, operating in the ...'

Donna was only vaguely aware of her mother filling the kettle and Lee nattering about being famished and how he felt sick because he'd had nothing to eat and why was there never anything to eat in this house.

'Drugs are thought to be involved in the case.'

Donna's skin prickled with coldness.

'I'm making peasant omelette,' her mother said, 'and it won't take long, so stop whinging, Lee.'

'I'll be too hungry to ea

'Nonsense.'

The phone started ringing.
her body knotted itself with sho

'Can you answer that, love?' h
cooker, where she'd begun to fry oni
shoving chunks of sliced bread into h
ing like a maniac.

'OK, but I bet it's for him. It'll be one o

Donna went into the hall, wondering w   ɔice she
would hear on the other end of the phone, she braced
herself.

'Oh, Gran, it's you . . . Two days together, this is a
record . . . Yes, she's fine, just a bit frazzled, cooking. Is
there anything particular? . . . What? . . . And the bastard
tried to get your bag. Fuckin' – sorry, bloody hell – that's
terrible . . . You're OK? Really OK? . . . You didn't let
him? Let me get Mum . . . I'll come up there after we've
eaten. See you soon.'

Donna rushed back into the kitchen. 'Mum, that was
Gran. Some bastardly kid tried to mug her. He was on his
bike, but she hung onto her bag and he didn't get it. A
fellow in a car stopped and blew the horn and the bastard
scarpered.'

'Damn me, I've just about had enough this week.'

'Look, it's OK, I'll belt off up there as soon as we've
eaten, no sweat.'

'Are you sure?'

'Pos.'

Donna's gaze was dragged back to the newspaper. So
Joanne had become a heroin addict and had turned to
prostitution to fund her habit. That was how it went. On
the surface it seemed so mundane, but beneath that
surface lay heart-stopping pathos.

olved', 'a known prostitute' – those
                      ...es hid so much . . . all the desperation, the
                      Her head swam; her stomach ached with tension.
                      ...e made another attempt to remember when she'd last
seen Joanne. Bits of it came back to her – it must have
been not long after Joanne left school. One Saturday in the
shopping precinct. They'd had a coffee and sat by the
window looking out onto what was left of the old dock.
Joanne was poured into a white sheath dress and her white
shoes had dagger heels, all ultra smart, only the outfit
made her look miles older than she was.

They both chomped down doughnuts and told each
other that they ought not to because it would make their
bums stick out.

Joanne went on and on about this new boyfriend she'd
got and how he bought her French perfume and fantastic
underwear. Donna felt quite envious: Joanne seemed so
sophisticated and she was still a school kid, though not
wanting to be. She was going through an ugly phase where
she felt fat and ordinary, but she managed to keep up with
the other girls in her group when they got wrecked on
Martini lemon and brandy Coke when they held parties or
went clubbing.

One evening around that time, when Donna was babysitting for Lee, she'd invited several mates in and they raided
the booze cupboard and could barely stand up by the time
Mum returned. Fortunately, Mum and Nick, who was still
part of the household then, were fairly drunk too, so they
didn't notice – well, not until they'd invited friends for a
drinks party and half the bottles were empty. Nick kicked
off then and Mum went quiet. Not a good sign. Though
really, until then, she must have got away with quite a lot.

Mum's preoccupation with Nick was another reason
for her to feel frumpy. For ages there'd been just the two

of them, herself and Mum, and suddenly Nick appeared on the scene; kept being smuggled in, there in the morning. Finally came the Big News: Mum was pregnant – and eventually the birth of the Big Nuisance, the Sprog, Lee. Lee, ten years her junior.

People, including Gran, said: Oh you'll be able to help your mum. You'll enjoy that, won't you? Be a second mother to him.

But a baby at such close quarters put her off reproduction for life. Babies were howly, messy, idiosyncratic creatures and you spent your days pouring stuff in one end just so it could spurt from the other.

It unsettled her, all this delving into the past when Lee was a baby and Joanne her best friend. Joanne – so high tensile, always after the ultimate thrill – probably started injecting just for the hell of it. And then found she couldn't stop. Before long she'd have gone out on the streets trying to earn the money for the smack. Donna knew this story backwards; she heard it every day. Only there was another bit to this one, a vital piece of the jigsaw.

Someone had killed Joanne.

Was it a punter, one of those guys from out of town in flash cars? Or her pimp? Donna wished she weren't so familiar with such stories. They never seemed to leave her head.

The woman whose dismembered body was discovered in the drain had been a prostitute killed over some drug palaver. A face in a newspaper: you shuddered but then let the story sink away. This was different, though. This was Joanne. And Joanne had joined the ranks of all these other women, her own age or a year or two younger, who had tried smack for kicks, through boredom, a hunger for something to wrench them out of the everyday – and it had killed them.

'The police are following certain leads . . .'

The sentence ran in her head like an advertising strip in the post office, selling insurance and holidays. It zigzagged back and forth, winking.

'The police are . . . certain leads . . .'

She lost the illuminated tape once they sat round the table with the peasant omelette on a wide brown plate. Mum sliced it into wedges.

'I need a lot,' Lee said.

'Your eyes are bigger than your belly – eat that first,' Mum said.

Donna looked into the shiny blackness of the bay windows, through which she could make out the jumble of bricks from the collapsed wall. They were caught by the living-room light, ominous with stark shadows.

'Why don't you ever close the curtains, Mum?' she asked.

'There's no need, is there really? I mean nobody's going to look in, are they?'

'You don't know,' Donna said, thinking of the eyes staring in at her in the late afternoon. 'Now that the wall's down, it's all open – anyone could look in.' A shudder jerked through her.

'Pack it in!' Lee said.

'Well, I'd best get off to Gran's,' Donna said, rising from the table.

'Thanks, love,' her mother said.

'You look buggered, Mum, try to get your feet up for a bit. Don't worry about Gran, I told her I was planning on dropping in anyway. See you.'

Quick kiss and a hug for Mum. Lee squirmed away in mock horror.

After a fifteen-minute drive Donna reached the middle of the estate, with its row upon row of raw-faced pinkish blocks, metal clothes poles stuck in piddling front gardens, open-plan lawns where scraps of paper and crisp packets bowled and dogs ran in packs shitting. The tower blocks hit you in the eye like those hastily thrown up hotels in places like Benidorm. They didn't seem to fit in with the crabbed houses squatting round their bases.

After a lot of incidents with druggies breaking in and shooting up in the flats, the council had secured the entrance. Now Donna rang Gran's bell and waited for her to release the door catch. She'd first come here when she was very small and learned to know the lift's zoom and slither. The space specially designed for coffins made her shiver now. She remembered clattering in there as a little kid and bouncing up and down until Gran said, Leave off, Donna, that's not for playing in – that's where they put coffins. Donna wouldn't leave it there, wanted to know why they needed coffins in lifts, and Gran talked about people dying in the flats and how would they get the bodies down if they didn't have a special coffin area. Nowadays Donna couldn't travel in the lift without thinking of Gran dying up there and her coffin being manhandled into that oblong; it made her want to cry.

Gran's flat reassured her with its smell of air freshener and lavender polish.

'Hiya, Gran. You OK?' Donna's question was drowned beneath Squawker's excited rumblings. The male laugh rang out, followed by a clatter as his perch crashed against the side of the big wire cage.

'Oh yes, I'm fine, Donna love. You shouldn't have come all this way. Will you have a sup of port, eh?'

'Go on then, Gran, just a teaspoonful – I'm driving.'

Out came the port bottle and two ornate glasses. Up there, six storeys into the sky, with the curtains closed and in the orangey glow of the standard lamp and the rushing of wind hitting the tower block and Squawker adding trills and watery noises, it all seemed very cosy, like a sealed bubble drifting above the earth. Gran's was where she'd come when she was poorly and Mum had to work – times lying in Gran's big soft bed, hearing the comforting drone of the vacuum cleaner in another room and gazing at the jug of lemon barley water on the bedside table and the picture in the silver frame of a man in a flying jacket and helmet. The bed smelled of Gran, cinnamony and faintly perfumed. Donna remembered dressing up in Gran's jewellery; standing in front of the dressing-table mirror and admiring the blue glass beads round her neck. Ruby, azure, pearl and jet beads twinkled in a square glass ornament on Gran's dressing table with clip-on earrings that nipped your earlobes. Everywhere smelled of powder and Max Factor 'Mystique'. She tried on Gran's heels, and stumbled round with a feather boa draped about her neck. Mum didn't have the same magic – she didn't go in for jewellery, her life governed by a sensible streak. You're like me, Gran used to say, looking at Donna and smiling. But then of course, Lee, the nuisance, the sprog, had come on the scene, and Gran transferred her attention to him.

Gran described the attempted mugging and showed Donna her wrecked handbag. 'I s'll not use this bugger again, it's done for now. Perhaps pick up something at Cancer Research – they have some real bargains in there. I got this pair of grand shoes for me dancing from there – silver, you know.'

Squawker burst out singing in a deep male voice, the voice that Donna had heard so many times over the years.

'Gran, whose voice is that then?'

This time Gran didn't pretend she hadn't heard. Often she'd refuse to go over the old stories again. I've told you, she'd say when Donna pleaded for more. Tonight, though, was different; perhaps the struggle in the street had made her want to talk. 'Ernie,' she said. 'Squawker belonged to

Ernie and he was your grandfather, your mother's dad, as you know.'

'Oh, right. So what happened to him then?'

'Heart attack. He was one of those to set a girl's heart in a flutter, though I'm not saying he was the right one for me. It was hearing him sing "I'll take you home again Kathleen" that did it. At one of these street parties when the war finished. What a voice he had! He was an airman, bailed out over enemy territory – some French peasants hid him. He was a good dancer an' all.'

'Gran, what about my dad? What did you make of him?'

'Didn't know him, did I? Your mother was in London when she met him, at university, I suppose. Next thing I knew she rang up and said she'd married him – I'd never met him. Then he'd left her just like that. She had to come back home because you were a babe in arms. After that there was that tripe-hound she got caught up with – Lee's dad. Maggie always chooses men who'll do for her. I hope you'll do better than that, Donna.'

Donna found her grandmother's canny dark eyes on her. Gran couldn't be doing with kidology. She'd ferret until she unearthed the truth. No way did she want Gran going on about Joanne – because she was bound to bring up all the old stuff about how she'd always thought Joanne was a bad influence.

'Well, I'll try to, Gran. But I'll tell you as of now there's nobody and I'm not planning on there being somebody – not yet anyway.'

'Mm. I never know with you. Did you love that Rob then, lass?'

The question made Donna pause. 'No, I don't suppose I did – it sort of happened. I think I wanted somebody and he was there and well, he seemed to have certainties –

I mean, he had these very definite likes and dislikes. People like that, though, are a real pain – but I didn't understand that at first. I got like I didn't know who I was any more. I just did what he said. And then one day I thought, I've had enough, and that was it.'

'Aye, well, next time make sure you choose better.'

'Yes, Gran, but I'm not into boyfriends just now, so there's no need to look at me like that.'

'That girl in tonight's *Mail* again, Donna, she was that friend of yours, wasn't she? After you'd rung last night I saw it in my paper.'

'Yes,' Donna said.

'I always thought that girl knew more than was good for her. She'd have her skirt up her backside – and the way she looked at you.'

'But Gran, she was lovely, she was full of life – I've never had a friend since who was so much fun to be with. OK, she'd do anything, she was amazing how nothing scared her – and I can't believe this, that somebody's killed her.' To her embarrassment and relief Donna found tears running down her cheeks.

'Oh, lass, don't get upset. Here, have another nip.'

A long time later Donna drove home, her head full of pictures: Gran as a young girl; now a widow after the death of her first husband Billy, who was washed overboard in Icelandic waters; going dancing with her friend, Lil, the bottle blonde. Lil died when Hull got bombed during the war – entombed under mountains of bricks and mortar from something called the Provident Building.

Then there was Annie, another best friend, who fell pregnant to a black GI and was spat on by her soldier husband on his return from war. And Leroy, Leroy who danced the war out with that young widow, Gran, and whose body was music. All merged with Joanne lying dead in the city morgue. And there was guilt and regret too at the way a university education, three years away from home, and a new way of life had made her forget Joanne's friendship.

As she drove home through the eleven o'clock night, the skin of frost on the road and pavements, the rows of boarded-up houses and the empty areas where the grass was frozen stiff, she resolved to find out what really happened to Joanne.

5

Another evening and Donna strode down the road by the lines of cars squatting on the rubbed-out verges. She glanced at the rusting Ford propped up on bricks in what would once have been a garden. Around here people seemed to use the little front gardens as repositories for dead cars; or cars that their owners hoped one day might be revived.

A clutch of youths in baseball caps dawdled by on the other side of the road, dragging at privet hedges and cuffing one another from time to time. A couple passed, cramming chips into their mouths. The chippy round the corner sent out inviting messages. The hermaphrodite person with the chamber-pot hat lurched up gabbling to herself. 'Have you seen them?' she asked.

'No,' Donna said, 'sorry, I haven't,' and kept going. The woman, who Donna often bumped into wandering the streets, always alone and dressed in peculiar gear, could hold you up for a good half-hour if you didn't escape, talking about 'them' and 'they' in a very mysterious manner so that you felt another reality yawning before you. Nobody seemed to know who she was or where she belonged but she was accepted as a feature of the landscape, like the elderly man in a Highland piper's rig-out, hefting all his possessions in black bags and invariably to be seen on the stretch of road near the former convent.

Donna was on her way to the pub to meet Lisa and talk about Joanne. She wanted to get drunk, disgustingly drunk, just so she wouldn't have to keep on churning through the whole ghastly business. It had stuck in her head, repeating over and over.

Turning right, she passed the second-hand shop, Lew's Corner, which declared guarantees on all goods but would slide out of honouring them if the article broke down shortly after purchase. The rambling shop sold all sorts of dodgy oddments at prices often higher than the articles would cost brand new. Lee had been ripped off by Lew over a defunct digital recorder and was muttering about 'giving Lew a clatter'.

The chippy was packed. A middle-aged man, a really creepy, geeky type, stared at her.

Seven o'clock and the main road flashed with the zoom of cars into town for a night out. She rounded the bend into an avenue of plane trees. On one side the park was in deep shadow. She used to love that park as a child. It hid the Victorian conservatory where mynah birds honked and screeched and red-cheeked lovebirds swung on a wire or pecked at halved oranges and seeds on the floor of their aviary. The smell of hyacinths and the massed banks of cinerarias in the spring made her dizzy, tickling her nose so that she sneezed.

The swings and the slide and the whirligig would be motionless behind the screen of trees.

The public lavatories in the park had been closed down because men were 'doing things' in them. Donna always wanted to know what 'things', but of course nobody would be explicit. Gran said Donna was too nosy for her own good. Mum thought the lavs ought not to be closed. Sheer prejudice, she said, but Gran was horrified. Now the park was apparently swarming with drug dealers.

Donna kept to the other side of the road where the handsome redbrick Victorian terrace stood. Most of the houses were split up into flats; one was a big medical practice, one a nursery, another a nursing home. They had a dignity and assurance lacking in the houses in Donna's square.

Knots of students sloped by, making for the offy. Donna sniffed curry from the Bangladeshi restaurant. That competed with the Italian pizza parlour opposite. The little shops along the road changed hands repeatedly, only the take-aways and restaurants staying in business. Three boarded-up premises were flanked by a couple of salons, one owned by a real poseur. Donna frowned across at it; just the white and gold décor made her pull a face. At last she reached the pub, one of a new chain which served meals and had a reputation for fights.

Lisa was nowhere to be seen and Donna went up to the bar and bought a Martini lemon. Already the pub was quite full. Fleshy men in football shirts dominated with gusts of laughter and raucous voices. She pretended she couldn't see them and selected a secluded corner. No sooner had she sat down than a voice said, 'Hi,' and she found herself looking at Shane.

'Saw you come in here,' he said.

'Oh well . . .' Donna's cheeks felt hot and uncomfortable.

'On your own?'

'No – well, I'm expecting a friend.' Hopefully that would drive him away.

'I'll shove off when your friend arrives.'

If she said OK, she might be stuck with him, but while she was still hesitating, Lisa walked in.

'Sorry I'm late, Don. I'll get a drink.' She obviously liked the look of Shane and assumed he'd joined them because she asked him if he wanted a drink. He smiled and said if she was sure, then he'd like a pint of bitter. Donna

54

was furious. Why couldn't Lisa use her brains instead of jumping in with both feet?

Had he been following her from her street, Donna wondered, and if so, what did he want? She struggled to find something to say. He turned to look at her and smiled.

'Must be quite tiring, labouring?' she threw out. She stared at the logo on his black sweatshirt.

'Yer. Not ideal.'

'What would you like to do?'

'Got an NVQ in carpentry, done a painting and decorating course as well, but can't get a job with them – I mean as soon as they know, well . . .'

'Yes, it's a massive problem.' She pondered how on earth someone like Shane could ever escape from this trap, and her annoyance softened into pity, sympathy for his plight.

'He's a right bastard, the one I'm working for. You're casual, right – nothing official, right. He hires and fires, no questions asked.'

Lisa was back with the drinks and Donna knew she couldn't expose Shane's past to her. She'd have to keep mum. It wouldn't be right to talk about Joanne either, not in front of a stranger. But then a thought started to niggle away at her: what if he had some inside knowledge? In nicks a lot of talk went about. A coldness prickled her arms.

They'd known who had battered that girl to death when she'd called for petrol at the all-night garage, known it long before the trial. They talked murder all day long. They knew hideous secrets, things that nauseated you and brought the bile to your mouth.

Shane said, 'Cheers!' and sipped his pint. Lisa beamed. She was clearly quite taken with him.

'Do you come here often then?' Lisa chortled and patted her blond hair.

'Not really,' Shane said.

He threw Donna another smiling glance, a covert look excluding Lisa and drawing Donna into an intimacy with him which terrified her. He was over the line; someone from the other side. What if a member of the prison staff saw her in this pub drinking with him? Questions would be asked; she'd lose her job. They'd warned about mixing with ex-inmates. A previous drugs worker had to leave because someone had seen her in the city centre with an ex-prisoner. She posed a risk, the head of security said, and they couldn't afford such things.

Donna herself had once received a covert warning – nothing had been said to her directly but she had found out. She was working in a Doncaster prison and interviewed a chap who'd just received news that his daughter had died. He was being released into the community, where she'd been assigned as his case worker. In a spontaneous show of sympathy, she'd placed a hand on his arm. A prison officer evidently reported the information to the drugs unit where the man would be a client. They were told to watch Donna and make sure she wasn't having a relationship with the ex-inmate. Donna escaped any further repercussions by arranging for a colleague to supervise the man so she wouldn't have to see him again. But the whole episode had shocked her. She knew now that even the most casual gesture could be misinterpreted.

She didn't want to lose her job – she loved the work. OK, it was a love–hate relationship, but that didn't change anything. Even as a child she'd been fascinated by people like some she'd seen on Gran's estate. At university a girl in the same hall had taken Es at a party, gone into a coma and died. After that she knew she was going to work with drug abusers. On some days she'd feel a great surge of love for the moth-eaten, sour-smelling, sparky mob she saw around her day in day out. They were loveable in a weird sort of way. Taken as individuals you could sympathize with them, admire them for their determination. But . . .

As she glanced around, scared of encountering some work connection, the other voice cut in, a cool, calculating, reasonable voice: Perhaps he can help you find out about Joanne. You can play this to your advantage if you're careful.

Lisa rumbled on about some concert she'd been to and Shane listened. Donna gulped down her Martini lemon and decided she'd have a Castaway next round.

'Me and Donna went clubbing the other weekend,' Lisa told him, 'and you should have seen the men – God, navelhigh, a right load of prats as well.'

Shane smiled. Donna had a vision of C wingers and burst out giggling.

'What's wrong with you?' Lisa said.

'Nothing, nothing at all.'

C wingers effing and blinding; their cells gassy with the odour of feet; walls papered with ugly pictures of knickerless women exposing their genitalia, women with bladder breasts. C wingers, vulgar, crude, basic: men stripped down, without a civilizing gloss. Was she being too hard? Were the officers any better? She had a gut feeling that they weren't – that they all infected one another with this crudeness: men together, men at their worst.

She got up. 'I'm having another drink. Who wants one?'

'Let me,' Shane said.

'No.' She came on firm. 'This is my shout.' With relief she stood at the bar, scanning the pub to make sure there were no familiar faces in the hubbub. She couldn't see anybody she recognized but she couldn't believe she wasn't being watched. In prisons you got the habit of watching and noting and mentally filing things away – you never knew when you might need the information. It was spooky, just like the constant security alerts. You stopped trusting people; you acquired a habit of checking and rechecking.

Donna set down the drinks on the table and found Shane studying her. She tried to dodge his glance.

'My boyfriend will be plonked in front of telly,' Lisa told Shane. 'Can't be bothered to go out – sooner just sit there goggling. So boring.' She giggled and fluttered her eyelashes.

'Yer,' he said, 'but it's usually the women who like telly.'

'Sexist,' Donna said, setting off an argument as to whether watching television was a predominantly female pastime.

Donna wanted to come out with something about heroin users being too busy robbing and shooting up to have time for telly, but she bit back the words. She watched Shane's mouth, took in the slide of his straw-coloured hair and the scar on his cheekbone. He didn't give the impression that he was a practised liar, seemed oddly matter of fact.

'Which school did you go to, then?' Lisa asked when the TV argument had petered out.

'Didn't do much school, like.'

'How come?'

'I was always twaggin' off, you see,' he said. 'We'd be down by the docks . . . always wanted to go to sea. On a weekend we'd walk along Hessle Road – we lived just off it – into town and get jumping on and off these barges on the river. You'd nearly miss a mud bank when you jumped. There used to be a rope tied to a tree and we'd swing on it over the water. I'd look down and think, Bet there's crocodiles in there, lying in the slime. It, like, terrified me but I loved it.'

She knew the paradox: you're scared shitless but you enjoy it, have to test things to their limits. Joanne was like that – or was she? She never seemed to be afraid, as though she couldn't see where her actions would land her. Or even if she'd realized what would happen, she didn't care. It could be a sort of bravery, or was it desperation?

The evening flowed by and everything was easy. You might imagine the murky, druggie undertow wasn't there but it was – she saw what the sludge of it did every day.

Last orders. They emerged into the night. Donna looked up at the electric whiteness of the stars and Shane pointed out the Plough. Frost glittered on the pavement and the wind was blade sharp. Lisa stumbled with drink. The druggies who begged outside the 24-hour supermarket had taken up position. A security guard barrelled at the door, making sure none slipped inside.

Donna considered how she could get rid of Shane.

'Shall I walk you back home?' he said.

'No, ta. Thanks for the offer but it's fine – anyway I'm going back with Lisa.'

'You don't have to.' Lisa grinned.

'Oh yes I do.'

Shane disappeared. Instead of a sense of relief, Donna felt even edgier, dissatisfied. His mouth, his laugh, his teeth, his off-hand way of talking hung about – they prickled her. She wished they didn't.

Lisa asked why she didn't let Shane take her home.

'Not my type,' Donna said.

'He was after you,' Lisa mumbled, 'and he's all right.'

'We couldn't talk about Joanne in there. I got a bit worried you might say something, though.'

'I nearly opened my gob, Don, and then I looked across at you and I thought better not. Oh, Christ, did you see, it said she was on the streets? I mean to say – you can't believe it, can you? It blows your mind. School and then that.' Tears ran down her cheeks.

They linked arms as they walked up Lisa's street and Donna found herself crying too. For several minutes they stood outside her terrace going over and over what they remembered about Joanne, but always coming back to how she met her death. The words 'prostitute' and 'murdered' seemed ungraspable.

Donna spent ten minutes in Lisa's house. She exchanged greetings with Andy, still immobile in front of the telly, and then left.

As she strode down the night-time avenues, hearing now and then the echoing moo of an owl, she imagined Joanne at night, waiting for a client. How scary to be out in the darkness, hanging about, waiting, wondering. Cars sliding by; you gazing at the drivers, a smile stretching your lips. You offered an invitation, though your legs were frozen up and you just wanted a coffee and a fag. The car slowed – a Jag, which meant money. The man was grey haired, old enough to be your granddad; old blokes were usually all right, at least he was unlikely to be violent like some of the young ones. But you never knew: any time you climbed into a car could be your last.

The next car might be a red Toyota. No dents, no mud splashes, just shining immaculate enamel. Driver, a man knocking forty with a rough-hewn face but a weak voice; the sort of man who had strange fixations; a cleanliness freak who hated what he was about to do, thought it was dirty and wanted to degrade the women he used.

Could it have been someone like him? Donna quickened her step. She hurried by the park. Cars shot by at intervals and each time she heard one, a shiver tensed her neck and shoulders. She was Joanne out there, watching, waiting.

6

The silver shoes from Cancer Research were a luxury. Sometimes Ruby felt she could splurge her entire pension on shoes, but in order to add the ultimate touch of giddiness, she decided to visit the chiropodist, a double bus ride away. During the ride she mused on Donna's visit, and the newspaper story about the murdered girl. She never had cared for that Joanne – her eyes were all over and she had that pouty look that made her seem old, too old. It always worried her that Maggie let Donna play with Joanne, but then that was Maggie all over: Oh, Mum, they're poor, that's all. Just because they're poor it doesn't mean we can't associate with them.

Common more like, was what Ruby said. That girl had a common look. Maggie was always too wafty, never had any clue about real things. Sometimes, Ruby thought, everything Maggie did was book talk – how things ought to be, never how they really were. Of course she'd never admit that; as far as she was concerned Ruby was a back number.

The chiropodist ran his business from his yellow house. The ritual always progressed in the same way. He met her at the door, ushered her in and indicated she should go behind a screen to remove her tights and shoes; then she stepped onto the big leather chair, which he pumped up until she was reclining.

'Ah now, Mrs Er . . .' and he fluttered pages in his appointment book. 'Not seen you for some time.'

She swooned into his hands stroking her feet. He examined her toes and snooped after bunions and hard skin. Then the paring process started. For a big chap his hands were surprisingly delicate, nails manicured into perfect filbert arcs. He picked away at the lumpy bits on her little toes with a scalpel and while thus engaged he told her stories. She knew how he ran away to join the Foreign Legion . . .

She heard about the Indo-China war and the spear that went through his groin and how fellow soldiers wanted to pull it out but he said on no account. When he arrived at the hospital, the doctor said: No more jigger-jigger for you, young man. Ruby often speculated as to how this lack of jigger-jigger affected the chiropodist's life.

When she left, her head dizzied with tales of arrows through privates and executions and swarmings in the undergrowth, she always felt light and airy. Her corns didn't pain, she could enjoy her shoes again and besides, she could mull over the chiropodist's tales, amazed that he hadn't stabbed her to death. The thing about the chiropodist was that he allowed you to toy with the possibility of the ultimate horror while sparing you the reality of it. It was rather like watching a horror film on TV and knowing that when she pressed the off switch, she could return to the world of Squawker, her three-piece suite, the gulls shimmying past the windows, and a cup of tea and a ham sandwich on a tray.

That afternoon she'd break in her new silver shoes at the tea dance and give her Sue Ryder Lurex top and jazzy skirt an airing.

Ruby could see Ivy waiting on the City Hall steps for her. She shouldn't wear that red coat, Ruby decided; it made her face look like old sheets.

'You've took your time,' Ivy said. 'Thought you wasn't comin'.'

'Just missed me bus,' Ruby explained, lying. She didn't go in for apologies. Gave that up years ago. People had to take you how you were and she was often late. Timing was never her strong point.

They clattered down to the cloakrooms and it was just like years ago, with girls standing beside one another in front of mirrors – except that these girls were a lot older than those other phantom ones and they had learned how to jab with their elbows. Now they talked of operations and how so and so had it all took away and such and such had lost her husband.

Ivy got chatting with an acquaintance. 'Oh yes, it was his you-know . . . yes and he couldn't . . . so then he . . .'

Ruby half listened as she sprayed herself with a fruity number Donna had given her at Christmas. It came in a basket with a purple soap the size of a fried grade one egg and a little plastic bottle of hand cream. Body Shop stuff. Donna was into all sorts of environmental matters, which she liked to explain to Ruby in great detail.

You ought to be taking your bottles and tins to the Eco Dump, Gran, she said. You're helping to destroy the environment by throwing all these bottles away. They could be recycled, you know.

And how am I going to lug that lot over half the town? Ruby responded. I'm six floors up in a high rise, lass.

Donna couldn't quite work that one out, could she? In many respects she was just like her mother. With Maggie it was all wild gardens – of course that meant you didn't bother about weeding. Mum, the insects are being killed off. That spray you want me to use, just think what it will do to the environment.

Ruby snorted to herself and turned to look for Ivy. She seemed to be mesmerized by a gruesome tale involving loss of bowel control and a constant washing of sheets.

'He wouldn't let me out of the room.'

'Is that right?' Ivy said.

'Shall we be getting along then?' Ruby intervened.

'Aye, I think we'd better,' Ivy said, looking relieved.

Ruby hoped Ivy wouldn't feel the need to relay the conversation to her. She thought instead of Leroy, her GI love of many moons ago, as they mounted the red carpeted stairs and entered the magic portals.

Of course there wasn't a big band brassing up. You just had to imagine that. Now they had to make do with a DJ bellowing out and playing records. Still, better than nothing.

Leroy had smooched with her to slow foxtrots. His hand on the base of her spine wouldn't let her stumble, had transformed her into an accomplished dancer. But now there was a new problem: with more women than men, you had to be able to take the male part, and she couldn't. She didn't know how.

Ruby waited beside Ivy and they surveyed the dance floor. 'Don't know as we'll get a dance,' Ruby muttered.

'Well, we can dance together.'

'Not this,' Ruby snapped.

But a chap did hoik himself across. Ruby watched him, wondering which of them he'd choose. He addressed himself to her.

'Like a dance?' he said, and gave her a Sterodent-white smile.

The chap had grey hair, slicked back and longish, but it was his voice that intrigued Ruby. It was soft as feathers. She imagined talking to him on the phone. What you would call a swoony voice, a voice to take your breath away.

The DJ put on 'In the Mood' and off they went, launching out across the gleaming surface. Ruby loved her silver shoes and she let herself go in the sway of the beat. Again she sensed the nearness of that other world. Leroy from New York crooning above her head and his limbs shaking with the rhythm that swung from his pelvis and absorbed the whole of him. Nights of passion. Nights that made her impervious to all those looks of disgust and the mutterings: How can she? Our boys fighting and dying and she's nobut a tart . . .

He gave her silk stockings and Hershey bars – the sweet things you lusted after when everything was rationed and unobtainable. He took her to clubs and somehow managed to get whisky, even when there wasn't supposed to be any. He taught her things she could never have dreamed of and she found he had a hairless body and the soles of his feet were yellow like the palms of his hands and he could make her yowl with pleasure like a tomcat at night. The bombs fell and the old city's contour shifted. Youngsters like Donna nowadays had no idea of that world, nor, for that matter, had Maggie. They took the city's shape for granted and couldn't imagine how wars and poverty had gouged out hollows in it.

The dance finished and the man introduced himself as Frank Prentice. In his brown suit and tie he was quite smart. A slight cast in his left eye lent him a certain slyness. A lot of elderly men just looked bald, bulgy and belligerent, she decided, whereas this Frank Prentice had another quality, which was heightened by his oozy voice and squinty eyes. He might be a chancer – Ruby had a weakness for chancers. They didn't spend their days debating the state of their bowels or their indigestion and counting their tablets with satisfaction. Nor did they bore you with tales of their sainted dead spouses.

'Not seen you here before, Ruby,' he said.

'Nor would you have,' Ruby countered, 'because I've not been here for a long while – just felt like a change.'

'You're a good dancer.'

'Aye, they used to say I'd a good leg on me.' Ruby gave a dirty laugh. The man joined in.

'I'd have to have a closer examination to know about that, love.'

It turned out Frank used to be a porter in Kingston General Hospital. Ruby could just see him pushing bodies stretched out under white sheets on trolleys and tweaking up the sheet to have a quick squinny at the legs beneath it . . . oh, yes, he'd be into all that. Bound to be with a voice like his.

They continued dancing, moving into a waltz and then a rumba and then modern stuff, the things they played in the fifties and sixties. There was 'Singing the Blues' and 'Rock around the Clock'. It turned out he was a master jiver and again she remembered Leroy. He could throw her over his shoulder, her dress flaring round her thighs, and people would be gawping with their mouths open, practically dropping their dentures.

When the dance finished a couple of hours later in mid-afternoon, Frank's voice silked, 'How about a little refreshment, Ruby? I don't mean tea.'

'Well,' Ruby recollected, 'I'm with my friend.'

'She can come as well.'

'I'll have to find out.' Mustn't be too eager, Ruby thought, don't want him to think I'm a walkover. He hadn't once referred to piles, biliousness, constipation or rheumatics, which was a major plus. The last feller she went out with had everything under the sun wrong with him and what he'd had cut off must have occupied umpteen surgeons. By the time she parted with him, she'd begun to feel ill herself.

Ivy didn't look too pleased but she agreed to a quickie. 'Said as I'd be back to mind the great-grandbairns.'

He took them to their usual haunt beside the art gallery and bought them a stout each. He had a whisky.

'Bit early for that, in'it?' Ivy said, staring at Frank's drink and snorting with laughter.

'Never too early, lady,' he said.

Ruby could see Ivy's nose was out of joint. She contented herself with a chortle. That red certainly didn't suit her, Ruby noted, and she only needed a couple of sips of stout to start her screeching.

'This is like our favourite,' Ivy let drop. 'We come in here on a Thursday dinner – they do a good meal.'

'I'll have to join you then, ladies, if you'll permit me?' he said.

Ruby nodded and the matter was settled, though she had to admit she'd have preferred a date on her own with Frank, who she quite liked. Still, that might come later . . .

He bent down in front of Ruby, seized her right hand and kissed it. Ruby was astounded. With that he swept on a brown trilby and gawked out.

'He's a proper tinker,' Ivy pronounced, half in admiration, half disapproval.

'Hope me hand smelled clean,' Ruby said, staring down at its veiny back. She ought to have had firm-fleshed, small white hands, not these shrivelled claws. Then she dismissed the thought with disgust. She had to see her Ordnance Survey face as it was, take it straight on, with its concertinaed upper lips, craters around the eyes and parallel corrugations on the brow. There was no other way. She wasn't Donna's age, nor Maggie's come to that.

'Another half?' Ivy suggested.

'Aye, go on,' Ruby said. She was in a nostalgic mood and the past seemed so close she could almost touch it. Perhaps over there in the United States Leroy (if he was still alive) would pause sometimes and think of the young woman he promised to marry but never did. One day those gum-chewing, hunky-bodied GIs packed the Wenlock Barracks and the next they'd flown. All gone, pulled out.

On her homeward bus journey Ruby fell again into specu-
lation about Donna. Instinctively she knew that the lass
was in bits underneath but most people wouldn't realize it
because she smiled all the time and acted happy. She
seemed to be a girl who'd never know romance. Stars had
never got in her eyes with that tripe-hound Rob. It made
her dread who the lass would fetch up with next. Watching Donna was like scrolling back the years to her own
young self: Ruby caught glimpses of the same torment and
fragility in the girl and she was afraid. Donna was thin
and white faced when she finished with that Rob, and
Ruby knew she'd been just the same herself after Billy
drowned at sea and she'd realized that now he'd never
give her a baby. It had been worse when Leroy went. By
the time she was with Ernie and saw how Ernie couldn't
keep his hands off women, she understood that rapture
only came in moments; that it didn't last – and now she took
it where she could.

7

Donna looked across at Joe Langly and asked the usual questions. He began to tell her why he wanted to give up heroin.

'Been on all this time, like – no sooner do I get out and I'm in again. But there's me mates, like. They was only twenty-three. They goes in this toilet and shoots up together like and that was it. Both of 'em dead . . . OD.'

He couldn't look at her but gazed at the rim of the table.

'We was at school together, been comin' in here for years. I have to stop usin'. I think it's the pinnin' I can't stop – just the pinnin'.' He met her eyes then.

'Yes,' she said. This would have been Joanne's story too; she would have been locked into this craving, this endless compulsion. Donna felt the tears wanting to spring to her eyes – lately she kept finding herself crying. Even the smallest, stupidest thing could start her off.

'I mean, I'd get out – like I went to see me mam. It was her birthday the day I got out. Wayne, one of them who's died, met us. He'd got a pin. Here, he says, I've give up. We go into me mam's. All I can think of is a turn-on and I know me mate's got this pin. In the end I have to go in our toilet. Me mam knew I was off again and she threw us out.'

The interview continued, rambling back and forth. He said he had to stop, wanted to, must. She listened, and all the time Joanne floated near the surface of her thoughts. This was Joanne's story, this story of slow, insidious leaching away.

At lunchtime she ran into Wes, the prison officer, in the canteen. 'Can I join you?' he said, approaching the table where she munched a cheese and salad sandwich.

'Sure,' she said and smiled, but really she wanted to concentrate on her own thoughts.

'How you doing?'

'Managing,' she said.

'Don't envy you.'

'No.' She couldn't be bothered to ask what he meant.

'It's like an epidemic.'

'Too right,' she said.

'What made you choose this job?' he asked.

She stopped mid-bite and thought. 'I knew I never wanted to work in an office. I like working with people, plus somebody at uni overdosed and that kind of got to me. Loads of my year at uni seemed to be doing drugs and I began to see what a problem drugs are . . . like major. I mean they can wreck you and I suppose I wanted to do something about it. Anyway I've always been fascinated by deviancy, and why people do what they do.' She grinned at him, trying to bring the conversation onto a lighter level.

He laughed too. 'Get plenty of that in here for sure.'

'Why are you working in here then?'

'I wanted to make a difference.'

'How can locking and unlocking doors make a difference?' Donna said, immediately wondering whether he would think she was taking the piss.

'I didn't quite see it as that.'

'No.'

'No? What about a drink some time – like next Friday?'

She was so surprised that she didn't have time to extricate

herself from the situation and agreed, experiencing a throb of excitement – after all it was a long time since she'd had a date. Next Friday at the Queens.

After work she decided to call in on her mother and see Lee and find out what was happening there. She also had another motive – perhaps her chief one – though she wouldn't let herself examine it.

Amazing to be driving home in daylight; she noticed the pale lemon sky and the twirls of dark birds. Galaxy thumped away.

Another thing that drew Joanne and her together was the stepfather business. She used to complain about Nick and his kids and Joanne would go on about John and his stinking cowboy boots and how he'd come in late at night from the pub, smelling like a brewery and touching her up. Donna didn't know at the time what Joanne meant exactly by 'touching up'; it didn't happen with Nick. Now it all seemed important.

Joanne's mother always wore too-short skirts, which looked odd on her old, knotty legs. Being a top-heavy woman, she dwindled to broomsticks lower down. She must be in this equation too, Donna thought.

She parked. No sign of Mum's car. She let herself in. No sound from upstairs either; Lee must be out. Dumping her bag on the table, she turned to stare out of the window – and encountered a direct look from Shane. She unlocked the back door and went out to him.

'You're getting on well with it,' she said, pretending to be surveying his work.

'Yer, coming on. How are you then?'

'Fine. You?'

'Yer.'

'Do you want a drink?'

'Thanks.'

She went back in, made two coffees and filched the two remaining chocolate digestives. Mum had this thing about biscuits being full of hydrogenated oils and fats. Mum put the dampers on loads of comfort foods.

She handed Shane his mug and held out the biscuit plate.

'Hands are mucky,' he said.

'Oh, come in and wash them at the sink,' she said without thinking.

Now she had let him in. He was in her mother's kitchen. She tried not to be aware of him near her drying his hands on the striped towel, as though this were a normal scenario and they were just two everyday types having a coffee break.

She could hardly shoo him out after this, so she offered him a seat at the table and they sat facing each other – he with his back to the window and she gazing out.

'Where's your mate?' she asked.

'Left me to finish off.'

'Oh, right.'

'Not done anything like this before – quite nice being in the open air.'

'Yes,' she said.

'You been at the nick?'

'That's right, nothing changes.'

'Places like that don't.'

'They're all still saying they're going to give up – and then three months later, or less, they're back.' She wanted to make him face it, get an idea of what her feelings were. She had the urge to hit out at him because underneath he was probably just the same as the rest, but part of her willed him to be different.

'Yer,' he said, 'that's how it goes.'

She proffered her tobacco tin and he nipped out a pinch. She watched him lining his Rizla. His fingers finicked about, aligning the brown squiggles. Then, as he licked the edge of the paper, his eyes drilled her.

'Do you know,' she said, 'your eyes remind me of Rupert's? He's my cat.'

'Oh,' he said, 'I haven't seen him about.'

She realized she'd made a mistake – Shane didn't know this wasn't her home. 'No,' she said, 'no, you won't. I don't live here.'

'I see. I wondered why you never seemed about much.'

'That's right.' She hoped he wouldn't ask her where she lived – if he did then she could hardly refuse to tell him. Agitation beat up in her. She found those pale eyes fixed on her face. 'I guess you'll be moving on soon,' she said. 'Another job?'

'Yer, the gaffer's got a fair bit of stuff lined up. Just doesn't like paying.'

'Yes,' she said, thinking how she must stop herself erecting barriers each time she found herself in close proximity with a man. Working in a male world had made her cynical but, since the news of Joanne's murder, she'd felt as though a protective layer had been peeled away and now the dangerousness of men was never far from her thoughts.

'He's getting another feller in for the brickwork – we'll be off then. We've just been cleaning up the bricks. Said we'd to use the old bricks.'

'Yes,' she came in, on safe territory, 'it's the original wall and the bricks are a lot nicer than modern ones – not that garish colour.'

'See what you mean – they're like, softer.'

She tried to avoid meeting his eyes again. He was wearing a sweatshirt, so she couldn't see his arms – she wanted to check for needle marks, traces she saw on so many arms.

'Shall you look for something else then?' she said, desperate to keep on ordinary topics.

'Can't get anything else – they don't want to know once they find out you've been in nick.'

Silence fell. They puffed their fags. Donna slid into panic because her mother might appear at any moment and she wouldn't like this – but she couldn't tell Shane that he'd better hurry up and leg it. She wished she hadn't mentioned to her mother that she knew Shane from the prison, but when Mum had asked, How do you know that chap? she'd blurted out the truth.

'Like to come for a drink, then?'

She found her face burning. If she said yes, she might find out more about Joanne's world; if she said no, she would seem to be shunning him. She tried to dismiss the sweetness in his face when he smiled and the way he could switch into a haggard watchfulness. At the same time she wanted to laugh: twice in one day – couldn't one admirer at least have been unconnected with the nick!

The probation notes always said: 'poor self-image'. Poor self-image, as though it were something unnatural, a disease and not a logical outcome of poverty and lack of education, chances in life, everything . . .

Her answer hung for a sweating, panicky, agonizing moment inside her head – and then she exhaled and heard her own voice jollying along in a matter-of-fact way, a way that reminded her of her mother's tone when she dealt with Lee.

'Yes, that would be nice – when were you thinking of?'

'Tonight?'

It would have to be tonight – instant gratification. If he said next week or in two days' time, he'd forget. Her cynicism horrified her. She wasn't a girly girl: no, she was hard, gristly, and didn't believe three quarters of men's guff – a lot of it was patter, for effect, to con you, a come-on.

They arranged to meet at eight thirty at an Irish pub in town. She was glad it was in the city centre because she was less likely to be noticed – but she still felt nervous.

Then he went back outside and not long after, she saw him knocking off for the night.

Now she just wanted to go home, feed Rupert and get ready for the evening. She was sure that this drink with Shane was crazy: it could only lead into an area which could destroy her. If the prison staff found out, she would certainly lose her job, there could be no other outcome; but even if they didn't find out, she still risked becoming enmeshed in the druggie world. Listening to those men day after day sketched in an outline of what went on: the weak were preyed upon, used, squeezed, rendered useless, killed. Everything was up for grabs and nothing could be ruled out; all moral barriers fell.

It was the same from all of them: When you have to have it, see . . . when you've got a rattle on, you have to have it.

Lee came banging in and for once Donna felt relieved to see him. 'Hiya,' she said and grinned at him.

'Have you scoffed the last biscuits?' He scowled.

'What about, Hello, Donna, nice to see you?'

'Yer, yer. Have you then?'

'Lee, hello.'

'Donna, hello . . . satisfied? If I don't get something to eat I'll be sick, don't you understand?'

'If you weren't stoned all the bloody time, you'd not be having the munchies. You just about drive Mum spare, whining after food every minute and being off your face with dope.'

'Give it a rest. I'm fucking ravenous.'

'Watch your mouth, you nerk! I might, just might, make us some cheese on toast. Not that you can't do it yourself, but of course you're the little prince, aren't you? I was forgetting.'

After some ridiculous squabbling, Donna grated Cheddar cheese and placed four slices of bread under the grill. She watched the cheese bubbling and spitting. Lee sat opposite her at the table, and she remembered Shane's light eyes: pale with pupils the size of pinheads. Pinned, the smack addicts called them. Was Shane still using? Lee's eyes were cornflower blue and his pupils were dilated from the cannabis he'd smoked. She supposed he might be quite handsome if he weren't such an uncoordinated yob . . . because yob he was.

'Have you just got up?' she said. She'd assumed Lee was out. Now she realized she'd had a lucky escape – he could have come barging in and seen Shane.

'What is this, an interrogation?'

'Just wondered.'

'Where's Mum?'

'Oh, doing something with the inspection or something. Anyway, I'm off in a minute – things to do. How's school?'

'Crap.'

'How come?'

'That cow Lidell just shoves these handouts in front of you or tells you what page to read in the fucking text book – that's it, that's the lesson. Then she got arsy with me because she said my essay was crap. She's a real cow. I'm sick of it.'

This was a long speech for Lee, who was always very secretive, but Donna only half listened. She couldn't stop worrying about the evening ahead. Now she wanted to cop out of it, say she was ill, anything to escape, but it was too late. If she didn't turn up she'd be bound to run into him again. He wouldn't let her escape. But it'd only take one person on the staff to see her with him and she'd be finished. She saw those pale green Rupert eyes gazing at her, the pillar of his throat, his blond hair, and he was like some fallen angel.

'Must dash,' she said. Lee looked a bit put out.

'You aren't going, are you?'

'Yes, got to – busy.'

*

She drove home in a fever of indecision, running through all the excuses she could think of to disentangle herself from the invitation. She wouldn't turn up, that's what she'd do. Some people were always saying they'd do things and didn't. There was no reason why she couldn't be an unreliable type – but she knew she wasn't. Her mother always said: If you've promised something then you've got to go through with it.

After she'd fed Rupert, made herself another pot of tea and gobbled down some salt and vinegar crisps, she sat glaring at her sunflower clock. Six fifty. She bounded upstairs, with Rupert leaping behind her thinking this was some new game, stripped off and rattled back the curtain over the lines of coat hangers to study her clothes. When she'd selected an outfit – denim battledress top, checked shirt, straight-leg jeans, leather jacket – she dressed, spraying herself with a new musky scent. The next ten minutes she devoted to her face. Sand-coloured wings shaded her eyes, her lashes spiked with mascara. She used a lippy brush to make her lips bloom geranium red. Her hair rose in pink tufts from her scalp. This was her war paint, her shield against the world.

She'd walk into town and get a taxi back. Whatever happened Shane mustn't discover where she lived.

All the evening paper said was that the police were questioning people and that the murder was thought to be drug related. Every time they published a piece about the case, the same picture of Joanne appeared: Joanne in a white T-shirt, smiling into the camera; Joanne with a shadow behind her eyes. It made Donna shiver. She'd searched in the shoeboxes where she kept old school photos and found one of Joanne standing between her and Lisa, beaming at the photographer – not an ordinary smile, because Joanne had bet them she'd pull faces, only at the last minute she didn't do it, and anyway Miss

Thompson shouted at them to stop being silly. All that larking about seemed so innocent.

Donna passed the park. The trees and the play area were in intense shadow. She carried on past the little Italian restaurant, where people sat at the window sipping pre-dinner drinks and chatting. The offy was packed with kids in for cheap litre bottles of rotgut. Lee frequented that place. He could despatch a bottle of the stuff in a few minutes, literally pouring it down his throat. She wondered if her mother really knew how bad he'd got. They'd discussed the cannabis but Donna had told her there was no point in trying to stop him smoking because he had to want to stop it himself first.

She crossed a road well known for its druggie community who sallied forth, particularly in the evening, to beg in front of the supermarket. She cast an interested glance at Gwenap, where models lounged in red PVC minis, rubberized knickers and black lace things. Once when they were about thirteen she'd dared Joanne to go in and look round and of course she had, but had been disappointed because the assistant was quite normal and motherly rather than some wild sex bomb.

On her left now was the tattooist's shop. The owner was good; he'd done some nice stuff for her. She fancied having another design on her arm but she wasn't sure what . . . she just liked the adrenaline buzz that a new tattoo gave her.

Her and Joanne had their first tattoos done together. Donna found herself grinning at the memory. Nobody at home had known what she intended to do. Mum would have freaked out and stopped her. Or she would have pulled one of her crafty tricks: Well, it's entirely up to you, but if you do, then . . . laying on the guilt, which was just as effective as a direct ban. So Donna had stolen out on the sly. In fact, having that tattoo done seemed, when she thought about it, a major landmark: she took her own decision quite independently, did what she wanted to do and wouldn't let anyone stop her. Of course, Joanne started the whole thing off. She thought it'd be a laugh and look stylish. She chose a heart for her upper arm with an arrow through it and a scroll with 'Love' and 'Death', and the tattooist gave Joanne a funny look and said: Are you sure you want them words on, love? At the time the sadness of those words shocked Donna, made her wonder about Joanne.

Having that dragonfly put on her shoulder hurt like hell but she didn't cry out – that would have been babyish. They had lied about their age, not that the chap cared whether they were eighteen or not; he just wanted his money.

When they emerged onto the pavement, Donna began to feel terrified as well as exhilarated, because the time of reckoning was fast approaching and she imagined Mum's face. Only it didn't go like that. She kept the tattoo hidden and her mother didn't spot it until Donna wore a sleeveless T-shirt that summer. In fact, Mum didn't say much at all; Gran was the one who made a fuss.

Joanne never said whether she'd got into trouble over her tattoo, but maybe nobody realized she'd had it done – maybe they didn't care either way.

Lots of the shops en route had turned into charity outlets. They squatted beside the Chinese take-away, the kebab counter, the taxi place that had a notice on the window saying RUNNERS IN WANTED. Donna always wondered what work 'runners in' did. Next came the barber's, a trendy hairdresser's, a boarded-up place, a tat shop, and Readers' Exchange where people could swap their tatty and often porno paperbacks.

Donna tensed as she strode into the city centre. She began glancing around her, nervous at being observed by anybody she knew.

Girls in little vests and minis thronged the nightclub entrance opposite, their arms folded, shivering. Groups of men wearing white shirts and no jackets hung round outside the club eyeing up the girls. Even from across the road Donna could smell scent and men's body sprays; the aura of sex hung heavy in the air. She loved the night-time city streets. Their shoddy glamour drew her in no matter how hard she resisted. The potency was at its strongest when she was fifteen or sixteen and she ventured forth secretly with Joanne. She felt most alive in the rush of the clubs. What was forbidden, hidden, beckoned. Fear deepened its appeal. It was difficult to know where pleasure ended and terror began. But sometimes Donna could dismiss it all as tawdry – she knew it through and through: daft kids posing and geeks whispering clichéd nonsense that irritated and didn't fool.

Only on this night, for some reason, the old pull returned and held her captive.

Perhaps he wouldn't show and then all this nervousness would have been for nothing. She could ring Lisa on her mobile and see if she wanted to come into town for a drink. But he was bound to be there – he'd be able to manage something which didn't demand too long a wait. Instant gratification – no frustration tolerance.

She passed the public lavs and stared up the street, conscious of the pattering of her heart. She took a deep breath.

Just this once, then she wouldn't need to see him again; she could be evasive. But what if she needed to see him? Supposing he really was able to throw light on Joanne's murder? Of course, she could be facing instant dismissal from her job – putting her whole future in the balance.

Her sense of alarm subsided as she strolled up the street to the pub. A burst of Irish music greeted her. She stared into the gloom and found Shane looking at her.

'Hiya, Donna,' he said. 'What are you drinking?'

Should she accept a drink in view of the slave wages he must be getting for his labouring job? But she realized he might feel patronized if she immediately offered to buy the drinks.

'A Malibu and Coke, please,' she said and gave a loopy grin.

She wandered off into a corner and subsided onto a settle against which she rested her back. The sepia twilight of the pub's interior and the wailing lilt in the Irish voices caught at her own feeling of loss, giving her an urge to cry. Her neck tightened with the effort of controlling her tears. The music sang of lost times, suffering, disinheritance . . . Joanne's lost youth, death before she was thirty.

Shane stood in front of her with the drinks.

'Here,' he said, 'you looked a long, long way away.'

'Yes,' she said.

'Cheers!'

'Cheers!' she returned. What the hell were they going to talk about and how on earth would she steer the evening in a useful direction? 'Nice music,' she said, 'but sad.'

'Sure. I don't like to hear too much of it, not with the sort of life I've led.'

Donna wanted to ask what he meant but couldn't. She caught an expression of intense sadness on his face: it aged him, slackened the edgy, blond handsomeness, made his cheekbones jut beneath the skin.

'You did say you come from round here, didn't you?'

'Yer – that's right. Me and a mate used to spend loads of time down by the old factories.'

'I used to twag off as well,' she said, 'with a mate of mine.'

'Wouldn't have thought you'd do something like that, Donna.'

'Ah, well, appearances can be deceptive.'

'I can see you're a bit of a rebel though, what with the hair and the piercings.'

Of course he couldn't see her tattoos and she'd keep quiet about them.

'So what did you do when you twagged off?'

'Have a few blasts with the perfume testers in Boots and try on clothes in the Quay. If we'd not spent our dinner money, buy a drink and sit in a café goggling at everybody.'

'You weren't bad girls, then?'

'Depends what you call "bad girls". We were bad in that we were truanting.'

'I hardly went to school. Didn't like it. Outside was a lot more interesting. It's real good being out in the open. Was on this scheme like, one time. Community Service, actually – planting trees on this estate. I really enjoyed that. But then the kids went and vandalized the trees after. You know, if I could have, I'd have been a forester, sommat after that fashion. Do you like your job then?'

Were his pupils dilated because he'd been smoking dope? At least dope wasn't heroin, she supposed, loads of people smoked it. She lost her train of thought and found him looking at her with a question on his face.

'Sorry – no, I was just thinking about what you were saying. My job, yes, very challenging.' At the mention of 'job' she was back to worrying that somebody from work might see them and she was glad of the gloom.

He kept asking her about herself, what did she think and feel – always edging her into personal things. She laughed a lot and tried to be her laid-back, extrovert self but she watched him all the time.

When she was at the bar, buying the next round, she half turned to get an overview of the other drinkers. Mercifully, they all seemed engrossed in their own conversations.

Their talk drifted onto fathers. He had only seen his dad once and that was in a police cell. 'I'd be about fifteen and this chap was in with me and there was another feller as well. At some point they came for the first chap and the other one says, Eh, that was your dad, you know. I think he got lifed off for murdering some chap in a club.'

'Oh,' Donna said, trying not to betray her horror, 'that can't have been very easy for you.'

'When he told me it was my dad, I didn't want to know.'

'I've not seen my dad since I was little, either,' Donna couldn't help saying. 'I mean, I was a baby when he cleared off. I can understand that you weren't interested – I'm not about mine. If he turned up tomorrow, I'd just think, So what? Do you still see your mum?' She was sounding like her interviewing self: cool, pleasant, detached. If you weren't detached it'd break your heart.

'Nah. Not seen her since I was fifteen and left home. She'd got this new bloke, right. Him and me didn't hit it off – couldn't stand the sight of each other. I had to keep out of the house or he'd belt me, liked to give me a good braying the minute he caught sight of me. He'd a studded leather belt that he used. Well, I got a bit big for that . . .' He laughed.

Donna thought of Nick, her stepfather, Lee's dad. He and her mother had had no time for anyone else – or so it seemed to Donna – and she was useful because she could keep an eye on Lee, who was a total pest when he was little. Then Mum and Nick started rowing – usually about things like who should wash up and clean the house. Nick didn't think he should do anything apart from be there, while Mum worked full-time and was expected to do the domestic round as well. Nick was supposed to be working on a novel, though he groaned incessantly of writers' block and nothing ever came of it. In the arguments, saucepans were thrown, plates got broken, and Nick would retire in an impenetrable sulk. Mum became more and more absent-minded and remote, and everyone snapped at one another.

Disputes centred round mealtimes.

Mum: I have cooked the meal and shopped. Perhaps it wouldn't be too much to ask you to wash up?

Nick: Don't nag. I can't bear it when people nag. It's very destructive. I've told you, I'll wash up when I get round to it. Why do you have to use so many pots anyway? You make the job much harder – using every pan in the fucking kitchen.

The pots would still be piled in the sink next morning.

'Relationships can be a minefield,' Donna found herself saying.

'Too right. You had a bad time then?'

She didn't want to have this sort of conversation with him. 'I suppose so. What about you?'

'I've not always been on the out very much.' He gave a little laugh. 'I mean, I'll just be getting going with someone and then I get nicked and by the time I come out, everything's changed. I was real keen on somebody once, thought a lot about her, but while I was inside she moved in with my best mate.'

He paused and took a swig at his pint. 'She'd come to the visits. I'd spend a week longing to see her, thinking of her all the time, and she never said what was happening. But it's a small world and guys would whisper things: What about her and Andy? Didn't I know? That was the worst – not knowing, the jealousy. It ate me up.'

Sadness shadowed his face again. She could imagine the ferocity of the jealousy. At the end, when Rob was secretly seeing someone else – or she suspected he was – it had obsessed her. She'd run through pictures of him and the mysterious woman as though she were watching a video. Her heart banged, her blood glowed with fever. She could see Shane in the visits hall, gazing across the table at the girl and knowing she was hiding something that he couldn't find out.

'Oh well, it's all water under the bridge now. Andy's always in and out. Things don't change.'

She seized this opportunity. 'Can't he give up then?'

'Nah.' He met her eyes. In the half-light his face was closed in mystery. 'Mind you, a death on smack is one of the nicest deaths.'

'How do you mean?' Sweat broke out on her palms and under her hairline.

'You just drift off. Real peaceful – like dying in your sleep. I've lost four mates with it.'

She wanted to put the question now: Have you stopped using? But even if she asked him, he wouldn't tell her the truth. 'If you really loved that girl, why didn't you stop using smack?'

'She used as well.'

That was it. She wanted to ask where the money came from for the drugs, but something held her back. Here was a short step to prostitution. Did the girl work the streets? Was that how she paid for her heroin? She retreated from the shadowy world full of hints and intimacies where everyone was locked in an opacity of lies and double-dealing.

'But can't love ever defeat addiction?' she said, in a sudden determination to fight her way out of the silence. The question fell into a crooning song of lost love. I've never loved a man, she thought, not ever, and no man has ever really loved me – it came on her in a flash as she waited for his answer. He didn't seem to know what to do with her question and he simply smiled across at her, his opalescent eyes shining.

'I reckon it could,' he said finally and his voice was blurred as a whisper.

Donna's chest burned. She wanted to get out of the bar, away from Shane, and escape.

'Another drink?' he said.

'No, ta. I must make tracks – work tomorrow.'

'Can I take you back, Donna?'

'Thanks for offering but I'll call a cab.'

They were out in the street. The usual groups of lads trailing flags of aftershave were in pursuit of perilously young girls with gleaming stalk legs and little skirts that hugged their bums. Sparks dithered in the sharp air that was mazed with hysterical laughter and the click of stilettos.

'I think I'll not bother phoning, I'll just pick up a cab at the train station,' she told him. 'No need to wait.'

'When do we meet again?' he said.

'Oh, well . . .' The crunch. What did she say, how could she slip out of it?

'Saturday? Here again?'

She couldn't say no. She hadn't achieved anything yet. She'd almost got there, but not quite. Next time she'd be bolder.

'Fine,' she said. 'Eight?'

He nodded. Before anything else could happen, she strode off towards the station. She felt his eyes on her back, watching her.

In the taxi, she relaxed back against the upholstery and tried to work through everything they'd said to each other. She reproached herself for not delving into that shadowy world he must know so well. Next time she wouldn't draw back when there was a question to be put.

8

Each evening Donna bought the paper and scanned it for news of Joanne's case but at the most there were a couple of paragraphs saying that the police were still searching for leads – they hadn't arrested anybody yet. She phoned Lisa and they had long conversations about Joanne.

'She was a nice girl,' Lisa said, 'just a bit mad, wasn't she? Sort of dilly?'

Donna thought back. Yes, she was crazy. 'But only like the rest of us,' she said, wondering.

Joanne seemed to have got stuck in Donna's life. With the usual run of unpleasant stuff, Donna obsessed until she'd consumed it and then its impression faded and she was free once more to junket along. But Joanne's death was different. No matter how much she centred on it, she didn't lose it. Lisa was obviously obsessing about it too.

'I keep saying to myself, if she was a proper drug addict, how did she get that way?'

'She'd have been bored, Lisa, you know what Jo was like, she had to have something going on – and then she'd have met somebody who was using.'

'Well, yeah, but we wouldn't go with people like that, would we? Though at first she might not have known the bloke was a druggie?'

During the day everything trundled along in the same old way with a constant succession of men talking about their addiction, their stories a mixture of longing and self-disgust. The men were in love with the needle, which they referred to as a pin. They fantasized about the needle puncturing their skin and the orgasmic flush of euphoria as the hit struck. After that the gruesome details of the rattle: uncontrollable limbs threshing in withdrawal, vomiting, diarrhoea scouring the bowels and convulsing them in agony . . .

When you have a rattle in here, they just leave you, the men said. You can't know how bad that is. They don't give you owt.

The pin was the centre of their lives; their obsession incredibly boring, banal, lacking in imagination. Yet on another level the nature of obsession itself intrigued – but could you really call it intriguing? What shocked was its absolute power over people and the way it cancelled out all human ties.

As Donna walked to the pub to meet Wes, she worried away at the tales she had heard that day.

Been pinning since I was fifteen. You don't realize that it's taken your life . . .

I've got this three-year-old, beautiful boy, but his mother, well, she's skagged up most of the time and I mean, now I've got clean . . .

The unstated thought: she'd infect him again. It was like a fatal disease, totally contagious and once you had it, it condemned you to a living death.

That was her last client of the day and his parting words were: You see the worst is, I got her to try it in the first place.

Wes smiled across at her from the bar and she joined him there, composing her face.

'What you drinking?'

'Martini lemon, please. I'll go and sit down,' she said,

and made for an unoccupied corner. She caught herself scanning the bar, looking to see if anybody was watching her. This is crazy, she thought. What does it matter? I'm not doing anything wrong.

'Here we are,' Wes said, sliding a drink before her and tossing a bag of plain crisps and one of peanuts onto the table.

'Oh, don't tempt me,' Donna said, 'have to think about this,' and she patted her gut.

'Looks all right to me,' he said, grinning.

'Yes, well, it might to you.'

He offered her one of his Lambert and Butlers.

'No, ta. I roll my own.' She fished her tobacco tin out of her silver rucksack.

'Don't know how you can,' he said, still grinning. 'That's what *they* do.'

'Who?'

'The inmates.'

'Oh, right, so?'

For a couple of seconds he looked a bit at a loss and then it passed and he laughed.

'I keep saying I'll give up,' she said, 'but I haven't got round to it yet.'

'I've started jogging – got to get fit – and after this week I'm quitting this,' he said, staring at the lighted cig in his hand.

'A lot of prisoners say they used to be footballers and rugby players before they took up the pin.'

'Yer,' he said, 'more than likely. They'll not play much football now, will they?'

He told her he'd just split up from his partner. 'We kind of got on one another's nerves. She said I was always on about the nick and she was on about patients – she's a nurse – and she'd be on shifts and knackered all the time or in bed asleep. Anyway, we've called it a day.'

89

Donna reflected that this was what happened when you met someone new: first you had to have a run-down on the story so far and offload the poison of your last partners. Only then were you free to move on. Whole evenings could pass while you enumerated and embellished their monstrous misdemeanours.

'Been living together four years.'

'Right. It ought to have been seven – you know, the seven-year itch.' He'd be moving onto her story soon, she imagined, and she braced herself.

She bought a round of drinks and gave in to several gobbles at the peanuts. Wes had an open friendly face and splendid teeth, which was a distinct advantage. After days of seeing mouths crammed with browning stumps, it was refreshing.

'Do you like working in the nick?' she asked; after all, this was something they had in common.

'Most of the time it bores me silly and then there's the hairy bits and you never know when they'll come, and that can get on your nerves. Then there's being shut in.'

'Yes,' she said, 'yes, being shut in. Sometimes I feel like one of those ponies they used to use down pits. Bloody dire.'

He looked at her. 'You're a funny girl.'

'Woman,' she said and exhaled deeply, smiling.

'Woman, then.'

'Yes, when I come out into the air again, it feels kind of odd at first – makes me see how you could develop a phobia about going outdoors if you'd spent years locked up.'

'It'd be claustrophobia as far as I'm concerned. But you get locking mania. I mean, Kirsty, my ex, she says I've got locking mania – that security is more important to me than anything else.'

'I suppose that can easily happen.'

'I get this nightmare and I wake up sweating – it's that I've left some vital door open and they've all done a runner.

Or I've let the VPs get battered by the C wingers – though between you and me, they do my head in.'

'Anxiety dreams,' she said. 'Tell me about it. Mine is I've parked my car but I can't remember where.' She kept quiet about the one where the walls were caving in and pressing the life out of her.

They had several more drinks, all quite cosy, and then she said, 'Do you think smack addicts ever kick the habit?'

'Nah, once a smack addict, always a smack addict.'

'As simple as that?'

'Oh, yer. They go on those rehabs but it doesn't make a blind bit of difference. I'm not giving a dig at you because, after all, you're the one working with the druggies. Look,' he said, 'let's stop talking shop. Tell me about you.'

She gave a potted version of her past without dwelling on Rob, the Demon King. She could see he was quite interested and even sympathetic.

'I've nearly talked to you quite a few times,' Wes said. 'Noticed you first week here – I've only been at this nick couple of months. You wanted that kid's pad unlocking and that was my chance.'

Donna laughed. It was quite flattering, she supposed, and she was touched by his confession. She couldn't help being drawn in by his openness.

They had come to last orders and the talk still dodged pleasantly along.

'Want to go clubbing?' he asked.

'Why not?'

He called a cab and they whizzed down streets crowded with the ever-present young lads in white shirts and girls with skirts frisking around their buttocks and arms hugging their breasts against the cold; it was a dagger-cold night with a navy-blue sky and no wind. The take-away outlets spilled orange rectangles onto the pavements. The taxi turned into an industrial area with scrap yards and paint factories and builders' merchants and decaying warehouses whose black eyeless sockets gaped at the street. Not a place to walk at night. Donna shivered. She'd told him she wouldn't go to mainstream clubs, the ones where you found the shallow town poseurs. It would have to be the type of club where they played reggae or ska. Music was a major thing for her. He didn't seem to mind but she could see he was a chart type . . . his leather jacket, dark trousers, pale blue shirt and black slip-ons slotted him into that compartment. He'd have a shock if he saw her tattoos. She smiled to herself in the darkness, liking the smell of his aftershave. He hadn't tried to touch her and she didn't know how she'd react if he did.

The taxi ran along for a while beside the river; she could make out the coiling water and the slumped barges and she thought of Shane leaping down onto their decks. When she was fifteen or sixteen and sneaking out with Joanne to nightclubs, a lad they knew got drunk – or so it was said – fell in and drowned.

The bouncers let them into the club with barely a glance. They recognized Donna, and Wes was obviously a respectable citizen with his neat, spotless clothes. He gave the impression of a policeman in plain clothes. They were invariably big chaps in leather jackets or sharp suits, their clothes exact and new-looking, almost as though they were still in uniform, a uniform that had put a permanent stamp on their lives.

More drinks and then they danced. Donna threw herself into it, her hands flying, her shoulders shaking. She was away. Wes stomped about near her, obviously not used to reggae. She could go on all night. The alternating darkness and the shafts of spinning light heightened the pulse of the beat. At some point she realized she was drunk.

Then it was the end of the evening and everybody shoved out into the night and streamed across the black shiny road. Frost sparkled on pavements. Cars swished past. Donna looked up and saw the spangling of stars. Wes took her hand. She knew he would want sex – you did after a long-term relationship collapsed. You were used to sex and you expected it, liked to sink into it after a night out. Although she'd drunk a lot, Donna was quite sure that she didn't want sex with him. She wasn't clear why. For one thing she hadn't been out with him before, but it was more than that – something to do with Joanne, Joanne selling sex: naked sex, sex without love. Sex with Rob had become a habit and there was only one glitch, one deviation from that monogamous state: she got drunk, Rob was away and she'd done it with a chap at a party. It proved to be a frantic, excited grabbing but nothing more. Rob never knew. She lived with her guilt and almost forgot the episode, but now it returned to her. Though that wasn't sex as a commodity, was it? Tendrils of fear twined about her; she felt them constricting her breathing. He could rape her here, it was so isolated. She mustn't think that way. Her heart juddered. She forced her panic down with a show of jauntiness and a resolve to keep him involved in conversation.

'Wes,' she said after they'd been walking for some time, 'Wes, would you ever go with a prostitute?'

He turned a surprised face on her. 'Bloody hell, you must be joking.'

'Why not?' she persisted.

'Think of what you might catch – HIV, Aids, hep C.'

He could list them all. Yes, she would have expected his response. 'But I mean, if it wasn't for the disease angle, you'd have no problem?'

'God, you do say some weird things. I don't know – haven't a clue.' He clearly didn't want to pursue that subject. 'You enjoy dancing, don't you?' he said, smiling.

'Yes, great, love it.'

'Yer, you're a proper wild one. First time I ever saw you in the nick, I thought, She's one on her own. There you were with your pink hair and big boots.'

She sensed this intrigued him. They continued trekking past the warehouses and derelict sites, moving through the shadows and emerging now and then into the orange streetlights. 'I'll call a cab,' he said. 'We'll be walking for miles.'

'But then we'd have to stand here and it might take ages.' Donna looked up at the dense shadow of a warehouse and shuddered. She was back in the afternoon of the newspaper headline and her body was clenched with fear, fear of what a human being might contain. This man might murder her. What was to stop him? He could attack her; nobody would come to her rescue, the place was deserted. She broke out in a wave of clamminess.

'I'm phoning.'

As they stood waiting, he started a conversation about privatization. 'The POA's fighting back, but I mean it's happened in some places.'

She just wanted him to go on talking about work, that way she might survive. Her eyes scanned the road, praying for the sight of the taxi.

'What would you do if you found out privatization was on the cards for us?'

He didn't know. 'No clue how it would affect us – but I've heard from this kid who's in a private prison they get paid less. Plus the conditions of service aren't so good and the regime's different. A lot of us could get made redundant.'

When they'd finally installed themselves in the back of a taxi, he kissed her and moved into a clinch. Through the alcoholic haze, this felt good and she fell into the lushness of it. His leather jacket slid against her flesh and his mouth was hot and wet. A rip-roaring urgency throbbed between her legs and she could have gone with him there and then, but something cold and still dragged her back and she pulled away gasping.

'I think,' she heard herself say, 'we'd better leave it at that.'

His mouth, she could see even in the dark, was smeared with her lipstick. He wiped the back of his hand across it, breathing heavily as if he'd been sprinting.

'If you say so.'

'I do.'

They reached her road. 'Just drop me off here, please,' she said. 'Been a great night.'

'Don't I get to come in?'

'Not tonight,' she said. 'Things to do.'

Then the taxi was gone, coughing into the night.

Rupert met her at the door and rubbed against her legs and she sighed, muttering greetings to him. She flung her jacket over a chair and they thumped upstairs to bed. All she could be bothered to do was visit her newly painted, scarlet bathroom for a pee and to clean her teeth. The removal of make-up would have to wait. Tomorrow she'd regret it when she found brownish singe marks on the sheets. I'm a proper slut, she thought, pulling on the T-shirt and old baggy leggings she'd taken to sleeping in and climbing into bed. Rups was already curled up in a gently breathing, striped orange coil.

No sooner had she got her head down than it started to big-wheel and she shot wide awake. Four a.m. Saturday, later on today she'd be meeting Shane. This was getting a bit complicated. On the one hand, Wes; on the other, Shane. If Wes were to find out she was seeing Shane, he'd no doubt tell the chief of security . . . and if Shane knew she was socializing with Wes, a screw, what then? Her heart banged, her head ached and she felt sick. Hidden behind all this was Joanne, and Joanne didn't go away.

Rup's eyes, those strange, light eyes that reminded her of Shane's, stared at her, as much as to say: What's the matter? Go to sleep, you're disturbing me. He could pick up vibrations and knew she was upset.

She was thankful she hadn't let Wes come in – she must hold him off too.

Once sex entered into a relationship, she always felt that in some way she'd lost control of it. Wes was likeable, quite attractive, but he wasn't her type – at least she didn't think so. Just the fact of his being a prison officer made him suspect; they all seemed to have very rigid ideas.

I'll look bloody grotesque if I don't get some sleep, she thought.

After three quarters of an hour listening to the wailing of the wind in the hawthorn bushes, terrified that a murderer might be waiting to break in, she went downstairs and made herself a mug of tea and a slice of toast and jam. She decided she'd stop trying to sleep: everything was too freaky, too unsettling – pictures kept sliding through her head of decapitated women, women in plastic bags, severed arms floating among weeds in the drains. And if she slept, her dreams might be just as bad. Anyway, she wasn't meeting Shane until evening, so there was lots of time to sleep later: once it got light the house wouldn't be so scary and she might drop off. She went back up with the toast and tea, slid into bed, balanced the tray on her knees and flicked the remote on her portable telly. For some time she watched an old movie; it occurred to her that in the past, in Gran's youth for instance, life must have been a lot simpler. Pondering that, she at last fell asleep. When she woke later the telly was still chattering away.

Ten o'clock. Not bad. She stretched. Sun stole through the crack in the curtains. Rups yawned and showed spiny teeth and his pink emery-board tongue arched. He rewound his tail round his paws and settled back down. She pushed the duvet back and got out of bed. Perhaps she'd walk round to her mother's to clear her head.

The sun glinted on decaying cars. Billy, the macaw who belonged to Lew, stood on his perch in the shop doorway and examined his bendy claws with interest. Donna loved the black markings like laughter lines around his eyes and down his cheeks. His feathers were strike-me-down scarlet and blue reminiscent of her bathroom walls. She fully approved of him. Animals, and more particularly birds, were her passion. Gran's Squawker had set her off on that track. He'd always been there. When she saw the Vs of wild geese flying from the pond in Pearson Park and heard the crake of their voices, shivers shot down her spine. At fourteen, much to Gran's and Nick's annoyance, she'd decided to become a vegetarian. In sixth form biology she landed in trouble because she wouldn't dissect a rat.

On past the stationery shop she went. Sun, oh bliss! She felt like a tortoise shambling out from hibernation, blinking. Summer was the best time of year and today just hinted at it – never mind that tonight there'd perhaps be frost and that on Monday and Tuesday snow flurries and sixty-mile-an-hour winds had blasted so that she could hardly keep upright on her way into the prison.

Last night they'd played a bit of Northern Soul. She hummed Al Wilson's 'Snake'. The lyrics in songs often chimed with her mood, said things to her. And now the music churned in her head, reminding her of Shane.

The woman took pity on the injured snake and invited him into her house to recuperate, then he bit and killed her – the scorpion and the tortoise legend all over again: the tortoise helped the scorpion, who then killed his saviour. Of course it was in the nature of snakes and scorpions to bite and sting. Was that how it was with some people? A rush of coldness made her shudder.

By the time she reached her mother's it was almost midday. She resolved that if Shane was still working on the wall, she'd renege on the evening with him. How would she phrase it? Oh, I say, Shane, sorry about tonight, I can't make it after all. Something's just cropped up.

She wasn't a good liar; she was too straightforward. She sweated as she strode up the avenue, past the Victorian fountain where cast-iron mermaids held conch shells aloft. The mermaids – fish women – had implacable faces. They wouldn't have taken pity on the snake; they'd have drowned him more like, just dragged him down with them five fathoms under where he couldn't inflict any further damage. Are people born implacable or does life make them that way?

Donna paused in the rambling front garden to smell the viburnum. Hundreds of tiny bells made up blooms the size of a fist. Their scent was deep and sweet and searching like that of hyacinths.

Nobody seemed to be about at first. Then she heard some banging about upstairs and Lee emerged, his face bleary. 'What time is it?' he groaned.

'After twelve.'

'I knew it. Those bastards have woken me up – fucking noise!'

'Ooh, handbag, handbag!' Donna said fluttering her right wrist.

'S'all right for you.'

'I beg your pardon. Some of us actually work.'

'Oh, don't tell me.'

'Where's Mum?'

'How should I know?'

'Look, Lee, just be a bit civilized. You haven't even said hello.'

'Hello, Donna!' he chirped in a high, prissy voice.

'Hello, Lee. I'm going to look for Mum. She's probably on the allotment.'

Donna clattered through the house, taking a deep breath as she approached the kitchen door. She braced herself for the sight of Shane . . . but no. Outside the kitchen window she saw a small cement mixer and two different men laying bricks. Already the wall stood several feet high. So he must have finished his part of the job; he'd said he couldn't lay bricks. Perhaps he wouldn't turn up tonight.

She went out the back door and made for the allotment at the bottom of the garden. More viburnum and daffodils stabbed the border with brightness. Through the gap in the fence, and in front of her lay the patchwork of plots, surrounded by a circle of sycamores and the backs of houses so that they seemed like some magic island. Donna had always loved the place.

Her mother dug, head down, expression concentrated.

'Hiya, Mum!' Donna yelled.

'Oh, hello, love.' Her mother looked vaguely shocked at first. 'How are things?'

'Too much to drink last night but otherwise not bad,' Donna said, taking in her mother's old jeans and saggy grey sweatshirt.

'Ah . . .' She stopped, blew her nose and focused on her. Donna couldn't read the expression on her mother's face.

'What's up?'

'Well, actually, Donna, I was wanting to have a chat with you.'

What could this be? Donna didn't remember anything similar since she was a teenager.

At that point they heard a hoarse squawking coming from the gap in the garden fence and Lee came into view, his garments flapping and his shaven head a shine.

'What are you two doing? Is there any food?'

'Just a minute.'

'Mum,' Donna said, irritated, 'you shouldn't pander to him. He'll never get himself together at this rate.'

'I'm starving.'

'All right, all right.'

'What did you want to ask me?' Donna asked.

'It's OK, love. We'll talk later.'

'Lee,' Donna bellowed, 'you are a total pest.'

'Who's handbagging now!' he chortled and hopped away up the garden.

'You'll catch your death,' her mother pronounced, while Donna seethed with exasperation and suspense. It was always the same – particularly with Gran. Whenever she saw Gran or spoke to her on the phone, Gran's first words were: How's Lee? What's that boy doing? Life fell into two distinct periods: before and after the Nuisance.

In the 'before' period she sometimes used to stay over at Gran's during the holidays and Gran would take her shopping down Hessle Road to Boyes, a shop full of interesting bargains: discounted designer gear, piles of knickers and bras you could rummage through. Gran scratted through slippery scarlet and black underwear, holding knickers up with a practised hand, running her fingers along the fabric. Toys overflowed counters and hung from the ceiling. It was like a gigantic bazaar. Down Hessle Road they'd trundle, past the pawnshop and the stalls where fruit and veg tumbled onto the pavement. They would visit Gran's friend Ivy, and Donna would sit sipping a lemonade through a straw and licking the jam out of the centre of a biscuit while she listened to Gran and Ivy discussing forbidden, exciting things.

In the 'after' period that exciting, off-beat Hessle Road world had vanished. Driving past now, she'd seen shops barricaded with scrolled-down metal grilles at their windows.

A lot of them stood empty. Gran didn't go down there any more. Hessle Road had lost its pull and whoever was left spent their time fortifying their property against druggie hordes, tramps and vandals. Lee, she thought, in his irritating stoned haze just seemed part of it all.

9

Maggie knew she'd have to get Lee fed and watered or he'd continue to whine and pester and she'd never be able to have a word with Donna, which she wasn't going to enjoy – Donna could be very spiky sometimes.

'Oh God, Ma, I don't want anything greasy.'

'Well, what do you want, Lee?'

'Tell me what there is.'

'Beans on toast.'

'I always have beans on toast.'

'Scrambled egg, boiled egg, bacon . . .'

'Why can't you stuff some cornflakes down your gob?' Donna snorted, wild with irritation. 'You're a spoilt little scrote.'

They heard the flipping of the letter flap in the front door. 'The postman,' Donna said. 'He's late.' Maggie noticed how she flinched, and then strode to the front door to retrieve the letter. 'It's for you, Mum.'

Maggie looked at the headed notepaper. More trouble.

'Lee,' she said, 'this is from your school, about your attendance. I've got to go in and see them.'

Lee growled and began to fume. 'I've told you that woman's a cow – says I'm no good and I'll never pass.'

Maggie began whipping eggs in a basin and stirring them in a pan. Two pieces of bread in the toaster. Hey presto, scrambled egg on toast. She slid the plate towards

Lee, who started eating while still on a fulminating jag. Maggie had become adept at the use of such ploys. With Lee everything had to be indirect; full-on confrontation achieved nothing.

'I'm going to have to answer this letter.'

Donna always complained that Lee was a spoilt brat, but she didn't appreciate that bringing up lads on your own wasn't easy. You always let him get away with things, she said. He's not stupid, just bone idle. Maybe Donna was right, but Lee was in a teenage rebel phase. It was all perfectly normal, only . . .

'I've told you, they're all wankers.'

'And you enjoy shocking them. You and I are going to have to have a talk about this.'

His answer was to drum his fingers on the table and nod his head to some inner rhythm.

'Going round to Jasy's,' he said, jerking up from the table and almost tipping milk over.

'Some time there might be some revision. And I meant what I said about the talk.'

'Might there!' He gave a smile. 'Chill! See yous.'

'What about the washing-up?' Donna shouted.

'A little job for you.'

'You must be joking, you scrote. I never got away with stuff like this.'

'Tonight, if you want any supper, it'll have to be fish and chips brought in by you,' Maggie called. She simply hadn't time at the moment to be dreaming up some dish which he might leave or scoff to the last morsel, even scraping the dish, you could never tell.

He exited, still chuntering.

Maggie listened to the stairs reverberating under his heavy boots as he blundered for his room.

'They're sixty quid a throw, those Caterpillar boots, easy, little bastard,' Donna grumbled.

'Honestly, Donna, that boy really infuriates me. I know there's going to be big trouble at the school, all because of his truanting, and then the drugs. I'm so worried about him – he just doesn't care.'

Maggie had lain awake a lot of the night, listening for Lee. He went out at times when most people would be going to bed. She'd had show-downs with him in the past, but she couldn't keep on having scenes; that way she'd alienate him entirely and he might never be able to find his way back. Like that poor Joanne dying: there was a girl who'd run right off the rails because nobody cared enough. Am *I* caring enough? she wondered. Could I have helped her more? Should I have reported her mother to the NSPCC? But surely children were better with their families, unless they proved totally horrific. The bruises on her arm, what had they meant?

'Mum, you can't do anything – he has to sort things out himself. He'll stop when he's a mind to. Your telling him to stop won't make any difference. He has to *feel* it and until he does, there won't be any stopping him.'

'But it might be too late then. I can't just stand by and watch him going crazy.'

'I know, but unless he wants to co-operate, nothing can change.'

'I'm just hoping the school don't know about all the cannabis he smokes, because if they suspect it, he'll be out on his ear and bang go his A levels. They just think he's lazy, I assume. I'm not going to enjoy the interview with his teacher.'

'Bloody hell, Mum, I don't know what to else to say . . .'

'I'd better stop thinking about it – the whole business depresses me too much.'

'OK. So what did you want to talk to me about?'

'Oh, yes. Look, Donna, when those chaps were repairing the wall and you were chatting with one of them, you said you knew him from the prison. That has worried me quite a lot ever since. You seemed so matey somehow and –'

'Mum, for God's sake, just because I talk to someone I know from inside – it's no big deal.'

'Yes, I know, but I keep thinking about Joanne – her murder's changed everything somehow. I'm suddenly aware of all these dangers. I think to myself, there you are, constantly exposed to threats of all kinds, simply because you work in the prison.'

'If these men are going to be rehabilitated they've got to be absorbed into the non-criminal world.'

Listening to Donna, Maggie thought she heard herself talking, only now this wasn't theoretical, it was nearer to home. Donna was bridling already and really there was nothing more to be said. Her head pounded and she felt disconnected from the day. Why were her kids so difficult? She sensed that her whole family was lurching towards an awful crisis from which nothing could deflect it. Abruptly, Donna swung round and Maggie watched her leap out of her chair and rush to the kitchen window, then she was out into the garden. Maggie continued to sit at the table, exhausted, but then, hearing voices, she stood up too and followed her. Two men advanced up the lawn. They had come through the gap in the fence which led to the allotments. One might have been in his forties, the other was much younger.

'This is private property,' she could hear Donna shouting. 'You're trespassing.'

'Well, love, my aunty sent us down, she wants her allotment fencing.'

'This is private property and you have no business here and if you don't leave now, I'm calling the police.'

Maggie was outside in time to see the men turning tail and retreating through the gap in the fence, forced out by Donna's fury.

'What on earth's happening?' Maggie said.

'Aunty's fence, my foot! They know damned well that there's no fencing on council allotments. No, they'd just come to see what they could nick. They'll be druggies. Mum, you're going to have to get that gap closed off.'

'This is all I need. I'm just sick and tired of it. Oh, don't bother about the blessed fence – I'll get round to it some time. I've too much to worry about to tackle that now. Things are too desperate at work,' Maggie said. 'God, I've got such a headache, right over my left eye. No, this inspection thing has driven everybody crazy. I mean we've been on special measures for ages. We're all pulling our guts out with it but when the kids truant all the time and the head's an idiot what can you do? And there's so much violence – every week something. Now, to cap it all, those two chancers have shown up. It's what I was saying, you're working with these people and it makes me frightened for you.' Maggie looked at Donna but she received one of Donna's I'm-cheering-Mumsie-up, bracing smiles.

'Mum, you're too dramatic. It'll be fine.'

'I just hope you're right,' Maggie said, zigzags of light shooting down her left eye – this was going to be a fully fledged migraine.

'I'll have to get home – things to do. But first I want to see what we can do to barricade the gap at least.'

'Honestly, love, I'll sort it eventually. But stay for lunch.'

'Ta, but better get off. Remember what I've said about the gap, Mum. You don't want them getting anywhere near the house.'

'All right, Don, but don't forget what I've said to you now, will you?'

Maggie stood at the door watching Donna's figure dwindle down the avenue. Once she turned and waved and gave a cheeky smile, and Maggie found her eyes full of tears. How would it be if you could never wave your daughter off again – if she'd disappeared off the face of the earth, been battered to death? She'd always felt that she and Donna had a special bond: Tom, Donna's father, had been the love of her life and sometimes a way Donna had of smiling, even the shape of her hands, would bring Tom back. Children weren't in his scheme of things – he wanted to pursue an academic career. When she was abandoned with baby Donna in that London flat, Maggie had felt that the two of them were together against the rest of the world. Having to come home had hurt; London had been her escape and she'd never intended to live back in Hull.

Maggie turned back into the house, still trying to throw off the shadow of the past – she'd made a conscious policy over the years of never regretting anything. For all their sakes she had to keep steady. No good collapsing now with everything about her toppling and lurching.

10

Out in the street Donna heard the grinding of the police helicopter as it dithered. Sometimes it woke her in the night, sounding so loud she almost expected it to land on the roof. People liked to complain about it: Taxpayers' money, that's what they squander it on. Who do they ever catch? Every time they have the thing out it costs thousands. No point in phoning the pigs if you get robbed.

She sauntered down the tree-lined avenue, staring in at the gardens. Three mallards squatted on the grass verge in a patch of sunlight. They must have flown there from the pond in the park. The males' green and blue plush feathers flashed with white and black; the tortoiseshell female wasn't half as dramatic as her companions.

Joanne and she used to sit on the swings, flying up into the air so high they could see people way over the trees on the other side of the road. They visited the shabby overgrown conservatory, a strange lush place, to gawp at the exotic birds, and wandered in the green gloom staring at the banana trees (could they pinch the weeny bananas forming?) and the palms, whose fronds pressed up under the glass roof. It was green and mossy and fragrant. Sometimes weird men skulked in there and the parky stared at them pointedly until they moved on. Couples sat on the benches snogging, lads with their hands up girls' skirts and girls writhing with pleasure, pretending to be completely unaware of passers-by. When they came out of the conservatory it felt as though they'd left a tropical island to emerge into a land of scabby grass and chill winds.

Then they'd roamed without feeling scared. Nowadays, Donna realized, it was different. A few years ago a group of lads beat Lee up in the park and he hobbled back home practically incoherent, with mud all over his clothes and a black eye and cut lip. The yobs had also nicked his bike. He'd had his bike snatched on several occasions and even with a massive lock it wasn't secure – they'd go at it with bolt cutters.

In the Joanne days they played in the bushes and kicked a ball across the grass, and the parky, a big, lanky chap with a navy blue traffic-warden's cap, yelled at them for hiding in the shrubberies: Come out of there, you lasses, I can see you. He banged a stick at the rhododendrons and they ran away giggling fit to bust with Joanne screaming that she'd wet herself.

On one side of the road stood well-kept family houses, Victorian terraces, their front gardens bright with daffodils and sometimes magnolia trees aglow with buds opening into pearl lightbulbs, viburnum, lily-of-the-valley, mauvy-blue periwinkle. But on the other side the gardens were swallowed up by raggy privet hedges and rank grass. Rows of doorbells studded the walls by the doorways: multi-occupancy places, benefit-dweller territory.

As Donna passed, three scrawny, raddled dogs barked at one another. They had shot out onto the bay outside the upper windows and sniffed and snarled at the air. They needed regular food and exercise instead of being confined up there on the roof of a window. She called to a man who appeared at the open window. 'Are you sure your dogs are all right?' No response. She hesitated and almost rang one of the doorbells but didn't. A police car was parked in the road. Probably some drugs saga, she thought resignedly. She went by the house where a chap had grown cannabis under the roof and somehow managed to set fire to the place when the electric wiring shorted. It was still being repaired.

At the bottom of the avenue she turned left to go past the second-hand shop. Billy stared at her from his perch on the pavement and pecked at his claws in a fastidious fashion.

'Hiya,' she said. He didn't respond but continued with his preening. She lingered in Skeltons, trying to decide between a malted wheat loaf and a Danish white with its shiny golden-brown crust. The potato, leek and cheese pasties looked inviting but that way lay calories, cellulite and a huge bum. In the end, she succumbed and bought two, together with a small malted wheat loaf.

Worry about the evening griped her stomach: would Shane turn up and, if he did, what would happen? She was frightened about where this might lead. Mum might be right, she ought not to take chances. Were the blokes in the garden part of the dodgy builder's network? Tonight she must listen carefully to what Shane said, watch out for an opportunity to bring up Joanne's story. She shuddered, hearing the whispering in her head of all those half-heard tales of women battered and mutilated.

When she got home there was a message on her answerphone. Lisa's sobbing voice: 'I think Andy's having it off with somebody – I've told him to find somewhere else to live.' Crying blotted out the end of the message. Donna sighed. Lisa had lived with Andy for about six years and they were always up and down, but this sounded more final.

Donna phoned Lisa back – after all, what were mates for? Lisa cried into the phone.

'I'll come round, Lise, be there in a minute. Got anything to eat? OK, I'll bring something.'

Lisa's face was puffy and pink with crying. Donna made a pot of tea and put the pasties in the oven to warm, while she scattered some prepared salad on two plates.

'He's cleared off.'

'Well, you told him to.'

'Yes, but –'

'You need a breathing space.'

'I'm frightened he'll come back and wreck the place while I'm at work.'

Donna pictured Andy, his red boozy face and his hectoring way when he'd been drinking – it was quite on the cards that he could turn on Lisa. 'Can't you change the locks?'

'No, it's a double-glazed door with integral locks – it'd be too expensive.'

'Are you sure he's having an affair?'

'Well, twice he's said it was a boys' night and I shouldn't come along and then his mate told me it wasn't. I can't ask him. And then there's all this drinking. It's become like a pattern, Don. I mean every time I get home after a day slogging my guts out at work I find him pissed as a newt sprottling on the settee, cans all round him and telly on. I gave him an ultimatum. Oh, yes, he said, he'll get back to work, but he's hurt his back. Fucking back, my arse! And he can get very funny over little things – if he can't find his rugby shirt or his boxers aren't clean, he goes spare.'

After promising to ring later, and telling Lisa that if Andy were to turn up and cause trouble, she should spend the night at her house, Donna left.

Late afternoon now and nerves were clenching Donna's stomach. Perhaps he wouldn't turn up. She couldn't compete with smack and if he was back on it, he'd be out robbing or shooting up. Maybe he was the one the police helicopter was after? No, of course not. He wouldn't know anything about that . . . she was kidding herself about her anxieties.

*

Six thirty and she tried on various combinations of clothes – in the end it was khaki cargo pants and a striped candy-pink and khaki top, a battery of blazing earrings both drops and studs, and her lovely big boots with their metal insets and decorations. She adored those boots. Gran said she had a shoe fetish – though she'd not like Donna's prize boots. Donna wondered whether this was something a person could inherit; perhaps it was embedded in the genes like blue eyes and big noses? When she was little Gran had some scarlet stilettos that Donna enjoyed stroking, gazing at the way the shoe fronts plunged and ended in an oblique point. She loved to follow the spike of the heel with her fingers.

She took the bus into town, arriving dead on eight, and made for the pub. The evening had turned cold again and silver stars spotted the sky. Donna felt the acute edge of the night and shivered. If he didn't turn up, she'd wait a while, have a half of lager or something and then clear off.

He was there already, spotted her and walked over. She hadn't time to think.

'Hiya,' he said, moving up close. 'What would you like to drink?'

'It's all right,' she said, 'I'll get them.'

'No, come on, Donna, I'm not a beggar.'

'OK, half of lager, please.'

When he went to the bar, she glanced about the pub trying to make out the faces of people gathered round the tables or standing chatting in groups. Was there anybody she knew or who would know her?

From the back Shane was just a good-looking bloke in black chinos and black sweater. You would have no idea about his other life. If this were true of him, what about all these other people in here? What were they hiding? She looked away just in time to avoid meeting his eyes as he returned with the drinks.

'Oh, great, thanks,' she said. He sat down beside her.

'Cheers,' they said in unison. Then silence into which a voice sang about the green hills of home.

'How've you been?' he said.

'Fine.' She wanted to tell him about the two men in the garden just to gauge his reaction, but she didn't know how to start. 'Well,' she said eventually, 'there was a mini-drama this afternoon. Two chaps came into my mum's back garden, obviously on the nick.'

'Oh,' he said. She watched his face for signs of embarrassment but could see none.

'I told them to clear off – I was furious.'

'Yes,' he said, giving nothing away, and grinning.

'I'd be very upset if anybody broke into my mum's.' She couldn't say any more without it sounding like an accusation.

'I bet you scared 'em,' he said and laughed.

She didn't know how to interpret that. 'Why, am I such a monster?'

'You can be quite tough.'

'Oh, come off it.' She found herself laughing now too. 'Surely I'm not as awful as that.'

'Bad enough.' He was still laughing.

'Well, men can be so obtuse.'

'What's that when it's at home?'

'Pass. So what have you been getting up to – or shouldn't I ask?' She kept her tone light.

'Worked this morning.'

'What sort of work?'

'Clearing a building out and dumping the rubbish.'

'Sounds fun.'

'Was filthy – full of crap.'

'You can't go on with this sort of temporary work indefinitely, can you? I mean, from what you say the boss just hires and fires at random. You need something proper, don't you?'

'Can't get anything – not with my record.'

'What about Nacro?'

'Nah.'

Then they got to talking about their early lives again, speculating how things might have been quite different.

'I thought you might not want to know me, Donna, with you having seen me inside.'

Her throat tensed and her mouth felt dry. His talking like this made it difficult for her, because it was partly true.

'Yes, well, it isn't too easy but we'll not go into that. Tell me something,' she said, concentrating on a matchstick so she wouldn't have to look at him, 'why do so many men in the nick say, after a while on the out, they can't wait to get back in the nick again?'

'It's the robbing and shooting up routine gets so boring. There isn't anything else.'

'Just such a waste,' she said, looking at him. 'If you want to know, it makes me mad.'

'You don't know anything about it,' he said. His voice was low and smooth, making Donna flush.

'I've got a pretty good idea.'

Their eyes met. His glinted like a blade.

'I'll tell you something,' she blurted out. 'I get utterly fed up with the hopelessness of it – all this floundering about.' She felt herself vibrating with anger. He didn't say anything. 'Let's get out of here,' she said, surprising herself, 'and have a walk down by the pier. I could do with some fresh air.'

'Cool you off,' he said, with a bleak smile.

'That's about right. If you want to know, which you probably don't, because I've already told you, it makes me feel so angry and useless.'

They strode out, past the public lavs and ran into the usual groups of kids. The evening bumped with chart music pumping from a pillared stone building next to the library, once a reading room, now a nightclub. Two bouncers glared out at the street.

She wanted to reach the pier where the ferry used to cross to New Holland. Gran often told her about travelling across on her wedding day with trawlerman Billy. Thinking of Gran and Billy and the weaselling of the water calmed her.

They walked by King William on his golden horse at the back of Holy Trinity Church and along Lowgate, where the banks had been turned into nightclubs and eateries, and the city darkened.

As they were waiting for the lights to change at a crossing, a blond woman called out. 'Hiya, Shane,' she said, coming forward out of the shadows. 'Where you off to?'

'Hi, Jade. Just out for a stroll,' Shane said, looking a bit taken aback.

'Not clubbin', then?'

'No.'

'Introduce me, then,' Donna said, grinning.

'My sister, Jade, Jade, Donna.'

Jade's scent flaunted itself. Her skinny black dress clung to her figure and in the orangey light her skin shone like white gloss paint and her mouth was a red gash. Thin and wasted-looking, she tottered on her high stilettos.

'Must ger on,' Jade said and turned away, her attention focusing on a black Mercedes.

'Right, take care,' Shane said.

'Nice to have met you,' Donna called.

Jade didn't reply. Donna's head swarmed with questions. She tried to keep cool, working out the obvious conclusion from what she'd just seen.

'She seemed nice,' she tried.

'Yer, she's got a good heart.'

'You never mentioned her before.'

'No, well, I didn't see her for ages, did I? After I left home, like. She's not had it easy – got three bairns.'

'Goodness,' Donna said, knowing she sounded like her mother.

'Yer, not at all easy.'

They crossed the renovated square and Donna went to stand by a low wall facing the estuary. The wind coming off the water smelled of ozone and open spaces, a fishiness. She concentrated on the slapping and sishing of the waves on planks and stone.

'She must struggle if there's no bloke to help as well. It was hard for my mum my dad clearing off – we were always short of money when I was a kid,' Donna mused. 'And of course there was only me for ages. Your sister's got three to provide for.'

'Mind you, she's better off without some of the men she's had. They were bastards like my dad and if he turned up, I'd tell him to go fuck himself, if you'll excuse my language.'

'That's all right. It's how it goes.'

'Want another drink?'

'Come on, then.' Donna felt a lightening of her spirits. 'Drown our sorrows.'

They walked across the cobbles and into the Minerva. As usual, Donna had a good look round. She bought the drinks this time and they managed to find a spot by the bay window. Enjoyment at being near the water seized her; she loved feeling it just out there. Most of the time she hardly thought about it, but tonight it seemed important. She felt its blend of wildness and peace: it could kill, it could restore. Gran could tell stories about the sea, stories she'd listened to since she was little; Gran believed that the sea birds were really the souls of dead mariners. She told her tales of seances where the medium communed with

Mary, the Red Indian guide in the spirit world, and then gave out messages in an eldritch, piping voice. Mum used to hush Gran: You'll scare her stiff with all that stuff, Mum, she said. It's all old wives' tales, anyway. But Donna loved to hear them. They made the goose pimples rise on her arms, particularly the one that your husband would drown if you did the washing before he went to sea; nor must you ever go down to the quay to wave him off.

'You feeling better now?' Shane said.

'Yes, I am – funny what a bit of sea air can do for you.'

They started walking back after last orders had been called.

There was something comfortably relaxing about Shane. She liked his easy way. Tonight she could believe he was what he seemed to be, though she wanted to keep a distance between them. She mustn't get emotionally involved: it'd be too dangerous, could wreck her. The very thought brought a clamminess to her chest and armpits. But when she glanced at the side of his face, she was caught in an eddy of attraction. He was pale in the shifting illumination from the streetlights and his strong cheekbones lent him a remote, sharply etched appearance.

A moon dangled over the city. They walked through the old town, where the clubs and restaurants buzzed. The streets were a collage of laughter, heels clicking on flags, long shiny legs and lipsticked mouths, gelled hair and white shirts.

At a corner people spilled out of a club onto the street and for a scratch of a second she thought she saw a vaguely familiar face and shuddered. She searched her memory. Was it a prison officer, a former inmate, or just someone she'd met in a different sphere of life? She kept going. Perhaps she'd just imagined it. She couldn't mention it to Shane; it would tie her into complicity with him.

'Sure you don't want to get a taxi?' he said.

'Oh, no, I'm all right walking for a bit, thanks.'

'What about dropping by mine for a coffee? It's crap, like, but you're welcome.'

She ought not to do this. If she went with him, she would see where he lived. She could ask about Jade – she might find out other things, be able to ask questions.

'OK, thanks, I'll drop by yours for a while,' she said, the drink making it easier to agree.

Shane lived near the city centre in an area of old houses. Gran said her nan had told her that in the 1890s the doctors, solicitors, wealthy businessmen lived there. Somewhere in the seedy tackiness vestiges of the splendour still lingered. Donna noticed pillared fronts, big bay windows, curved lintels with noble façades, curlicues. Part of this street had been renovated, the houses done up by graduates from architectural college wanting to restore panelled doors, rip out the hideous flushed monstrosities. They wrenched out lowered ceilings to expose handsome ceiling roses, tried to return the splendour of the past, but they were beaten back – Donna knew because the mother of one of her mates told her the story of how in the end they'd sold up and quit the area. They couldn't win against the incursion of the druggies, so the reclamation stopped.

Donna glanced around her – late at night it looked ordinary enough, except for the young men slinking by, in beanies or baseball caps, moving in the shadows . . . but then you could see that anywhere. Lee and his cronies might look the same on their night-time prowlings.

They walked slightly apart, not touching – they'd never touched. Donna was very aware of this and she knew he must be. She struggled with shock waves of attraction and revulsion: he was a druggie, injecting, might be still.

Lots of prison inmates now had HIV – he could even have Aids. She couldn't just put it to one side. There couldn't be any innocent fumblings; everything was loaded.

Joanne might have come down here with a boyfriend – it'd have been exciting in the beginning, a way of escaping the boringness of the everyday. Did she walk down this street, flinching at shadows? Once the drugs had got hold, she'd have been desperate, desperate for unconsciousness because she couldn't cope with the reality of living. She'd have been so far gone that the day-to-day surprises – the exhilaration of a spring morning, the call of the wild ducks in flight, or a ginger cat sprottling on her feet at night – none of these small, perfect things could call her back.

'We're here,' Shane said, stopping before one of the big houses.

Discoloured curtains, more like sheets, were tacked across the bay windows on the ground floor. The front garden was a little square of bricks, broken bottles and tufty grass. Donna glanced at it as she mounted the stone steps, and then stared at the array of doorbells.

He turned his Yale key in the lock. A naked bulb drooping on a long wire illuminated the hall. She smelled urine, damp, rot. He climbed the long staircase, which would once have been imposing. The wallpaper was a greasy beige spotted with damp. Up she went after him. Closed doors. Sounds of telly sometimes, then a woman's voice shrieking and a deeper male voice answering, whether in fun or misery she couldn't tell. He paused two floors up and unlocked a door. His room was just a single bed, a telly on a low table, two easy chairs and a wardrobe, one of those huge, old-fashioned ones that turn up in the sale rooms – in fact it still bore the auction number on it – and a chest of drawers on which squatted a small expensive music centre. No pictures, nothing personal.

She let her eyes shoot about for signs: silver paper, needles, discoloured spoons . . . she dared not think what else. He put on a small lamp by the bed and the room was warmed by a tired orange cosiness. She shivered. He noticed and put on the gas fire.

'Sorry. It's always freezing in here but I've got used to it.'

'Have you?'

'Yer.' He grinned. 'Right, so you're up for a coffee, are you, Donna?'

'Yes, please, two sugars.'

He went into an adjoining room. She sat down in an armchair and waited, spooked by the place and wondering what she was doing there.

'That all right?' He handed her a chipped mug.

'Thanks, this'll wake me up a bit.'

'You all right?'

'Yes, fine, just had a smidgin too much maybe. What about you?'

'Great,' he said, 'it's been a great night. You aren't in a rush, are you? I mean, you can stay for a bit, can't you? It's early.'

Donna found her voice coming out too quickly. 'Oh, it's nice of you . . . but I'll have to get moving, it's late, really. Anyway, can't leave my cat – he pines.'

'Go on!'

'I'm not kidding. Rups will be waiting for me, he does.'

'I always wanted a pet – a dog, a cat. Never did have, though.'

The conversation dried up. Donna tried another tack. 'I'm intrigued by your sister. Tell me about her.'

'What is there to tell?'

'She looks incredibly young to have three children.'

'Boyfriends – she got caught real early on, like, when she was fifteen. They've always been wankers, the ones she's been with. She got put in care, right, when our mam took up with some guy. To tell you the truth, I don't know all that much about what happened when I cleared off, because she's seven years younger than me and she was still at home.'

Donna had an urge to ask another question but could not; embarrassment held her back, but something else as well – she didn't know whether she wanted to hear the truth.

He sat opposite her in the other armchair. 'You got a boyfriend then, Donna?' he said, smiling but intent.

'No,' she said, 'not at the moment.'

'Just had to find out whether the coast was clear.'

'Oh, did you!' She laughed – it started as a gruffish bark and turned into a hysterical titter. He was infected by it and laughed too.

'You're a hard nut to crack,' he said.

'You don't dish out compliments, Shane.'

'It's meant to be a compliment.'

She finished her coffee. 'Look, I'd best be going home. I'll ring for a taxi on my mobile.'

'They'll not come down here at night.'

'You don't mean it.'

'I do. They don't want to get mixed up with druggies. I'll walk you to the road.'

'I'll be all right. It's OK,' Donna said, knowing she'd be terrified.

'No way are you going back down there on your own. I'm taking you.'

They stood together and her skin shocked at the electricity leaping off his body. Excitement jostled with fear in her belly and a pulse throbbed between her legs. She wanted to work out why in God's name she was so attracted to him when she didn't want to be. The difference between neutrality and attraction was a nanosecond: at first there was nothing and then this tingling awareness.

He led the way back to the main road and waited beside her while she called a taxi. When it pulled up, he turned to her, grinning. 'Give me your number, Donna, and then I'll take you somewhere nice.'

She told him and he wrote it on his hand with her Biro. Fool, fool, she thought. I shouldn't be doing this.

11

Ruby gave Maggie's doorbell a good blast. The house vibrated with noise, which poured from somewhere upstairs. That would be Lee, bound to be, doing that business with records and the turntable things. What a racket! Why was it that lads always had to make a din or they felt they weren't living?

In the old days the doors were never locked – people just walked in. She gave another press on the bell. Not surprising Maggie couldn't hear. Then Ruby saw a figure moving behind the leaded lights in the top half of the door.

'Oh, Mum, there you are. Lovely to see you.'

Ruby received a hug and a mouth on her cheek. 'Didn't think you'd ever hear me with that racket going on.'

'Oh yes, Lee . . . I'm through in the back. Now then, cuppa? Got some teacakes in – like a toasted teacake?'

'Go on, then.'

Ruby surveyed the room. The place was always so messy – papers, magazines, books, coats, stuff in pots on the windowsills making sticky marks on the window and dropping black splodges, smudges on cabinets and on the light switches. Ivy's lass had spent thousands on a fitted kitchen but it was a beauty: all white and beige and not a speck to be seen – no mess, no crumbs, no grease. But Maggie didn't care, never had, and never would. She'd never cared as a kiddy either. When she got bought new things, she never had them five minutes before they were marked. There was that lovely little jacket – she went out in it and when she came back, she'd spilled blackcurrant or something on it and it was ruined. The stain wouldn't come out.

'They've about finished the wall, then,' Ruby said, glancing through the side window.

'Yes, it's all right, isn't it?'

'Donna's been round – bought me a lovely new handbag, bless her. But I keep wondering about that girl, Maggie.'

'How do you mean, Mum?'

'She's too pale and she keeps talking about that friend of hers, the lass who got murdered. It's shocking, but I never did think that girl was up to any good.'

Ruby couldn't forget that time when it had been Donna's birthday and they all went out for the day to Flamingo Land. Donna had insisted on inviting best friend Joanne. That Nick, Lee's dad, had still been around then and he'd driven them there. He'd been just like Ernie, cursing if he got jammed behind another car on the narrow roads – he had to be at the head of the queue no matter what. Of course, when they got there the kids went mad. Mark and Helen, Nick's kiddies by another woman, must have been there as well. Joanne shrieked the loudest; she wanted to go on all the rides. Lee was just a baby, but really demanding and cranky. The smell of burgers and fat burning had got on Ruby's stomach and made her feel sick. When she thought of that day it was always of that queasy smell and Joanne going missing. It was Mark who found her at the finish, when they'd been searching for an hour; she'd been away with a group of lads somewhere. Nick was mad at being held up and Ruby noted, even then, there'd be trouble wherever that girl went. Maggie dismissed her premonitions with: She just wants attention. It's a big family and she probably doesn't get enough at home.

'I'm sure Donna's all right, Mum. She was round here too as a matter of fact. She keeps telling me I must get a gate put at the bottom of the garden – two men appeared on the lawn, you see, and Donna thinks they were on the rob.'

Ruby felt Maggie was being far too casual about it – but then she always was, there was an excuse every time: poor deprived this and that, can't help it. 'Yes, you should, people can see right across here. They'll be in like a shot, and once they get in, they come back and back. Ivy told me about her grandbairn's home.' Ruby developed the theme. She maintained that National Service ought to be brought back to stop lads thieving. Ernie would have said that too. We fought for such as them, he'd say. In the old days the lads went to sea and once they'd done a trip on trawlers, when they came back, they knew how to behave.

'Yes, Mum,' Maggie said and Ruby could tell she wasn't listening.

'What's the matter, lass?' she said.

'Oh, nothing really.'

'So what's nothing then?'

'Just the inspection and everything. It's all been a quite a week and I mean the ramifications of it are tremendous. In the end we might find we've no jobs, but I hope to God it won't come to that . . . it's just the pressure all the time.'

'Yes. You've been talking about this inspection business a long time.'

Maggie got wired into all the complications. Ruby didn't understand why the inspectors couldn't get kids to behave better – they didn't seem to achieve anything except to give the teachers high blood pressure. She tried to concentrate on what Maggie was telling her but lost track and retired into her own thoughts – she reckoned she'd maybe ring Ivy up and suggest bingo on Monday.

'I hope Donna's not had any more of them tattoos done,' Ruby said, hoping a new topic would divert Maggie from the inspection. 'She never tells me, because she knows what I'll have to say.'

'No, I don't think so.'

Maggie still looked as though she was hiding something; Ruby had always been able to tell. She remembered when Maggie rang up that time and talked nonsense for half an hour while Ruby waited in dread and impatience for what she really wanted to say. Finally it came out: she'd gone and married that Tom, who Ruby had never met. It had all been London then; she'd no time to be seeing folks at home, wanted to live there permanently. Maggie was always ashamed of where she came from. Not smart enough for her. She'd got some very funny ideas.

'What about Lee?' Ruby asked.

'Well, I've got to go down to school.'

Ruby listened to the news about the letter and Lee's truanting. She sniffed. 'Why can't he stop looking like a convict? Don't you ever tell him?'

'Mum, there's no point.'

'You've never been strict enough. He runs rings round you.'

'Mum, kids reach a certain age and they have to rebel – it's how they are. It's growing up.'

'It looks like bad behaviour to me.' Ruby snorted and chewed on her toasted teacake, which was rather burnt. 'He'll never get a job looking like an escapee from a prison or a loony bin.'

'Kids have to be allowed to experiment.'

'Oh, you young people – can't tell you anything.'

'Mum, I'm middle aged.'

'Hmph!' Ruby slumped over her mug. They didn't even have cups and saucers nowadays. 'I'd just about got fed up with trying to get you on the phone, lass. You're either cooking and you can't speak or there's that answer thingy – and I'm not using that.'

'Sorry, Mum, but it's dead easy to leave a message – just talk as though I'm on the other end.'

'Well, I shan't.'

The noise from upstairs ceased and Ruby heard the stairs shuddering under pounding feet. The door burst open.

'Oh, hi, Gran.'

Ruby surveyed her lanky, bald-pated grandson, who grinned at her from the doorway. He really did resemble some asylum inmate, what with his shorn head and his awful baggy clothes.

'Mum, is there any food?'

'But you've only just had something.'

'That was ages ago.'

'Maggie, he's a growing boy. They need plenty.' Ruby could trace vestiges of Ernie in Lee – the shape of the face, a bend in the nose. These reminders both disconcerted and reassured her. When she looked at Maggie she often felt no link whatsoever. Head always in a book studying, not interested in anything, and the university business. Then off she went to London and when she'd come back in the holidays she'd been somebody else – even started talking posh. Since then it'd been no different. Maggie was just herself, somebody who hadn't a past. Well, what's wrong with that? was what Maggie would think.

Just as strange, though, were the times when she watched or listened to Donna and saw herself as she'd been all those years ago, with Billy dead and the war changing everything – it was sparkly one minute and shocking the next and she was confused. The girl had the same excitement in her and the sadness. When such glimpses opened up, Ruby wanted to say something to the lass, tell her it would all work out, be for the best – but she wasn't sure how to go about it.

'I'll do you something, then.'

'Not beans on toast or scrambled egg or –'

'Just wait and see.'

'How are your studies?' Ruby asked.

'All right.'

'You'll be finishing soon then, will you?'

'Could be.' He shifted his feet in their enormous boots.

Of course Ernie wasn't as tall as Lee and, being a grown man, he was much broader. Ernie had had style. He'd bought a big flash car with huge frog-eye headlamps and a walnut dashboard. It had a hood that pulled back and the leather seats gave off a whiff of luxury. When he came to call, all the kids in the street darted out and swarmed round to admire it. Ruby catapulted into a moment of remembering – that car, her and Ernie in the front seat, was just round the corner . . .

They motored out to the coast, down narrow lanes where the pink campions and purple cranesbill spotted the high hedgerows and everywhere smelled of wild honeysuckle and dogroses. On the beach they scrunched along the blue and grey pebbled shore and watched the waves breaking.

Going back in the dusk, he drove off the road into a concealed cutting and there in the froggy car they squirmed around on the seats as he pulled her knickers down and unbuttoned his flies. Then he eased over her and she had the rank odour of dead nettles and the sweetness of meadowsweet in her nostrils. She closed up with fear that someone might come by and discover them, but the thought of it caused her pulse to race. He hurt her as he thrust and then came the sudden sharp smell of bleach when he subsided against her.

That must have been the night Maggie was conceived. No wonder she was such a gypsyish woman, what with her trailing skirts and her lived-in clothes. She was never a pretty little girl – just messy and wild and rebellious. It would have been nice to have a daughter who behaved in a girly way, was a proper daughter.

The pictures dissolved as the present sliced through them and Ruby had to make herself attend to what Maggie was saying.

Maggie had evidently put a big pizza in the oven. 'You'll have some, won't you, Mum?' she said.

Ruby sniffed. Maggie liked to use this new-fangled bought stuff. Ruby supposed she didn't do much proper cooking – well, she never had been interested in domestic things. That was why the house looked such a tip.

'Might as well.'

'How long will it be?' Lee hovered in the doorway.

'About ten minutes.'

For a while Ruby had thought she couldn't have children. When she found she was pregnant, she couldn't believe it. At work in the sweet factory she wore loose clothing and complained of a bilious attack when she had to rush out to the lavatories.

Ernie's response to the news was, Oh, well, right, well, I see. And he went on to tell her that he couldn't marry her because he was married already and had four kiddies.

These sorts of details she wouldn't ever tell Maggie or Donna.

Ruby had kept quiet while he did his remorseful act; she knew with him the art lay in not carrying on scenes for too long, because that could make him lose patience. You had to know the precise point to withdraw the pressure. Go on too long and he'd make you feel guilty – you became the aggressor, the one in the wrong.

They all sat down to pizza with salad and malted brown bread. There was a white cob for Lee who refused to eat brown bread.

'She always wants to feed me healthy stuff,' he remarked to Ruby. 'Yuck!'

Ruby could understand his reluctance to eat some of those bean and seed things that Maggie went in for when she had time. If not she used bought stuff that was just as bad. What was wrong with roast beef and Yorkshires? Steak and onion pie, steak and kidney pudding? Maggie didn't know what a proper dinner was.

'We never get any real meat in this house,' Lee moaned.

'You'll have to come and see me, lad,' Ruby said. 'I'll cook you a nice bit of steak.' Maggie was frowning. Two parallel lines furrowed her forehead just above the bridge of her nose. 'You need feeding up,' Ruby told him.

'That's right,' Lee jumped in, pulling faces and watching his mum for a response, but she controlled herself and didn't say anything.

'Has Donna got herself a boyfriend yet?' Ruby asked. She did wonder whether Donna talked more to Maggie than she would let on to her.

'Not that I know of,' Maggie said. 'She hasn't mentioned anybody to me, anyway.'

Lee shovelled down his food in a flash and vanished upstairs, emitting noises like water burping down a plughole.

'I'll run you back, Mum,' Maggie said.

'What's the matter, Maggie, trying to shuffle me off, are you? Want to be rid of me?' Ruby studied her daughter.

'It'll save you a long journey if I take you – it's as simple as that.'

Ruby suspected Maggie had some ulterior motive for taking her home. She seemed very preoccupied.

'I do have some marking and prep to do for Monday – can't be caught flat-footed.'

'If that's how you want it . . .'

'Stop it, Mum, you know very well what it's like so there's no point in trying to manufacture something from nothing.'

Ruby realized she wasn't going to find out, not that day anyway, so she might as well accept the lift.

12

Donna tried to focus on the man sitting in front of her. Mick Wright. He was her age but looked a lot older. His teeth were gappy and decaying.

'Been usin' for years, like, but I know if I ger out there again like, and I don't stop, it'll kill me. It takes your life over.'

He told the same story; the story they all told. Donna could see how it must be: this need cancelled out everything else. The power of it terrified her. She could imagine how it ate the heart and soul out of them, leaving them doddering wrecks. It paralysed their will and took away any strength they might have.

He'd got his first fix from his older brother, now dead. In fact it was his brother's death which decided him to seek help.

'I can't go on, not like this, not any more.' His eyes stared at her, round with desperation.

At this point the door banged open and a prison officer barged in. Donna jumped with shock. 'Sorry about this,' the man said. 'I need Wright.'

'We haven't finished,' she said.

'Sorry, love, but I have to take him.'

The officer disappeared with Mick Wright in tow. Trying to reassure the prisoner, Donna called after him that yes, they'd continue the interview later on. She wondered what the urgency could be. Outside her office, she caught an officer on the landing just locking a cell door.

'What's happening?' she asked.

'Lock down. Somebody's missing.'

She spotted Wes coming down from the fours. 'What's the matter?' she whispered. 'Is somebody really missing?'

'No,' he said in an undertone, 'it's just an exercise to keep us up to scratch. Everybody's belting round like headless chickens. They're supposed to be looking for McKeogh and he's in reception having a coffee.'

'So what are we supposed to do?'

'We've to keep rushing round. You can kick your heels in the air. Enjoy the liberty!'

She hadn't seen him since their evening out and felt slightly embarrassed. She could tell from the way he looked at her that his thoughts were caught up with that evening and, more specifically, the moments in the taxi. Her armpits dampened. Get out of this, she told herself.

'It just means the work will pile up,' she said, pulling a face. 'What a pratting waste of time this is.'

He grinned. 'Yer, but if we don't practise and it does happen, we'll be in for it.'

'So you tell me.' She pulled an even worse face and his grin widened.

She remembered him describing the long boring stretches of work punctuated by incidents when everything began to skid out of control. You certainly never really relaxed. You might kid yourself that you did, but you didn't. You listened, watched, found your shoulders just about hitting your ears. You saw how laughter could switch into aggression before you'd caught your breath.

'You coming out with me again?'

'Might.'

'Don't sound so keen.'

'Oh, I'm just raring to go,' she said and gave a dirty great guffaw. Why oh why am I playing this dodgy game? she asked herself, feeling the hotness in her cheeks. But if I don't, he might get arsy with me. Anyway, he can be a friend, can't he? I don't need to make a big thing about it, needn't go any further than that.

A voice bellowed from the ones and Wes took off to investigate. The lock down meant that the wing was very quiet. Soon, she supposed, they'd start the count, which would mean looking into each cell to check who was there. She clomped back to her office and stared at the computer screen for a while, cursing to herself, then tapped out several reports.

She was still churning over two things that had happened the previous day. Her first interview had been with Gary Grayson, a chap in his mid-thirties. From his records she'd built up a picture of a chaotic person always overdosing. She'd spent ages doing this to prepare a report to prove that he desperately needed a rehab place. She'd known that if he didn't get on one, he'd be left to relapse when he was released after having been clean for two years in prison. She could see Gary's harrowed face when she'd had to tell him his application had been knocked back yet again. He'd seemed to shrink into himself. When she entered the interview room his face had been open with expectation – then she'd told him and a blind came down.

It happened again and again. She'd fill in forms for a man to get on a rehab, the assessment officer – a social worker who had to present his or her findings to an interview panel, which decided whether to recommend money for the rehab – would come on a special visit to assess the prisoner and, after another lengthy wait, a knock back would arrive. The men were shattered by it.

They gave up hope; they'd received what amounted to a death sentence in some cases. But what could you expect? The city didn't have an independent purse for providing residential care for drug users; no, the money had to be divided between them and the elderly. The chief criterion was always supposed to be need – and who could really make decisions about that?

Donna lit another roll-up, trying to calm down. The whole thing made her fume. What was the point in applying for any more rehabs, when the results depressed the men so deeply? She couldn't stand to see their hopelessness. Watch them getting locked ever deeper into resignation.

Another incident had disturbed her in the afternoon. She had a chap for interview sitting before her in the little room, not an officer in sight. She had opened his file and was going through it, asking him questions, when she realized that he was the instigator of a riot in another jail, and had just been shipped in. The officers must have known who he was, but hadn't bothered to warn her. Her heart banged. She went through the confidentiality stuff, asked as usual what he wanted from the service, got him to fill in and sign a couple of forms – all the time desperate to have the interview over and done with. When she was finally alone in the interview room, she sat for several minutes slumped with exhaustion.

Her thoughts turned to Shane. He hadn't rung. She expected him to immediately after their date at the Minerva but there was nothing. Just silence. This ought to have pleased her, but it didn't. Did it mean that he was gouching somewhere – drifting, full of smack. She thought the very word, gouching, sounded ugly. Of course if he really was trying to go straight, then he'd be hard at work.

You could imagine dying in one of those decaying rooms on the street where he lived, just lying on a springless sofa and floating away with the brown juice pulsating through your bloodstream and blotting out the sad wallpaper and the mildewed curtains and putting you to sleep for ever. It's an easy death, he said.

Had Joanne toyed with the idea of such a death? Or had she been too sucked down into the routine of shooting up, gouching, earning her drug money on the streets to have time for such thoughts? Still no reports in the newspaper. Everything seemed to have gone quiet. The police were 'following up leads'. What leads?

Dreams from last night flooded the now of the prison. Donna was sitting opposite Joanne in a pub somewhere. Joanne kept pushing at the broken heel of one of her white stilettos. Look at these stupid shoes, she said. I knew they were crap when I got 'em. I'll just walk barefoot. Like my nail varnish? Nicked it from this shop. She laughed and her eyes drew into slits. Donna laughed too, shocked but impressed. Joanne didn't know how to say no. If somebody offered her a dare, she took it on, had to. Dare you to jump in the dock. Dare you to swing on that rope. Dare you to climb into that haunted house. And she did. In the derelict property she came face to face with a wino. He reared up and ran at her with his fists but she screeched at him and laughed fit to bust so that he fell back, muttering obscenities.

Only Joanne wasn't really there. The dream peeled away and the sense of a live Joanne faded, leaving Donna with a curious feeling. It was as though Joanne must be around somewhere, perhaps in a parallel world, the sort of thing she'd read about in sci-fi novels. She shuddered.

After lunch she was about to leave the wing when a man slipped out of an open cell and positioned himself in front of her. She pretended she was unaware of him. When it became obvious that he wouldn't give way, she said, 'Excuse me, please.' He still didn't budge. 'You must think

I'm thinner than I am,' she said, trying to make light of it. 'I'd have to go on a diet to get past you.'

The sound of her voice and her eyes fixed on his face seemed to activate him. He stared back at her with hungry eyes but moved aside a fraction. She had her key in the lock as he made a grab at her, trying to drag her towards his cell, but she was already through the gate and the iron bars grazed his hand. An officer standing a few feet away blinked and seemed to wake up. Later, a colleague on the drugs team told her that the prisoner had been declared a danger to women, and she'd only found out by chance.

'Nobody bothered to mention it to me. It's almost like the bastards want us to get hurt,' Donna said.

An hour after the brush with the prisoner, she was at a briefing from the chief security officer. He had expressionless, parroty eyes. Donna, sitting two rows from the front, found him staring at her. She started to sweat. Had someone tipped him off about her seeing Shane? Was he trying to make her uneasy so that she'd give herself away? She let her gaze slip over his right shoulder and pretended to be concentrating. Her fear eased away.

There was the usual routine stuff. Don't let the inmates get a clear sight of your keys: some could easily be copied. Next, he produced various implements – which had been discovered in prisoners' cells; staff must keep a close check on any equipment. Then there followed instructions in the event of a hostage taking: you mustn't scream, call out, or draw attention to yourself because that could cost lives. You must stay calm and let the inmate talk, establish a dialogue. She had a strong impulse to put up her hand and tell him that she'd found a distinct lack of support from a number of his officers and that she'd experienced situations with an unacceptable level of potential threat. But of course she didn't. She listened to the pounding of her heart and kept quiet.

After her initial fear at the start of the briefing, Donna had daydreamed until the head of security got to hostage taking. It reminded her of times when, during interviews, she'd felt frightened but stifled it by thinking about Rups. She'd visualize him, a gently purring, hairy shape on her windowsill, peering down into her garden, and the panic would fade. It was all about concentration. Though she couldn't imagine how thinking about Rups would help her keep calm if she was actually taken hostage.

She lost the track of the lecture again because she began to wonder whether she liked being scared. As someone who had always enjoyed scary films and Stephen King books, she must get some sort of adrenaline rush from it. But in books and films she was in control; in real-life situations it was different. Joanne, of course, had been up for those as well. Donna suddenly felt cold in the stuffy room. The security chief was staring at her. She cleared her throat and picked her nails, shifted on the chair, wondered what she'd just missed.

They filed out. The afternoon was over. Hours and hours locked away in the fortress. She couldn't wait to escape. All you heard were doors clanging shut; keys grating; hoarse shouts; radios whining; the hollow ringing of boots on landings; cell alarms buzzing; sometimes the banging and clattering of an inmate smashing up his cell. Then there was the stench: the rancid, feet-body odour; the leaden metallic waft from heating pipes and ducts and cutting gusts of air when outer doors were unlocked down in the bowels of the prison.

It was cloying; she wanted rid of it and longed to be out of doors in the wind.

As antidote for her foul mood she drove into the city centre, parked her car and made for the Quay and her favourite shop. She could spend and spend on clothes, no problem, and the basement of this cut-price store selling catalogue ends of lines was paradise. Her mother couldn't stand the place. She was overwhelmed by the row upon row of clothes, not prepared to sort through them for the gem. But Donna liked the hunt. She could pass hours trawling through shrill orange numbers, lopsided purple garments, things with crooked seams, all in search of the miraculous, which must be there somewhere. The other incentive, a powerful one too, was the price – knockdown prices meant she could buy on impulse and reject soon after.

Donna cast a rapid eye over the water wrinkling in the old dock and entered the glass walkway that sloped up into the centre, where the shops rose in tiers, linked by looping escalators. A wonderland for kids twagging off from school. They could lounge on the seats or lean on the rails staring at the people passing up and down on the escalators, eyeing each other up.

She stood in the doorway of the store and looked with satisfaction at the mad array of rails. Off she went, her fingers nipping between harsh polyester, smooth nylon, and other man-made fibres. She pounced on some fluffy brushed cotton – but damn, nunty through and through. A minuscule velvety skirt, leopard print – wow, this was it! She held it up against her thighs, consulted the label. She might get into it. Some stone-coloured cargo pants looked promising. She fingered the material, inspected the seams. She couldn't afford more new clothes really, what with the mortgage and everything, but what the hell!

When she'd just about made up her mind to buy both garments, she saw a bleached face, one she recognized instantly: Jade, Shane's sister. The woman from the street noticed her too and stared across.

'Hi,' Donna called, 'found any bargains?'

Jade seemed to relax, and smiled. 'There's a load of crap in here – you have to know what you're looking for.'

'Sure, but it's fun.'

'Got anything?'

'Yes, look.' Donna joined her on the other side of the rails.

'Nice one! That's a great skirt.'

'Just what I thought. Want a coffee?'

Jade looked slightly fazed and then said, 'Oh, right, go on then, ta.'

Donna left the shop with Jade in a state of controlled excitement. She had no idea what Jade and she could talk about but it didn't matter – something had to come of this encounter.

'Two cappuccinos, please, and two toasted teacakes.'

Donna offered Jade her tobacco tin.

'No, ta, I smoke these.' Jade produced a packet of Benson and Hedges. 'When I'm rich, that is.'

'Oh, it's like that, is it? Won't go slumming with me!' Donna laughed. Jade's face unclenched.

'I can't stay long,' Jade said. 'Have to see to the bairns before I go to work.'

'I'm just on my way home from work, actually.'

'Right.' Jade looked vague and inhaled deeply. Donna stared at her hands. Jade's nail varnish, chipped at the edges, accentuated the extreme curves of her nails and turned them into claws.

'You known Shane long?'

The question thumped into the silence. Around them grey-haired ladies shared gossip over Danish pastries and coffee, all pleasant and companionable. This was different. Donna hadn't expected Jade to take the initiative like this.

'Not really.'

'Oh, right . . . well, just wondered.'

'Don't you get to see him often?'

'Not that much. I'm a bit busy, see . . . what with work and everything. You know.'

'Yes,' Donna said, but she didn't know at all.

'Did he tell you anything about me, then?'

'Only that you've got three children.'

'Yer, the bairns – Katie, Sheralee and Scott.'

'That's nice.' What the hell could she say?

'It costs. You've no bairns?'

'No.'

'Right.' Jade's eyes shifted about, while her left hand fiddled with her B&H packet and her right hand clutched her cig. It was as though she wanted to say something but didn't feel able. 'I'd best shove off. Ta for the coffee.'

'Cheers. See you soon.'

Jade tottered off in her stilettos and cream leather jacket. She could have been pretty if she wasn't so skinny. Donna decided that although she'd like to shed a few pounds, no way would she want to be like that.

No sooner had Donna arrived home, greeted Rupert and forked some rabbit and chicken in jelly into his blue and white dish, than her mobile rang.

'Hiya, Donna – it's me. How are you?'

'Fine. I just had a coffee with your sister, Shane.'

'Oh, right.' She fancied she heard a slight hesitation. 'How come?'

'Ran into her in town.'

'Nice one. Now then, are you up for a drink tonight?'

'Tonight? I've only just got in . . . I couldn't get sorted until about eightish.' Eventually she agreed to meet him at the Irish pub as before, but as soon as she had put the phone down, a wave of panic washed over her. What if one of the prison staff saw her? She knew that meeting him like this was taking a risk, but she couldn't stop herself: she was hooked by his haggard face and the stream of compacted energy that came off him. And then there was Joanne's voice whispering . . .

Staring at the fit of her new skirt in the mirror, she found herself back with Joanne – Joanne never seemed to leave her. The smack would have made her pale and hollow cheeked like the addicts who returned to prison. I'd have died if they hadn't brought us back in, they told her. That picture slid over the one of the pretty plump teenager who'd do anything for a dare.

Donna's mobile pinged again. Lisa. 'Hi, Don, er, how are things?' The fact that she was putting this question must mean that she was all right, which implied she was back with Andy. Donna mumbled 'fine' and waited, contemplating her reflection in her bedroom mirror, which was festooned with long ropes of sandalwood and glass beads.

'Er . . . Andy's here. We're OK – for now, anyway.'

Fool, Donna thought, it'll go wrong again, bound to with a wuss like him. But she didn't say it, of course – you wouldn't to Lisa. Instead, she said, 'Great. Catch you later. Take care, mind how you go,' and rang off.

For a couple of seconds she paused, thinking about what she'd just said: Take care. Mind how you go.

It sounded as though she considered the world a very dangerous place, where only the worst could happen. Well, that was right, she did think so. Look what happened to Joanne; her body, crazily battered, found behind garages in a ten foot in all the oil spills and filth. But if you really let yourself dwell on it, you could be completely unnerved and start barricading yourself in your home. Andy was the sort of man who could just blow up, and when he'd been drinking, he might lose it. Men always said they didn't mean to after they'd murdered a woman. He wouldn't mean to batter Lisa, but he might. The sheer scariness of Lisa's situation brought her out in a sweat. She'd told Andy off once about how he was carrying on and it hadn't done any good. Later, when Lisa had got back with him, she'd accused Donna of going over the top.

She walked into town, striding out in her Docs and wearing her new cargo pants and her scarlet fleece, which clashed marvellously with her sea-anemone hair.

No sign of him yet, so she went up to the bar and bought a modest half of lager. She sipped her drink, feeling slightly disappointed. The next thing she knew, he was at her side.

'Looking sad,' he said. 'Sorry I'm late.'

'Oh, that's all right.' She flashed him a smile and twiddled one of her earrings. 'So what's new?'

'Nothing much.'

'Listen, I've been thinking about you . . .'

He'd fetched drinks from the bar, and the conversation continued.

'I'm glad you've been thinking about me,' he said, smiling.

'You might have second thoughts when I tell you why.'

'Try me.'

'I just wondered if you did any exams or anything at school.'

'Nah, never took 'em – I wasn't that sort of kid.'

'There's loads of different courses people can go on at the college in town – know where I mean?'

'What, with my background!'

'Look, Shane, for heaven's sake, don't give up before you've even tried.'

'Well, I might.'

'Why don't you say "I will"?'

'You're a tough nut – told you before. You want to save me, don't you?'

'Save': that was a strange word to use and she paused, turning it over. She heard her mother say: There's a certain kind of woman who always thinks she can save men and it invariably ends in disaster, because you can't change people – they'll do what they will do.

'I don't know about that. I just thought it'd be good if you got a chance –'

'So you're going to smarten me up a tad, eh?' He was smiling and she relaxed. She saw the tense watchfulness clinging about him fade, saw him cut clear of it. She was in that minute with the glass in her hand and his eyes smiling at her.

He kidded her about her hair, told her he liked it; liked the way she was, sparky, unusual. This could be a good evening and she knew it: she was happy; she wasn't moiling over the past but had let it go.

He took her hand, turned it palm up and traced the lines with his index finger. It seemed an incredibly intimate gesture and she felt the colour flood her cheeks. She couldn't look at him.

Then, when they'd been in the pub a couple of hours, she happened to look up and thought she saw Wes in the gloom. The shock pulled her up sharply.

'Hell's teeth, Shane, I'll have to be off.'

He looked surprised.

'I promised my mother I'd call round at hers and it'll be too late if I don't go now.' She extricated herself and pelted to the taxi rank.

Safely back home, she started to tremble. Had she blown it? Was that Wes? If it was then he'd be bound to say something – he must have recognized Shane. Prison faces weren't ones you forgot; they engraved themselves in your head. But she didn't want to treat Shane like a leper just because his drug habit had landed him behind bars.

She flicked the telly on and half watched a wildlife programme, something about predators. The commentary yanked her back to Joanne . . . predators lying in wait, prowling. But women were mostly murdered by people they knew. Her pimp, somebody she relied on, could have killed her because he thought she wasn't handing over enough cash. Perhaps she worked without a pimp. Donna imagined, as so often before, Joanne climbing into an unknown man's car, being driven away outside Hull, not suspecting that this was to be the end, that he'd suddenly strangle her and dump her body . . . Was it her daredevil side that had let her go night after night with strange drivers? Just being out in dark streets could give Donna the jitters, let alone going with strangers.

13

On the Saturday before her mother's birthday, after four days of sea fret, cod-grey sky and temperatures of seven or eight centigrade, Donna woke to see the sun prising at the bedroom curtains and to feel a delicious warmth. Rups stretched, yawned and exposed his rough pink tongue and white needlepoint teeth. Her mobile pinged. Shane. Would she like to go for a ride to the coast with him that afternoon? He'd bought a second-hand car. The shadowy pall of Joanne's dreadful death lifted. She'd get out into the open air and see the sun.

She thought of sea and sand and pebbles and she said yes.

She arranged for Shane to pick her up by the parrot man's shop. She still felt she mustn't let him see where she lived. In the meantime, she rushed out and bought some rolls, Cheddar cheese with a bite to it and four tomatoes for the picnic.

Dead on twelve thirty Shane pulled up outside the shop. The first hot day, a really hot May day. Donna grinned with pleasure. Today it was combats, a little black hooded top and a scarlet vest. She'd sung along to Galaxy all morning and was in a rare good humour. On her feet were her new flowered Docs – scarlet flowers of course, with yellow centres. She wanted to run and leap and skip and do crazy things. This was a day she had waited for all winter.

'Hiya,' she said.

'Hi. You getting in, then?'

'You bet.'

'Like your boots.'

'Ta. Not bad, are they? They make me feel happy.'

'Right. Now, where are we off to?'

'The moon.'

'OK, the moon it is, if the old banger will make it!'

They drove through the city centre, past row upon row of small shops, Golden Touch places where kids played the gambling machines, cut-price clothes outlets, charity shops, second-hand car lots, East Hull swimming baths . . . on and on across traffic lights, by a big square police station. Gradually the closed-in area widened out and gave way to bungalows, the sort with crazy paving and plaster gnomes in their front gardens and windmills and wishing wells, an odd assortment of buildings with none of the dignity of the 1890s yellow-brick terraces.

Donna didn't like this end of the city. It wasn't like her place at all; a foreign conglomeration of straggling houses and little newsagents, all conventional and ugly-cosy. But then at last they were out, passing farmers' fields and clumps of horsechestnut trees and sycamores, flat, low-lying country with redbrick farmsteads. Water glistened on surfaces, oddly out of place, and gulls boated on it. The earth was dark brown, moist like Christmas cake.

With the windows wound down, smells of grass and fertilizer drifted in. Donna relaxed, her head thrown back. Galaxy trilled on the car radio, music alternating with rough, chirpy voices. Shane drove fast and sometimes the car banged down an incline and whined round sharp corners.

He parked at Aldborough and they set off to walk to the cliff top. Donna shrugged out of her hooded top and fastened the arms round her waist. The sun warmed her face and she luxuriated in the unexpected heat.

'If we find a good spot, we can have the nosh,' she said. 'I love picnics, do you?'

'I haven't really had any,' he said, smiling at her. 'There was the one time when I was a little kid in one of the homes that my mam put us in. We got taken to Withernsea or somewhere and I was clouted for wandering off. The sandwiches tasted like grit.'

'Shane, you are a poor lost boyo.'

'Are you going to take me in then, Donna?' He gave her a teasing smile.

'No way. Lost boyos are slippery geeks.' She flinched away and began to run, while he chased after her. The rucksack with the food in it bounced on her back and she laughed until she coughed. He came up panting and roaring. 'Idiot, idiot,' she squeaked. He had hold of her forearms but let go as she pulled away. 'Come on, lost boyo, I'm hungry.'

While he was fooling about, she couldn't help noticing the scars on his arms, partially hidden by tattoos. The sight of them sent an icy dart into her chest, but she let it melt in the pleasure of the day. She told herself she didn't have to think about it now – it belonged in another compartment of his life.

They walked through tufty grass and a warm wind blew in their faces from the sea. Before them stretched the water, a misty blue expanse fading into grey on the horizon.

The path they'd been following brought them out where the cliff fell steeply away. Below them was a fringe of rocks on which the sea crashed and spumed. Donna watched the waves breaking on the spindles and falling back again in froth.

'It makes you realize about erosion, doesn't it?' she said.

'Sure, there was sommat about that hotel falling in, wasn't there?'

'Yes. Funny to think that all this will be washed away one day.'

The only sounds were the mewing of the gulls and the sea striking the rocks.

'Where shall we sit?' she said, looking about.

'A bit further along maybe.'

They found a less exposed gully of tufty grass and Donna eased the rucksack off and stretched her arms wide. 'Lovely, lovely world,' she breathed. 'Total, total bliss!'

He looked at her and smiled.

'Come on, let's get on with the food.' She unwrapped the sandwiches and handed him some.

'Cool,' he said, 'ta,' and started to eat.

They sat there munching and gazing out to sea.

'The North Sea never looks calm,' Donna said. 'Imagine the trawlers sailing out there for Iceland.'

'I think my grandad was a trawlerman, that's why we grew up round Hessle Road,' Shane said.

'Mine was as well. Just think, if we'd still had a fishing industry, you might be out there now. It's weird that we've both got our roots in Hessle Road. I can remember going there with Gran when I was little and her pointing out the chapel where she got married and telling me about the fishermen's statue and about all the people who lived in her street – and it was like something really precious had vanished.'

'Maybe it has.'

He didn't say any more after that. Donna watched an impenetrable expression cross his face and the icy spike stabbed her once more. She lay down in the grass and closed her eyes, concentrating on the sound of the sea way below.

One minute she was lying lulled by the sound of the sea and the smell of sun on grass stalks and the next she was alert, feeling his warm breath on her cheeks.

'You still don't trust me, Donna, do you?' he said.

His eyes were shining pewter, the pupils shrunk in the sunlight, like the pinned pupils of the smack addict. She saw him in detail: the scar on his cheek near his left eye; the pronounced V of his upper lip; the new beard shading his jaws.

'Why should I?' she said.

'Why shouldn't you?'

She couldn't spell it out.

'I know what you're thinking, you know; druggie, aren't you? Like I've got the plague.'

Of course that was the truth – but out there in the sun, the first warm day of the year, with the sea washing on the rocks and fallen spars and this beautiful emptiness, that world seemed remote, just a figment of someone's imagination. Here everything was wholesome, burgeoning . . .

'Oh, Shane, for goodness sake –'

'It's true, isn't it?' He touched her arm and that shocked her.

I'm up here, she thought, alone, nobody about – anything could happen. It'd be so easy. He could throw my body into the sea. People would think I'd slipped. For God's sake, woman, you're getting paranoid, she told herself, her faint-hearted self berating her devil-may-care self. Idiot, idiot, idiot! His hand stole up her shoulder. He leaned down so his face was over hers. She could smell his skin.

If she pronounced it, told him her fears, she might unleash something she couldn't control . . . but what? Anyway, could she really articulate what this fear was?

'Donna, you're beautiful. You're very special for me and you know I'd never hurt you. You do know that, don't you?'

His eyes were fixed on hers and she could feel her heart pattering and bobbing.

'I've been waiting for you, you know that, waiting for you to come to me.'

She smelled the herby grass and the earth and a dry spiciness and the keen tang of the sea. The long-running surge of the waves lulled her and fused with his mesmerizing voice. She lay there in the crushed grass, gazing up at him through half-closed eyes. A long while since she'd had sex and her body cried out for it – she felt open, longing. At the same time, she thought, What if he's got HIV, Aids, hep C – they could all be passed to her in saliva, semen, blood.

'Are you going to trust me?' His voice was urgent. She got the feeling he wouldn't take no for an answer. She was quite alone with him – nobody anywhere about. This was off the beaten track, isolated. She struggled away from the monstrous shadow of her fear.

'You don't have to make such an issue of it, Shane,' she heard herself mumbling, trying at the same time to smile.

'I'll wait as long as it takes, right – and in the end you'll come to me, whether it's now or later.'

He touched her breasts, slid his hand over them, still watching her face. The heat of his hand on the cotton made stickiness ooze between her legs. He lowered his face and kissed her. She felt his mouth probing and pressing. She could hear herself moaning. He fumbled with the button on her waistband and her trousers peeled down, then her pants. He was out of his jeans, his boxers, his T-shirt.

'It's all right,' he whispered. 'I've got something, you'll be fine.'

She waited in suspense, gazing at him as he eased the condom on. She knew she wanted this, had wanted it a long time in some perverse way. 'Come on,' she said.

'I knew you would,' he said, kissing her again on the mouth, then boring into her. She groaned and cried out. The sun was warm on her naked thighs. The smell of him was in her nostrils. His bigness hurt her, but he wasn't clumsy. A jolt of pleasure vibrated between her legs and hit her solar plexus. He controlled himself, she sensed, until she shouted and stretched and bucked. She clawed at his shoulders and sank her nails in. They subsided together.

Donna dropped into a trance. It was as though, before, there'd been a thunderous noise and now a deep silence reigned. She found tears running down her face.

'What is it,' he murmured. 'Donna, what is it?'

'I don't know,' she said.

'You aren't mad at me?'

'No.'

'I told you: I'd never want to hurt you.'

He drove back in the early evening. A coldness was in the wind and the sky was an intense dark blue. The trees and hedgerows stood out distinctly as though etched with a blade. Big black birds winged across the sky. She felt very quiet inside. Everything had changed. She knew that now there could be no turning back and she sensed he knew it too.

14

Ruby knew she would find Ivy rooted before a bandit, feeding in 10ps and pressing nudge buttons, her eyes boring into the flashing console. No use talking to Ivy when she had a game on. You might as well save your breath, wait until the whirring squeaked out in a final grunt signifying she had lost the game and her money.

'So you're there,' Ruby tried.

'Just hold on a tick, love,' came the response. 'I've not done yet. Still got a few bob left.'

'You're wasting your money, you know that.'

Ivy turned deaf and continued to slot and press. The line of apples and pears, bananas and oranges looked quite bonny with the lights winking under it, Ruby decided. In the gloom the consoles shed a freakish glow, enhanced by their eldritch singing and an occasional thump when some lucky punter caused them to disgorge a shower of tokens.

Ruby peered round at the figures crowding the machines. Mostly female, mostly white haired; they'd spend their entire pensions on the machines sometimes. Ruby had seen them stand at a loss once the final click and thump sounded and then stumble out down the steps in a daze. The same women creaked in week after week and everything followed an identical, inescapable pattern. One in particular would slot in £40 and more, Ruby knew, because she watched her. She arrived with the money in a bag and when she lost the lot, she collapsed the bag, folded it up and stowed it in a boxy mock-croc handbag with wonky gilt fastenings. She wasn't somebody you'd expect to do that, just a typical nana figure . . . but then people were never what they seemed.

Ivy had had a win, so her game would continue. At this rate they'd miss the bingo in the main hall.

While she was still rumbling with annoyance, Ruby spotted a familiar figure. It was that Frank Prentice, the feller from the tea dance, the betting bloke. He looked proper dodgy with his trilby pulled well down, and belted into a mac. Ruby went over.

'Hello,' she said. 'Won much, have you? Or should I say, lost much?'

He gave one final jab at the machine and then turned to face her. 'Oh, the damsel from the dance. How are you, then?'

'Same as before – well enough,' Ruby snorted.

'You've come to lose all your hard-earned shekels, have you?'

'No, not on your nelly. My friend has though. I just have a little flutter in the bingo but by the way things are shaping, I'll be lucky if I get there in time.'

'Oh, it's bingo you go for?'

'Within limits.'

'You're not one of these wild spenders, then?'

'No, I'm not. Folks like that have got to have something to spend first.'

'Not necessarily.' He gave a subterranean guffaw and shoved his trilby a bit further back on his pate.

'I used to come here when it was the pictures, did you?' Ruby remarked, suddenly glancing round in the beige twilight. 'Funny it never got bombed, a big place like this.'

'Aye. Yer, I've come here a time or two myself.'

Ruby was caught for a moment, as she sometimes was, in the surprise of how these buildings littered throughout the city were the sole reminders of all that past passion and heartache . . . and they too had undergone reinvention. This picture palace with the long flight of steps up to the swing doors and the wide foyer leading to the mystery of the auditorium, where you stood for the wheezing of the National Anthem and then sat spellbound in the darkness on red velvet seats to watch Errol Flynn or Alan Ladd, had been wrenched and vulgarized into a bingo hall.

They muttered to each other about the changes, which he tended to brush off, but she could tell he understood what she meant.

'You from round here then, like?' he asked.

'No. I was born off Hessle Road but now I'm on the estate. Got moved out.'

'Aye, they shifted the whole lot, didn't they?'

'I'm in the high rises.'

'How's that, then?'

'It's my home – it's just the others,' Ruby said. She had been waiting to tell Ivy about the latest crisis but hadn't had the chance. 'Opposite me was this young lad – I say "was", because you never saw him. Well, most of 'em's drifting round at night. They don't work, you know. Never have, never will. Anyway, there was this real bad smell – couldn't fathom what it could be. I said to the neighbour on the floor below that I thought the drains must be blocked. It was kind of gone-off sweet, you know.'

The man guffawed again.

'Anyhow, she said that we'd best ring the corporation to come and see – so I did. You'll never guess what it was.'

'Well, what was it, then?'

'This lad – dead. He'd overdosed with a needle – you know what they do. Next thing we'd the police and newspapers and photographers and everybody asking questions.'

'Bloody hell – pardon my French, love. I'm not a swearin' man.'

'He was only twenty-three – the only young 'un left in the block.'

'Oh, there's needles all over where I live – you can see 'em in the street. Come and have a drink while your mate's finishin'.'

Ruby felt traitorous but she yelled across to Ivy, 'Just goin' for a coffee,' and they betook themselves to a refreshment room where a flowered carpet blitzed the eyes and plastic tulips and daffodils stuck out of boat-shaped vases like funeral urns with side handles and bits of gilt scalloping. A pinkish light plumped up everything.

They settled into a good grouse about the state of modern life and Ruby felt herself warmed by a blast of fellow sympathy from Frank Prentice. He'd continued to steer clear of any mention of physical decay, much to Ruby's relief. She had long since noticed that most exchanges between herself and her male contemporaries invariably centred on bodily dysfunction. She had no time for it. She thought she must have inherited this attitude from Nana, who lived to be a vast age and never gave way to moaning about her aches and pains. When Nana had decided she'd had enough, she died, simple as that, one Friday afternoon. I'll just have a lay down now, Ruby love – and that was it. She was off, floating away with the seagulls, gone into the spirit world to join Mary, the Red Indian spirit guide.

Ruby was whisked into the swell of the past. It moved before her inner eye: Maggie's birth, Maggie, a lovely little bairn with dark hair and eyes the colour of treacle. She'd always had hair – Ruby never liked those bald-headed babies like skinned rabbits with wizened, elderly faces. Maggie was chubby with eyebrows like feathery arcs and lots of hair right from the first moment when she fought her way from the cavern between Ruby's thighs.

Oh, yes, of course there was the disgrace. After saying she'd never lift her head up again for shame, when Nana actually saw the bairn, she changed . . . everything was different then. She loved her; Maggie was her pet.

When Ruby got back to work in the goodies factory there were some who wouldn't speak to her. Ruby once heard one of the women say: She's common as muck. She'd go with anybody – doesn't know how to keep her knickers on.

Ernie had looked at Maggie snoozing in a drawer at the bottom of Ruby's bed and exclaimed in wonder. Her cheeks were pink as wild roses and damp curls clung in question marks to her forehead. An O of saliva darkened the white pillowcase under her lips.

She's a little beauty, he said. I'm proud of you, girl.

One Sunday afternoon Ernie turned up in his motor. Want to take you out for a spin, he said, and Ruby could tell it was something momentous.

Off they drove in the froggy car, with Maggie asleep on the back seat. She was a baby who slept a lot, only cried for her feed, but otherwise remained chortling and self-contained.

They shot out to Hornsea. Ernie drove cars like Ruby imagined he must have done aeroplanes. He swung the wheel and the car zoomed. They passed everything on the narrow winding roads and hurtled round bends on two wheels. No forty m.p.h. nonsense for Ernie – it had to be seventy and above. Maggie woke up and sicked on Ruby's best dress and everything smelled very sour, but Ernie didn't seem to notice.

Sitting in the front at Hornsea with the sea lumpy and fizzing before them along the blue pebbles, Ernie turned to her.

Ruby, I've decided something . . . He told, rather than asked her, that he wanted them to move in together. He'd got a new job opening up for him: pub landlord. She could be part of it all. But Ruby said no. His eyes bulged and his cheeks blazed. Ruby's knees shook. Maggie, now recovered from the sick episode, stared at her vibrating dad with interest.

Now come off of it, Rube, you've got everything to gain – you'll be respectable.

Ruby laughed. I'll never be respectable now. Too late for that.

She could see he absolutely couldn't believe it and wouldn't accept it.

I'll make you happy, Ruby, depend on it.

She didn't say anything, simply stared at the sea slamming on the pebbles and trickling down in rivulets between them. Not a warm day, not a day for paddling or walking by the sea.

So what's your reason then, Rube? Why won't you?

You're a married man, Ernie, with a family.

She hadn't known she could say that, but it seemed as good an excuse as any. Really, to tell the truth, she was scared. If he'd left his wife and kids, he'd be quite capable of abandoning her when he got tired. Ernie was too much. He might swamp her. Of course she wanted to live with him, but she had doubts. Ernie was clearly an either/or, a black or white type. He didn't deal in ambiguous grey areas – and she had only a dim idea of who he was or how he might behave.

He thought about that, drumming his fingers on the steering wheel and contorting his forehead. Come an' live with me, Rube, and I'll get divorced and marry you, as God is my witness.

Ernie never spoke about God and that quite impressed Ruby. She realized that she'd inadvertently hit on a very effective strategy for dealing with him. She stroked Maggie's hair and straightened her collar while Ernie pleaded. After a suitable show of reluctance, she allowed herself to accept. And then began the Mermaid years.

'You deaf or sommat?'

She became aware that Frank had been staring at her for some time.

'No, thinking.'

'Was you ever workin' in that Mermaid pub, years ago?' he asked, peering at her.

'You can read my mind,' Ruby said, amazed. 'I was just thinking about them times.'

'Was you married to Ernie, the landlord?'

'Aye. Then I took it on. What a life!'

'I knew as I'd seen you before. You was spinning the bottle,' he said and gave her a long look. 'Was a lock-in. You'd a good leg on yer – and other things besides.'

Ruby coughed to hide her embarrassment. 'So what would you have been doing at that time then?'

'Went to sea, didn't I, for a bit, then them Cod Wars started.' He told her about being rammed by Icelandic trawlers and gunboats hoving up, trawls being cut: rage on the high seas, in the middle of gales with ice forming on the rigging and the decks awash. The trawls cut, the catch lost, the living ruined.

'My God, when we got back there were some black faces – the bosses had made no profits that time!'

Ruby could see the gigantic green waves heaving up and curling over the trawlers, the shadow of the Icelandic gun-boats, the crew, great blond-haired Scrobs, shaking their fists and brandishing gutting knives . . .

She was well engrossed in Frank's fishing dramas when Ivy lumbered in, her face creased with exasperation.

'Won nowt. So this is where you've got to! I've been looking all over.'

'Sorry, lass. Want a coffee?'

Ivy wasn't interested in hearing about the Cod Wars – they were times gone thirty and more years ago. But Ruby wouldn't forget them: they'd changed her life for ever. When she thought about what those Cod Wars really did, she could cry with the pity of it . . .

With a scowl Ivy said she'd promised to mind the great-grandbairns and departed smartish. Ruby wasn't sure whether or not she was in a mood; she'd phone her later to find out. Meanwhile she and Frank decided to have a pub OAP dinner.

Most of the pubs round about were new ones frequented by students. They had wooden benches and seats set up outside where you would see groups of young lads and lasses lounging over their pints even on cold days. Every second shop was a student letting agency. People used to mutter about bloody students; now, without them, the city's economy would collapse.

They trundled along until they reached a pub that took Ruby back to the days with Leroy.

'Have this one on me – I've come up on the dogs,' Frank said.

'Ta for that, I don't mind if I do.' Ruby gave him a flirtatious beamer.

Roast beef and Yorkshire, roast spuds and peas, that was what it must be.

'I like traditional food,' she told him. 'Can't be doin' with fancy stuff.'

He settled into his pint and stared ahead of him. 'You know, the thing about going to sea, you never feel right on land and when you're out there, you can't wait to get back. Oh, aye, even now, all them years later, it comes on me sometimes.'

Ruby was a young bride again, buffeted by Billy's unease.

'The sea kind of unsettled you. My first trip I saw the sun at midnight – was at Greenland like . . . unearthly. And when I saw Iceland – everything white, a white waste. It was like when you look at the moon. And then you'd see these little wooden churches. But by God, when we were fishing it was solid work: forty-eight hours sometimes and no sleep.'

Ruby listened to Frank's growly voice sketching in moments of splendour and despair. 'I've seen men drowned – you could do nowt about it. Trawlers have sunk within sight of the lock gates. The lads in the engine room stood no chance. Aye, gone in a second.' He swigged hard and his Adam's apple jerked. He'd taken off his trilby and his longish grey hair lent him a rakish air. He was a chancer, she was sure of it.

'But it was the 200-mile limit that finished us. When I think how it was when I was a lad – fair buzzing down Hessle Road, and now, what's left? Maybe six ships out of a hundred and forty-six.'

'Don't tell me,' Ruby said. She felt they were survivors, living relics of a bygone age. He acknowledged this by lurching up and ordering more drinks from the bar. Ruby had a second port and lemon and drifted into a pleasant lachrymose state.

Their dinner arrived and Ruby cut into the crispy skin of a roast potato. This was an unusual day, a day to make you think.

'Yes,' she said, chewing and pondering, 'and the end came when the corporation told us the houses weren't fit – fit habitations, they said – and folk had to move to the new estate. My nana had been in that house all her life near enough. It killed her, you know. Everybody else was moving, but she said no – she was real old then. Always said she'd die in that house. They'd even started pulling terraces down and the tatters were round after the lead on the roofs. I wanted her to come and live at the pub and I pleaded with her, but she wouldn't. She just decided she'd die rather than go . . . and she did.'

Tears rolled down Ruby's cheeks and plopped into her roast beef.

'Never mind, love.' Frank patted her shoulder. 'All water under the bridge now. They say we ought to be glad fishing's over – killed more men than mining. But it was a whole way of life that went.'

Ruby heard again the thunder of falling bricks and saw the great metal ball swinging at the houses. The dust spumed up like spray as the structures collapsed. Fires burned. The blitz all over again. Buildings had a history, a living presence; demolishing them was like denying the past. The afternoon of Nana's dying: Nana wouldn't move, no way would she leave that house. Nana had been father and mother to her, seen her through Billy's death, Maggie's birth, storms, despair, hope . . .

When she went up with a cup of tea and a biscuit for her, she found Nana already dead, her face eased out, quite peaceful, all the agitated lines smoothed away.

It was seeing Nana's house demolished that made her know she couldn't pass Hessle Road day in day out. So she gave up on the Mermaid and off she went with the rest to the new estate – the estate at the end of the world. But that, too, in time became home.

They sat in the pub yarning away to each other until well into the afternoon. Ruby told him about Donna's friend, Joanne, how they'd found her body in a ten foot – she'd been battered to death. 'That girl never had a chance,' she said, 'with a mother like she had.' And Frank nodded and muttered that it was a bad do – but all sorts could happen, like that bloke he knew selling his wife for a fast buck.

'You'll maybe like to come with me to the dogs, like, would you?' Frank said when they were about to leave.

'Now that's sommat I've never done. Aye, that might be quite up my street.'

'You're on then, lass. Gie us your phone number and I'll gie you a bell.'

He left her at the bus stop and she pretended not to watch him lurching away, trilby plonked well down, brim undulating with the roll of his walk and mac resolutely belted, hands in pockets.

She still didn't know about his past, apart from the sea. She guessed there'd be girls sprinkled about with babies, by now grown men and women, who cursed their elusive dad. That was how it often seemed to be. It was the surprise of people she found endlessly fascinating.

15

Maggie wished it wasn't her birthday today. Fifty! She really hadn't time for it: birthdays called for elaborate arrangements. The family would all float in, expecting to be fed. If she didn't get away from school promptly she'd not arrive home before Ruby and Donna descended. Donna would help but Ruby was bound to be on a cleaning inspection – she wasn't above running her finger round the top of a jardinière and sniffing. There was sure to be a meeting that would drag on after school closed because the head was such a windbag. Oh, and the sodding cream cake for the staff room. If she forgot that as the birthday 'girl' – some girl – she'd never live it down.

The electric toothbrush whirred as she addressed herself to the sensitive pockets in her gums. Her dentist had warned her: More people lose their teeth through gum disease than tooth decay, and she'd undergone some painful and expensive deep scaling. It's over to you now, Maggie, he said. Behind the whirr of the toothbrush and the dental irrigator, she heard the telephone ringing. 'Damnation!' she said, turning off the apparatus and making for her bedroom.

'Happy birthday to you, happy birthday, dear Mumsie, happy birthday to you!' Donna trilled away down the phone. Maggie thought she sounded extraordinarily cheerful, but then again she might be putting on a front for her mum's benefit. Since the news of Joanne's murder, the comfort of daily routines and the certainties of everyday life seemed to have been eroded. Now strange spongy places opened up; she found herself staring into deep fissures. What must Joanne's mother be feeling, wherever she might be? For a mother to lose a daughter in this way was unbearable. OK, so Joanne had worked the streets, but that didn't mean her life was any less valid than that of any other woman – and yet headline after headline screamed 'prostitute'. Other young women had been found murdered too, and the press seemed to imply that, as they'd been working women, in some way the girls had 'asked' for it.

Maggie put on a black trouser suit; these days you had to look like some business wallah or they thought you couldn't do the job. Gone were the days of jeans or floaty skirts. She sighed. Her thoughts brought her out in a flush and she stood at the back door now, feeling the air on her face and throat.

The day at school shot by in a confusion of colleagues going under with bad backs and sore throats; kids truanting; fights needing to be split up; detentions handed out. None of it seemed even vaguely related to education. She managed to escape at four fifteen. No meeting, thank God: the head was struck down with a migraine. Jubilation. Everyone pelted out to their cars, cream cake crumbs still decorating their jowls, anxious to discover how many scratches their respective vehicles had acquired in the course of the day.

Maggie found Donna laying the table. She'd put out knives and forks and wine glasses frothing red and gold paper napkins. A HAPPY BIRTHDAY streamer was draped across the centre of the pine table. White carnations filled a cut-glass vase.

'Happy birthday, Mumsie,' Donna called and she rushed

forward to give Maggie a hug. Embarrassingly, Maggie felt tears pricking her eyes.

'That is so sweet. Thank you, love. I'm glad you got here before your gran. You've made it look welcoming. If she'd arrived and nobody was in she wouldn't have been best pleased. The flowers are beautiful.'

The doorbell tinkled. Donna went to investigate and returned with Mark. He was Nick's son by his first partner and had chosen to live with Maggie rather than with his own mother. He had a luxury flat now in a renovated warehouse looking out onto the River Humber, worked in IT and always looked very dashing. He went down well with Donna and Lee because, even though he was six years older than Donna, he was trendy. Maggie admired his lean dark suit.

'Maggie, happy birthday. Lovely to see you.' He kissed her cheek, hugged her and placed an oblong box wrapped in silver paper on the table, together with a bottle of wine. Again she found herself wanting to cry. It touched her that Mark had remembered her birthday and bothered to come round. He'd always been a special favourite of hers, because of his thoughtfulness and how he empathized with people – he'd got Nick's sensitivity but not his neuroticism.

'How are you, little sister?' he said, turning to Donna. 'You're looking extra well.'

'Oh, I am, I'm good – couldn't be better.'

Maggie was amazed at Donna's flamboyance under the circumstances. She pressed on with her paella preparations. First course was mushrooms cooked in cream and sprinkled with chopped parsley and lemon. She could rustle that up when the main dish was ready and they could mop up the juices with slivers of toast – she'd thought of garlic bread, but Ruby didn't like garlic; she said it repeated on her.

The doorbell let out a peremptory yelp. 'That'll be your gran, Donna. Can you let her in, please? She'll be pleased to see you, Mark – she always says you look like a gentleman. In other words you're dressed properly, not like Lee.' Mark laughed.

'Hello, lass, happy birthday. Buses, they never come on time.'

At that moment Lee catapulted into the room. Maggie realized he'd been attracted by the smell of frying onions.

'Is tea going to be long?'

'Only a little while, Lee.'

'That means half an hour at least. I want to go out.'

'Lee, it's Mum's birthday and she shouldn't be cooking anyway. Get some bread and jam,' Donna snarled, 'and don't be a pain.'

'Oh, fuck off!'

'Language!' Ruby shouted. 'I never thought as I'd hear this from my grandson.'

Maggie kept her head down and concentrated on the frying. She was relieved when Mark engaged her mother in conversation, and the spat between Donna and Lee died into a dull rumble. If only Lee could have been more like Mark. Lee reminded her of Nick's annoying sides. When Nick had broken down, gone on perpetual sick leave and finally resigned from the staff, she'd felt sorry for him, been taken in by his stories of the novel he'd write – *Ulysses* all over again, Nick the great talker. She'd sympathized when he told the story of his wife and her lover, and how his kids didn't like the lover. But Nick had had a penchant for lying on couches and screwing up sheet after sheet of paper, which missed the waste basket. Why must she always take pity on people? Nick was a leech. Why was she remembering this now, on her birthday? Another wave of heat pressed up her chest. She must think of something else.

At last they were seated round the table and Maggie served up the starter. Lee grabbed the spoon, once Maggie had replaced it in the dish, and prepared to finish the remaining mushrooms, but Donna snatched it from him.

'Hold on, Dog Breath, you've just about ganneted the lot.'

'Didn't.'

'That will do,' Maggie intervened.

'Did you see in the paper about that girl being found murdered?' Mark said, looking across at Maggie. 'When I saw the picture I was sure it was that Joanne we took to Flamingo Land on Donna's birthday.'

'Yes,' Maggie said, 'that's right.'

'They found her all battered,' Ruby said, 'and they ought to string him up, the one who's done it. They should never have stopped hanging.'

'Mum, capital punishment is barbaric and it doesn't change anything, it isn't the answer.' Maggie felt her cheeks going red. Her flesh had always flinched at the idea of hanging or electrocuting criminals. At the same time she felt exasperated with herself: she knew quite well how Ruby would react, but she couldn't bear to let her get away with it.

Mark started asking Donna whether she knew what had gone wrong with Joanne's life. Maggie could see Ruby was raring to go on the argument but she simply couldn't face it. She looked across at Donna, and again felt the fear in her stomach: here they all were, the same group, apart from Nick and Helen, who had spent the day at Flamingo Land. She'd been too preoccupied in looking after Lee to pay much attention to what Donna and Joanne were doing. She'd missed so much – missed the point where Joanne might have been saved, where her life might have been turned round. The seeds of the future were being sown then. She could see Joanne's mother and her awful boyfriend clearly. Oh, God, her head ached with the inevitability of it . . . abuse perhaps, and then the slide into prostitution. Joanne wouldn't have learned much at school – she hadn't worked, got no qualifications, nothing to give her a worthwhile career. Lee was heading that way too. At the rate he was going, he would fail his A levels. He couldn't see that only the most boring jobs would be open to him if he didn't study. This was Nick, his father, all over again. Maggie sweated with agitation.

The others talked around her. 'I feel awful,' Donna was telling Mark, 'that I just didn't bother to keep up with Joanne – I mean after she left school.'

'She was a funny mixture,' Mark said. 'On one level she was a really young girl but there'd be this other side where you'd forget she was only a kid. Do you remember I had to go and find her and she was with a group of lads? You could see they'd noticed the pull she had.'

'How do you mean?' Donna was asking.

'Kind of sexy and beautiful.'

Ruby finished another glass of wine and snorted.

Maggie listened, her head reeling, and watched their faces. What if even now they were heading towards another disaster – one that she ought to have foreseen?

Lee nattered to get Mark's attention. He got on with Mark because he never criticized and always seemed interested in what Lee was doing – and of course he was the only male figure in the family. Lee seemed to think that females didn't understand him. Maggie stopped listening; she couldn't think past the interview she'd just had with Lee's teacher, Mrs Lidell. First she kept Maggie waiting twenty minutes. I've been on bus duty, she said. Why arrange to meet me at that precise time, Maggie thought, if you knew you were going to be on duty? The interview proved to be an inventory of Lee's failings: he was disruptive, failed to attend, did not hand in essays – in short, was heading for failure. He was just a waste of time.

His truanting meant that he was out of touch with what the class was studying. The list ground on. Maggie could see that her best way out of this was abasement – she must apologize profusely, tell the Gauleiterin that she'd speak to Lee and that she was really very sorry for his behaviour.

The truth was she could imagine that Lee was right, Mrs Lidell *was* a boring, unimaginative teacher. But Lee would have to put up with that if he was going to get anywhere – only Lee hadn't got any goals. All he wanted to do was be off out on his bike with his mates, or doing his mixing and smoking dope. She'd have to have another serious talk with him, somehow make him listen. The problem was that he'd slide away from her; she could never pin him down. He was impossible.

Lee and Mark retired upstairs to listen to some of Lee's music. Maggie approved because at least it meant he had someone more sensitive to talk to than his dubious pals.

'I want you to open this, lass,' her mother said, pushing a rigid-looking parcel at her. Maggie had to struggle with an elaborate network of Sellotape strips. Mum was not good on presents, Maggie thought. She specialized in hideous reach-me-down cardigans.

At last the wrapping gave way to reveal a china figurine. 'Oh, how lovely – a partner for Lady B. Marvellous, Mum.' The bloke did look rather sexy with his neat aquiline features, cobalt blue eyes and black moustache. 'I'll put him in my bedroom with Lady Belinda,' she said.

'So that's where she is – thought as you maybe didn't like her,' Ruby said.

'Oh, no, Mum, I love her, that's why she's in my bedroom.' Lady Belinda was a tacky figurine in a red dress with a pug sitting at her feet and Maggie had hidden her upstairs out of the way, not daring to bin her or take her to Oxfam because Ruby might find her there one day.

After Ruby's present, Maggie unwrapped Donna's toilet

bag and collection of eye shadows and anti-wrinkle creams. 'Gorgeous, love,' she said. 'I feel I'm rejuvenated already – all my lines gone.'

'I just thought you could spoil yourself a tad,' Donna said. 'Hope you like 'em.'

'Yes,' Ruby came in, 'your mam could do with a freshen-up. I've always told her she never makes the best of herself.'

'Thanks a bunch,' Maggie said, trying to smile. 'You've always done a lot for my self-confidence, Mum.' She was back as a teenager listening to Ruby chuntering on about her jeans and why couldn't she smarten up and be more sociable – she didn't have to have her nose in a book all the time.

Donna started on the washing-up, insisting that Maggie sit down and drink another glass of wine. Ruby was well in her cups, Maggie could see, and she waited for another garrulous outburst from her. So she was relieved to watch Mark leave and Donna take Ruby back to the estate. Now she'd have it out with Lee before he could shoot off anywhere.

'Lee,' she called. No answer, just the throb of drum and bass. After repeated shouting his face appeared at the top of the stairs.

'Yer?' he bellowed.

'I want to have a word, Lee, please.'

'What is it? I've got to go out.'

'Lee, not at this time – it's far too late. You'll never get up in the morning and then I'll have Mrs Lidell on my back again.' Maggie struggled with desperation and anger. She wanted to yell at him to be more considerate, to stop being so self-destructive, but she bit back the words.

'Oh, Mum, give it a rest. I'm sick of being moaned at. You're all the same. Why can't you fuck off and leave me alone? Somebody always has to be on my case about something. What's your problem, anyway?'

He stood in the doorway, his face blurry, his eyes wide and dark. She didn't like the look in them. It seemed violent, hysterical. His voice had risen. She wondered who this person was . . . surely to God it wasn't the little lad who'd snuggled up in bed between her and Nick, who'd loved to run into the waves at St Ives and had to be restrained because he seemed to have no sense of fear. He'd had an open, laughing face. This was the mask of a dangerous, half-wild youth.

'Lee, please, this can't go on. You must go to school and work for your exams. You're ruining your chances.'

'What fucking chances? I don't want to be one of your fucking wanking teachers and have a nice little job. What fucking chances? There are no fucking chances.' His voice rose into an awful, screeching threnody, which tore at Maggie's guts.

'Lee, for Christ's sake, stop!' His answer was to race out into the night, slamming the front door. Devastated, Maggie delved in the cleaning cupboard under the sink and brought out the brandy bottle, which she hid there from Lee. She poured herself a shot and took it and the bottle to the front room. She'd never get to sleep for hours after this.

Fifty, fucking fifty – and here she was with a son who was out of control and a mother who had never understood her and clearly held her responsible for the way Lee was. Maybe she was right – maybe it was her fault. But having to be the breadwinner and bring up the children single-handed meant you ran out of energy.

At fifty you had to do a bit of stocktaking. She'd fallen under Tom's spell at university – Tom in his leather jacket and with his coal-black hair and enthusiasm for Hermann Hesse – expecting the relationship would last for ever. When he'd walked out on her, in desperation she'd gone on the hunt for a replacement. Those men sensed her neediness, she'd understood that very soon, and quickly disappeared. Then Nick. She'd been determined that relationship would succeed, but in the end she couldn't bear it, though it had toughened her. In the mirror that morning she'd stared at her face and noticed how the skin had coarsened, not lined, particularly, but grown grainy – like my life, she thought.

Then there was her mother, irritating but loveable. The problem was she could never tell Ruby what she really felt because Ruby didn't understand. As far as she was concerned, Tom was a tripe-hound – that was her word for him. She'd wanted Maggie to marry a nice man, someone with a steady job, to live in a modern house and spend every spare minute cleaning. It had been just the same when Maggie was young and they'd lived at the pub. Ruby couldn't understand why she'd longed for something else, a different world where people discussed books, politics, and didn't bang on about trivialities. Her dad hadn't been much different either – but he'd died when she was seven and she only remembered him as being red-faced and jovial, the sort who, if you asked him a serious question, would make a joke of it and give some gag in return so that all the grown-ups would laugh and you didn't know why.

Feeling woozy, Maggie finally made her way upstairs to bed. This had been a birthday she could have done without.

16

All the newspapers would say was that police were 'working on certain leads as to the death of prostitute Joanne Singleton'. Nothing conclusive had been achieved. Every time Donna saw the word 'prostitute' she boiled with rage – it seemed indecent to pin that label on Joanne. It took away her humanity, her personality, reduced her to nothing. And every time the caption appeared it was beneath that dreadful photo, a photograph that made Joanne look vacant, anonymous. The real person had disappeared.

Joanne's murder shrank to the inside pages; the front page was now dominated by a fraud case.

The horror of it was a counterpoint to her other life.

One Wednesday, a week after Maggie's birthday, she took a day's leave from work, and Shane had a day off from labouring.

'Let's go to Whitby for the day,' Donna said. 'I love it there.' Shane said he'd never been before – he rarely seemed to have left the city, in fact, except for a brief spell in London and some hitching around in Manchester.

A normal workday and the roads were quiet. The air was mild and bundles of white cloud rollicked over the blueness. Donna had packed cheese and tomato sandwiches; apples and bananas. She wanted him to see this favourite place and hear his first reaction to it.

When they crossed the North York Moors and the gradient wound up ever steeper until they reached an upland where sheep skittered away at their approach, he let out a gasp of surprise.

'Eh, this is all right,' he said, peering about him. Donna glanced at him sideways and saw his face relax. 'Wow. I'd like to have a walk across there.'

Everything seemed possible in that second up there. She concentrated on the road twisting down into a hairpin bend. Up they shot again, weaving about until, at last, on their right they could glimpse the sea.

'Can't wait,' he said. 'I told you, didn't I? The job I'd really like to do is forest ranger – some place where you could get away from everybody and just be out in the country. I never knew till I got on that scheme for planting trees on the estate. Didn't know anything about trees before – always been in towns, like. But I got a real buzz out of it. When the kids wrecked 'em, I was gutted.'

'Look,' she said, a while later, 'can you see that in the distance? It's the abbey on the cliffs – with the 199 steps. We'll have to go up those, it's obligatory in Whitby.'

Donna listened to him exclaiming as the orange pantiled roofs came into view, striped with chalky birdlime from the seagulls, wheeling and squawking overhead. Trawlers were moored in the harbour. Everywhere smelled of fish and chips.

'Let's get some,' he said. 'It's making me hungry.'

They sat on a wooden seat facing the boats and ate their fish and chips from the paper. The chunks of cod in crispy batter and the sizzling chips made her want to gobble as fast as she could, suck in the flavour, absorb every last morsel and lose nothing. Donna wouldn't let herself think of depleted cod stocks, seas out-fished or the amount of fat they were consuming – those thoughts were like a ball and chain. Life was crammed with moral questions and she knew she was doing dreadful things all the time – but couldn't stop. Perhaps she lacked moral fibre, that was what it amounted to in the end.

'That was ace,' Shane said, wiping his mouth on the back of his hand and squeezing the newspaper into a tight ball. 'Never enjoyed any food as much for a long while.'

They crossed the little bridge and sauntered through the old town, staring in shop windows, and then they puffed up the 199 steps. Shane got ahead of Donna and reached the top well before she did.

'I'm out of condition,' she said as she stood panting, and stared out at the sea below and at the chimney pots, where seagulls balanced on one foot and kept up their constant mewing.

'Wow.' Shane had turned to the church and the gravestones that stuck up at odd angles. 'These have been here a bit.'

They pushed open the church door and stood looking in. It smelled of age and old books. Donna could imagine the women in black dresses rising to sing 'Eternal Father' while the wind wailed and the waves slammed and trawlers were battered and fishermen clung on for dear life.

He caught her hand as they stood in the entrance gazing in. Neither of them spoke. The silence felt special; she knew she'd remember that moment later. She was in the feel of his fingers and his body standing close beside her.

'Do you think places get haunted by the dead?' he said. 'It's like all the ghosts of the drowned fishermen are around us.'

'Maybe,' she said. 'I know what you mean.'

As soon as they turned and went outside he wanted to be off again, exploring. It was as though he couldn't remain still, must see everything. They stared at the abbey ruins, but didn't go in, and set off again.

Halfway down the steps he turned back to her, his face

alight. 'You know, Donna, I've never been anywhere like this before. I've not done anything like this, either.'

He was like a caged bird that had suddenly been let out and must fly around, darting here and there in an attempt to encompass what he had never known.

They had tea and carrot cake in a café. Then they walked round the harbour and down onto the beach. He wanted to wade into the sea so they took off their trainers and paddled. He walked deeper and deeper in until a wave wet his jeans almost to the thigh and he ran back laughing and shivering.

'Fucking cold,' he called. 'Didn't bargain for this.'

'It is the east coast, you know,' Donna reminded him. 'But you've brought it on yourself, muscles. Who's a big man then!'

'Oh, you've had it now,' he said and laughed. 'But don't crow or I'll chuck you in.'

Donna sped off, with him pounding after her. He lunged at her, missed, captured her and they tripped and went down on the sand, rolling over and over, Donna giggling until she cried. He picked her up in his arms and staggered down to the sea with her and they kissed as they stood in the waves.

They lingered in the town, exploring back streets until evening. For a final few minutes they walked out on the harbour wall and gazed at the sea, turned to mother of pearl now by the setting sun, reflecting the pink sky.

'I shan't forget today, Donna,' he said. 'Thanks for bringing us here.' He squeezed her hand and smiled at her. 'You've given me something very precious.'

It was one of those rare moments when Donna knew she was happy. The feel of the day was so fragile and hedged around by disastrous happenings – and yet this was a day without a flaw, filled with open spaces and sunlight and nothing hidden or scary. She wanted it to last for ever.

Over the moorland the moon lit up the ribbon of road. The clouds drifted in the sky and mounded up into castles lit by a fairy phosphorescence. They sang along to a blues CD and now and then he talked about his life – the homes and the strokes they'd pulled; escaping and sleeping rough.

'Today I've wondered where my life's been until now,' he said. 'It's like I've been asleep or something . . .'

His voice was almost lost at times in the noise of the car engine. In the half-light, the only illumination the glow from the dashboard, Donna felt they had entered a confessional where innermost thoughts could be admitted without embarrassment.

That night Donna took him home with her. He seemed to fill her little house as he wandered about staring at things and exclaiming. They fell upon each other first on her shabby old sofa.

'I've been making love to you all day,' he said, 'and this is just the icing on the cake.'

In the early hours she woke to find him hard against her back and they turned to each other wordlessly, ravenously, and just as rapidly fell back to sleep.

17

The alarm clock buzzed. Donna turned over, encountering a blond arm. Her eyes lingered on the straw-coloured hairs and fixed on scars beneath them. She sniffed at the flesh. 'Mm,' she murmured. It smelled salty, of ozone, of him, with undertones of bleach. She looked at his face and the mauve shadows beneath the eyes, a slight haggardness in the folds running from nostrils to mouth corners. It was a face that had been battered. If only she could make life better for him, help him to a new beginning. It hurt her to see the scars, the emblems of the past. He might so easily have been one of those dead young men – part of a missing generation, a generation killed not by war but by heroin addiction.

His arm tightened round her. 'Don't go.'

But she scrambled out of bed and stretched. Rupert was in a deep sulk and had spent the night downstairs; he felt supplanted. Shane leaned against the headboard and took her in.

'Cool, your tattoos are brilliant,' he said, 'paradise. Come back to bed. I've got something to show you.'

'No way, tempter. Got to be off. Anyway your tattoos are tribal same as mine – weird that. Tattooed like our forefathers, only they had hearts and birds.'

'Mine haven't got flowers like yours. Come on, I want to have a closer look!'

'You don't really,' Donna said, smiling, as she rushed off to shower.

After that Whitby day Shane came around a lot. Several days might pass when she didn't see him and then, in the evening, she'd find him on the doorstep, sitting waiting. Driving home from work, she'd feel the suspense build – would he be there? If he wasn't, disappointment hit her, but she tried to pretend she hadn't been hoping to see him. In his absence she moved in a dream of him, yet when he was there she treasured her times alone, because only then could she think about what had happened between them.

When Shane was around the minutes whirled. It was as though he had to cram life in as fast as he could, grab it, suck it dry. 'I get worried about you,' she told him. 'I'm frightened you'll burn out.'

'Better burn out than rust out,' he said and laughed.

Only when he slept did he relax, and then his features became marble, like a face on an old tomb in a church.

Today, as she drove to work, uneasiness churned in her stomach. What would Shane do while she was away? She'd asked him about his labouring job and he seemed vague, even evasive. The boss didn't employ continuously, only when particular jobs arose. She pressed him regularly to try to get on a college course, retrain for something, work he'd enjoy. If he wanted to be a forest ranger, then why not go for it? But he always brought them back to the same point: criminal record. All the training in the world wouldn't change his lack of job prospects.

But they'd never discussed drug addiction. She dared not ask, yet sometimes she glimpsed the shadow of it skulking behind all their moments together.

Between her legs the skin was tender with what they'd done together. The memory harpooned her with a dart of pleasure. She was mad for that sweet, crazy vibration; the ecstasy, the pure pleasure of it was like nothing she had known before. In those moments she became it, it merged into her, and there was no gap between the two. Later she was left yearning for it all over again. She knew that this longing could make her take risks and might be her undoing. If she wanted to keep her job and her career, she must never walk through the city centre with him during the day – the relationship had to remain hidden and she must keep control of it.

Reggae chirped in the background as she drove. She peeked at her face in the driving mirror. Her eyes looked different: drugged, heavy.

She ran into a bevy of prison officers parking their cars and making for the prison. Some nodded or called out to her and she responded with Hi or Morning, stealing nebs to catch their expressions, wondering whether they had secret information on her. Had she been seen? She shuddered, sensing a difference – they didn't seem so matey; did that mean . . . ? If she looked furtive, she'd give herself away. Nothing for it but to brazen it out. Then she asked herself what she was guilty of. She hadn't breached security – but they'd consider she had: she'd crossed the line, the line that must never be crossed or you'd become one of 'them'.

Only a couple of days ago she'd been chatting with one of the probation officers based at the prison. When she'd asked about Tracey, someone from the same office, the probation officer had said, Oh, Trace, she had to leave, didn't she? She went to live with that fellow Bridges we had on C wing. You wonder at them, don't you?

Of course Donna had nodded and said, Yes, you do. The probation officer went on about what a fool Tracey was and how she'd regret what she'd done because these people were all recidivists and once they were hooked that was it. Donna didn't trust herself to speak out. She wanted to come on strong about the stupidity of vast generaliz-ations and how could drug users ever beat addiction if nobody believed they could. They were human beings too – and any one of us might become prey to addiction. But she said nothing and her chest burned with suppressed rage and fear.

She drew her keys, grinning at the men by the control panels, and called a greeting through the bulletproof screen. What am I playing at? she thought. I'm not one of them and I don't want to be.

Then it was out across the draughty yard. A white prison transport van had just arrived. She could tell them anywhere: big, ugly, unmarked vehicles with a series of small square windows set high along their sides. Their very anony-mity made them stand out. They bowled on, never stopping, and nobody would suspect they were carrying people. Soon the massive mesh gates would creak open and the van would trundle through to disgorge its contents at reception.

Not so long ago Shane would have arrived in one of those. As she unlocked the series of gates into the building, she understood suddenly the frenzy of those prisoners who babbled on half crazy with longing for wives and partners on the out. The awfulness of having to sit in the visits room facing your partner across a table, supervised by prison officers, unable to press the lover's body against your own, fling off your clothes, tear at each other . . . and then perhaps imagine your lover at liberty to do those things with someone else. It was enough to drive you mad with jealousy. She'd seen it, heard it, watched and listened, always detached, because it had never really registered with her before.

She reached her office, unlocked it, switched on the computer, dumped the referrals list on the table and sat back.

*

The morning raced by with her asking the usual questions, trying to ascertain what the prisoners wanted from the service and how they might best be helped. At the thought of running into Wes in the canteen, her stomach knotted. What if he had seen her out with Shane that night in the pub? If he knew, he could ask her straight out, or he could report her to security. He might be capable of doing that out of pique – he'd say she was stringing him along so she deserved it. Why couldn't she tell him straight out that she didn't want to see him again? It all came down to a mixture of not wanting to hurt his feelings, liking him anyway, and fearing what might happen if he suspected she was having a relationship with an ex-inmate. She'd been over this ground before but nothing changed – except that she grew more jumpy. Perhaps today she'd say it if she saw him.

She stomped along doing her loopy, extrovert number, moving by the maroon lads on D wing threes, who were about to stampede down for their lunches. Some already had their metal trays and she got a view of flabby chips, mushy peas and the usual unnameable thing in batter – fried panscrubber. She gave them a grin and answered their backchat with a bit of her own.

Entering the canteen, she didn't look around but made straight for the serving hatch. No sooner was she there, clutching a packet of cheese and salad sandwiches and a bottle of Evian water, than she flinched as a hand grasped her shoulder.

'Donna, are you ignoring me?'

'Wes.' She blushed and bumbled. 'Would I do that – am I so ignorant?'

'You tell me.'

They exchanged smiles. Donna tried for her looniest.

'Every time I've seen you, you've turned your head away.'

'I don't believe it. How could I ignore a handsome hunk like you, Wes?' He was having some obscene mince thing with spud jammed on top – shepherd's pie, she presumed. 'You could get poisoned from that,' she said to divert him.

'You want to convert me, is that it?'

They had a bouncy discussion on meat-eating versus vegetarianism and ended up trading insults and roaring with laughter. This attracted a group of Wes's colleagues to their table, which reassured Donna. He wouldn't be able to start on anything personal with the others around. She hoped to rattle down her sandwiches and rush off before he could ask her any difficult questions. She'd never been good at lying: she always started giggling, making the whole subterfuge transparent.

Every time she looked up from her sandwich, she found Wes watching her. His gaze seemed speculative, as though he were weighing her up. He must know. Now he was waiting for an opportunity to expose her. But this was stupid, pure guesswork. She must appear her normal self – bright, joky, all froth and feathers. What if he had set a trap for her? He could well be spying on her. Every day when she drew her keys, her eyes were caught by the dancing red letters in the moving strip: SECURITY AWARE-NESS – ARE YOU LOOKING? They had been instructed to be vigilant at all times; that slackness and routine could be your undoing. You started to let things slide, to trust, and then one day, hey presto, disaster. Nobody actually spelled out what the disaster might be – prison escapes, hostage taking, murder of staff and inmates. She ran through the alternatives and stopped. Wes had focused on her.

'Now then, you hulk, what are you wittering on about?'

'Wittering – I like that!' He laughed but wasn't going to be deflected. 'You aren't in today, are you? I've told her she's avoiding me. I think I'm in the dog house.'

The others guffawed.

'Abject apologies.'

'I'm not making much headway with her today.'

They all looked at her. She blushed, feeling idiotic and scared.

'I'd best be off – some of us have work to do,' she said and pulled a face.

'I'm coming. You aren't rid of me yet.'

She forced herself to appear pleased and walked beside him towards the door and then out into the narrow flagged way leading to the prison entrance.

'We're meant to be having a date,' he said. 'So when's it going to be, Donna?'

'Oh, right . . . yes. When had you in mind?'

'Tonight?'

'That would be nice but I'm doing my mate's hair for her.'

'Tomorrow?'

'Yes, fine, brilliant.'

They arranged to meet in a town pub. Donna hurried off to her room, cursing herself for her inability to avert the invitation, but still convinced that excuses would have made him suspicious.

Three clients to see. Everything they said pierced her. She felt she hadn't really listened properly before. Her head ached, she wanted to be sick. For days she'd lost her preoccupation with Joanne, hadn't rushed to the newsagent's to buy the evening paper and scan it for information. Now, while she sat concentrating on her last client of the afternoon, the thought of Joanne returned – Joanne smiling in an old photo in her album, Joanne just like any other girl, only she wasn't, she was already marked out.

Not until she was on her way into town, with Galaxy lolloping along, could she begin to relax. All this thought of disaster demanded a little comforter, so she parked up and made for Debenham's where a sale was going full belt.

Emerging from the car park she caught sight of Jade across the road, coming from the Drugs Advisory and Needle Exchange headquarters. Donna watched as she scrabbled in her handbag for a cig, fished one out and lit up, then raised her head and looked across the road. Their eyes met.

'Hi, Jade,' Donna called and went over.

'Oh, hiya.' Jade took a long uneasy drag on her cig.

'I've just come into town for a bit of retail therapy. Fancy a coffee? We could pop in here if you like.' They were just passing the library snack bar. Donna didn't know whether she really wanted this chat – she'd rather have plunged straight into her shopping binge – but it felt unavoidable.

This time it was self-service. They got biscuits and coffee and sat at a small table surrounded by an exhibition of pictures composed of black blobs and a few strategically positioned black lines.

'Never been in here before,' Jade said. 'Don't rate them pictures. Not bad though, is it?'

'No, I drop in here when I want a quick coffee. It's quite handy.'

'Are you still seeing Shane?' Jade asked after they'd been quiet for a while. Donna noticed the slight tremor in her fingers.

'That's right.'

'OK is he, then?'

'Seems fine to me.' Donna wondered what she meant. She detected a hesitation in Jade's question. Did Jade imply that he might be ill? No, it wouldn't be that, it'd be a question about the old enemy. Donna's chest felt tight. Was he back on smack? She nipped out her exhausted roll-up, opened her tobacco tin and dribbled a line of threads onto a Rizla paper. She needed to be doing something.

'You know about him?'

'You mean the smack?'

'Yer. Yer, that's it.'

'I mean, I know that he used to.'

Donna began to go under. It was as though she was submerged in water; drowning, her lungs bursting. Panic flipped her heart. Her palms sweated. She didn't want to hear what Jade might tell her.

'Yer, well it's like . . . it, like, takes you over. You know that.'

'Actually I'm a drugs worker in the nick.'

'Oh, right.' Jade shook out another a cig and lit up. She inhaled with real need, sucking like a vacuum cleaner absorbing dust. Her right hand shook; her left played with crumbs on her plate. 'I'm a user,' she said and her eyes flicked up at Donna. 'Correction, I used to . . . I'm on Methadone, like. I go to see someone every week. I have to beat it. I was just coming from there.'

'What made you decide you'd give up?' This was the old professional self surfacing. She'd automatically slipped into the question that would elicit the information.

'Yer, well – things happen. You, like, get to think things – and anyway if I don't stop I'll lose my kids.'

'Is that right?'

'Yer, the kids'll have to go into care. They take 'em away. The social workers say you can't cope, you're not a good parent. But, like, when somebody dies . . . that makes you think.'

'Yes – you mean from an overdose?'

'Yer, but you know, like . . . well, yer.'

She trailed off, but before Donna could ask a question Jade spoke up again.

'You see, I been on smack since I was sixteen. I started going with this kid – was a good bit older than me. He was a user. Half the time he'd be asleep. He was injecting. Well, I wanted to try it. You know how you are at that age –

you're into everything. He knew I'd have to do it . . . once you're on smack your partner has to be or you'd never stay together. So he gives me a washout and by God, did I throw up! After that I never looked back.'

Donna found herself listening hard, as though she might be hearing about Joanne.

'When I'd done it, like, for three months, I'm on my way into town to sign on and I get stomach cramps and I have to go into this pub and use their toilet and I'm shivering and hot at the same time like I've got fever.' Her chalky skin strained with tension. 'I felt like a space cadet and I was real irritable – it was like I was different from everybody else.'

Donna bought them another coffee. For the first time Jade was the one wanting to talk, and Donna knew she needed to listen.

'Ta, love. See, it was then I knew as I was hooked. I didn't realize it before – thought I could just pack it up if I wanted. You can guess what then – we'd be shoplifting together to get the money for the smack. I got sent down at the finish. Of course while I was in nick he was off then with everything – the cash, the drugs. After that it had to be the streets . . .'

Donna nodded.

'Didn't Shane tell you?'

'No, Jade, he didn't. I think I kind of guessed, though, that first time I saw you.'

'Yer, well . . .'

'Doesn't it scare you stiff?'

'Yer, sometimes . . . Yer, it's fucking awful.'

Donna was back again with the image of Joanne out in the dark behind the stores, standing on corners, watching the cars rolling by on the dual carriageway out of the city.

'It's never knowing who you're getting, that's what scares the shit out of you. Though I do have regulars – they'll be some fellers who stop on their way home from work, fellers in nice Rovers, Jags, fellers in suits with briefcases. But there's plenty from out of town, here on business. There's been times when I never thought I'd get back home alive. One feller, young chap, in a real flash car, he drives me out into the country. I've told him it'll be twenty quid, straight sex in his car with Durex, and he's said OK. Anyway, I hear warning bells once he orders me to get out and rams me up against the bonnet. He was real rough, like crazy. Afterwards he wouldn't pay me and started kicking me, slapped me around and roared off. I didn't know where I was. All sorts can happen. Mind you, I'm lucky it's not been worse. Me and this other lass, we used to work together sometimes – we used her flat. She's dead now, like.'

Donna heard the blood thumping in her ears. None of the men's stories had ever struck such horror into her as this. 'Why did she die?' she croaked, unable to look at Jade.

'She got killed – murdered, like.'

This blows your mind, Donna thought. This is where madness starts. 'Why?' She had to put the question, although her armpits ran hot with sweat and her heart banged as though it would explode.

'They haven't got anybody – they don't know who did it. But after that, like, I decided I'd have to pack it in. It'd come in too close . . . it's different when you know some-one real well.'

'Christ! It's monstrous.'

'Yer, that's about it. A few girls have got killed lately. I mean, it can happen. Nobody's bothered, though, once they find out you're a working woman.'

Donna smoked a roll-up, unable to speak, while Jade chain-smoked in silence.

'I don't want to upset you, love,' Jade said at last.

'Was she – was she called Joanne?'

Something flickered in Jade's face as she met Donna's eyes. 'Yer? Why you askin'? Seen it in the papers?'

'Oh, this does my head in. This is too much. She was my friend, the girl I hung around with all the time at school, and she was always larking about, and then to finish up . . .'

'Your friend?'

'Yes.'

'Like I said, we worked together. I'd known her a long while. God, it's a small world.'

'I can't hack this at all.' Donna's hands trembled so much that she had difficulty making herself another roll-up. She sat inhaling, staring unseeing at the blobby paintings with the strangest feeling that this encounter was unavoidable – the sensation that she had to meet Jade, hear this story.

'Look,' Jade said, 'I have to go – it's the kiddies' tea and everything.'

'Yes,' Donna said, 'yes, of course. Will we meet here again – I mean if you're going to be in town about this time?'

'I'm not very regular with things, but I'll keep a lookout for you – bound to see you huntin' for bargains. I always have to go to the exchange regular.'

She left, putting her fags and lighter into her purse and clopping away on her neck-breaking stilettos, looking from the back like a scrawny teenager. She was a blown-glass figurine, so slender she might snap in half. Blown glass – it conjured up a piercing feeling of loss. Donna had longed for blown-glass animals once. The craze was at its height when they spent a week at Whitby. A shop near the steps displayed fawns, cats, dogs and people, all made of glass and so fragile your fingers dared hardly touch them. Her mother bought her a Bambi with spindly legs and black bobbly eyes but on the way back home somehow it broke. She howled with regret and it was no good any-body trying to console her with the thought of a future visit to Whitby. She wanted the creature at that moment, not next summer, a whole year away. Oh, how the past and present intertwined and tormented.

For a long time after Jade's departure, Donna sat at the café table, gazing blankly at the pictures and turning over their conversation. There was so much she wanted to ask, felt she must know. She couldn't stop thinking of the scene out in the country at night with Jade and the crazed driver. That could have been Joanne – a flash young chap in a sports car could have killed her later. But Jade said nobody knew who had killed Joanne – or was it 'they don't know'? 'They' must be the police. Had Jade got any idea who the killer might have been? Most murders were after all domestic – women killed by their husbands, partners – and this case might not be any different, but for the fact that Joanne's work must have brought her into contact with all sorts of weirdos.

And taking that risk, day in day out, with your life, all because of smack, the craving – she knew she had never really felt the extent and impact of it on a person's life until now. With the men in prison their smack habit cut them off from other human beings, ruined them mentally and physically, but at least it didn't present them constantly with the possibility of a hideous death.

She left the café and instead of going shopping – the thought of looking at rails of clothes sickened her – she turned off to the right and, after a short walk, reached the remnant of the dock and followed it as it curved round. She was making for the old ferry point, where she had sometimes stood with Shane, gazing out over the estuary.

Once she crossed the frantic main road, she reached a much quieter area. The wholesale fruit and vegetable market had closed for the day, leaving a few lorries onto which wooden pallets were still being loaded. Soon she was striding by the low brick wall with the breeze from the estuary in her face. Today the fudge-coloured water was like a plain patterned with cappuccino-foam frills. She wondered how Joanne could possibly have lived her life driven by a craving so strong that even degradation and the threat of a violent death couldn't shock her out of it. And how could it start so easily, as a longing for kicks, a way out of boredom?

Impervious to everything else, she stood by the wall, gazing out over the water – it was a good place to think and the chunter of the waves helped calm her.

The terrible power of smack over Joanne's life brought her back once more to Shane – and made her wonder how on earth he could have conquered his addiction. She needed to tell him she'd met up with Jade again, talk about Joanne – but somehow she couldn't quite bring herself to do so. The shadow seemed to be drifting back. All this time she'd been able to disregard it, banish her many misgivings for long periods. Most of the time Shane seemed just fine, cut free from the tentacles of the smack and stealing . . . but how did she know? Smack squeezed the life out of people – it wouldn't loosen its tentacles. Look at all those dead women: they couldn't extricate themselves, could they?

She'd never asked Shane about his past drug taking; had never put the question: Are you still using? He must believe she had such confidence in him that she'd never dream that he might still be in the grip of heroin.

Would he turn up this evening? She wanted him to be there; needed assurance that would drive out her doubts; longed to spend one of their high-octane nights together. They left her exhausted, wanting to get away, but only hours later that fierce desire for him would be back. It'd had never been anything like this with any other boyfriend.

If he didn't appear tonight, she'd not get to see him tomorrow either because she'd gone and agreed to the date with Wes. She could have got out of it, but it would have been too difficult, too embarrassing; more than that, dangerous. Was she being melodramatic? She had to get things in perspective. So what if she was seeing Shane? It wasn't as though he was a murderer, a bank robber or a rapist, was it? He did a few drugs, stole because he needed the money for them. A few drugs? Heroin addict. If you said it like that, *heroin addict*, the picture changed. There could be mitigating circumstances, but was there anything that could put a person beyond the pale? Yes, obviously there was. Of course, the prison authorities just had to make sure that nobody was a security risk; they weren't concerned with moral judgements.

Donna's thoughts were interrupted by the purring of her mobile at the bottom of her rucksack. She fished it out. 'Oh, Lisa, hi.' They talked for a while about an ace top Lisa had just bought; about Lisa's hair, which, contrary to what Donna had told Wes, she was not going to cut and colour that evening. They made an arrangement for hairdressing the following week. 'Yes, you need it spiking up a bit more,' Donna said. Under the influence of Donna's pink tufts, Lisa was toying with the idea of either green or blue hair.

'Only teenagers launch out a bit with colour. By the time you've hit your twenties, you're meant to be a right old dweeb,' Donna said and guffawed. She was amazed how confident she sounded, when her insides clenched and ached as if braced for something unpleasant. She was reluctant to return to her car and drive home, but with Lisa's voice chirping away, she set off walking back to the car park.

Lisa went on about some woman at work. 'She's a real cow is that one.' And that linked Donna back to the ordinary world of clothes and backbiting and evenings messing with each other's hair, dressing up, videos – hilarious nonsense stuff. That was how it used to be with Joanne. Only the Joanne times were much crazier because Joanne knew no fear. There was the time they'd been babysitting for Lee and she'd drunk the best part of a bottle of cherry brandy – Donna had joined in but hadn't downed as much. By the time Maggie got home they couldn't stop giggling. Donna ended up vomiting in the lav, pissed out of her face, but not Joanne: oh, no, she played the sweet, caring babysitter.

Right at the end of the conversation Lisa said, 'Have you heard anything else? I mean about Jo?'

'No,' Donna said, the awfulness seeping back. She couldn't tell her about Jade, that was completely outside Lisa's experience. She'd be bound to pronounce judgements like Gran always did. And anyway, it was all too raw, something she didn't yet understand herself. To save herself from Lisa's speculations, she said she'd have to be going.

At home, Rups deigned to meet her at the door. He'd been playing it very cool recently, ignoring her, but now he seemed to have forgotten his sulk and allowed himself to be picked up and stroked. A baritone purr rumbled against her chest. She rubbed her nose on his stripy head and felt the silk of his fur tickling her nostrils. Everything would be all right – bound to be.

She dawdled from feeding Rupert to organizing her own meal. She didn't like cooking, never had. In the end she grilled three vegetarian sausages, which weren't too disgusting, fried some cold potatoes and boiled some frozen peas. Not too hideous, she decided.

Exhaustion dragged at her eyelids and her legs. She wanted to sleep but at the same time she was alert, listening for his feet on the flagged path beyond the window. If he didn't turn up this evening, where would he be? She floundered in the aura of the desolate street where he lived: the syringes lying in gutters, the boarded-up fronts, the rubbish piled up where once gardens lay. There was a watchfulness down there. Unseen eyes peered at you from behind stained blinds. Drug City. Smack Paradise.

In this world of hide and seek, where she was constantly braced for the unexpected, any definite time demarcations had disappeared. Days could crash by without her noticing anything but her own preoccupations. She moved about in a dream, all her senses mesmerized by what was happening in her head.

Must ring Mumsie, she told herself, in an effort to wrench herself out of it. Promised to call by . . . oh, hell! But then she heard footsteps by the window and jumped with shock – but the steps went on past. Perhaps he wouldn't come now, not this evening. She shuddered when the phone rang at nine thirty. 'Hi,' she breathed, wanting to hear Shane's voice.

'Hello, love . . .'

'Oh, hello, Mum. Sorry, I didn't manage to get round – been a bit busy, you know.' Mustn't let her guess anything, must keep her off the scent, she told herself. Mustn't let her find out about Shane. When Shane was working on the wall that Saturday morning and her mother asked why Donna and he were chatting, she hadn't been easy with it. Then there had been the little pep talk later, of course, and that had been unusual because Mum wasn't somebody who said things out straight. You were left feeling guilty and unsatisfactory and somehow in the wrong. If you challenged her it didn't make it any easier. Gran was much more straightforward. If she didn't like something, she declaimed; shot you down and wouldn't change her mind;

she was also quite capable of raising the roof if she thought she was being squashed.

'How are things?' Donna got in straight away. Her mother sounded tired. The school was chaotic; everybody was stressed. Some French teacher had broken down and loads of others were off sick. It was all bad backs, breakdowns and bronchial pneumonia. Sounded a bundle of laughs. Oh, and the school was being accused of having excluded difficult 'statemented' pupils because of the inspection.

Donna struggled to concentrate, still listening for footsteps. The questioning was turned on her now. How was she? Well, great, no probs. Yer, just eaten – Rups been fed too. Was Mumsie surviving then? Donna didn't listen properly to Maggie's response, because she could hear Shane's tread coming up the path. Hastily she excused herself, somebody at the door.

He was there, cheeks smelling of evening coldness, hands cool. He came in and she fluttered about him, going into her loony act. He was quiet and smiling. She realized she was tense, unnerved by what was unspoken between them, things she wanted to ask but couldn't bring herself to. At times she'd glimpse unknown areas in him and then they'd slide away and she'd dismiss them – Shane was a man with whom she'd shared experiences, reached a certain trust . . . but had she? Those scary, unknown areas moved beneath the surface, threatening to leap out.

She made him cheese on toast. They drank a couple of cans of lager and sat on the sofa, not touching. She knew that once she felt his hands on her, she'd lose her resolve to speak of what nagged away inside her head.

'Shane,' she managed, and he turned to look into her face. He'd been quiet for a while, abstracted, and she imagined she saw a wildness in his eyes that were now all pupil. He focused on her face but as he smiled, the sweetness of his expression lit the heat between her legs. He traced the tattoos on her upper arm; one finger stroked her throat.

Caressing, not yet kissing, they manoeuvred on the sofa. Her upper body was naked, reclining across him. His hands slid over the patterns on her shoulders, those brilliant tropical forests that extended down her back.

'You're a strange girl, Don,' he whispered. His hands were around her throat. The sensation was arousing. Hands on her neck – they could pleasure, they could kill, so easily. The thought settled in her head and she couldn't lose it. 'There aren't many people I trust, Don, but I trust you.'

Not until they ended up rolling to and fro on the carpet, did her mind move onto another track.

He surprised her then when he scrabbled in the pocket of his jeans jacket and pulled out a small blue box. 'For you,' he said. Donna found his slight embarrassment touching. 'Open it then, come on.' His face was eager, reminding her of Lee when he was a kid and used to be so enthusiastic.

'Oh, wow!' she said, holding up the silver chain. It would have cost him a lot of money, cash he'd earned labouring, doing hard dirty work. 'This is really fantastic,' she said, moved by his generosity. He fastened it round her neck and, kissing him, she told him she'd always wear it. Later they climbed the stairs to bed, arms around each other.

Shane slept as though he was dead, neither moving nor making a sound. She lay for a while, watching his face. Rups padded into the room. He peered at the bed, leapt into a basket chair and coiled his tail round his paws, settling into a breathing heap.

18

The next day Donna breezed about at work looking her most flamboyant in a long-sleeved purple T-shirt covered with pale blue and candy-pink tie-dye blobs, and navy cargo pants. Hysteria powered her through the afternoon. She'd told Shane she'd to meet a work colleague that evening and not to come round.

At lunchtime in the canteen Wes waved to her and mouthed 'tonight' and she nodded in acknowledgement.

Her stomach lurched. She was sure he would challenge her about Shane. From fear of a confrontation she switched to certainty that she was merely overreacting. He wouldn't have seen them. She'd give herself away if she didn't stop making assumptions. Whatever happened she'd brazen it out, laugh him into submission and then freeze him off.

By evening she felt sick with suspense. She'd already lost her job; been blacklisted by the Home Office and couldn't pay her mortgage so her house was being repossessed. When she was little they'd lived in a series of flats and never seemed to have enough money. Mum bought her school uniform from the second-hand sales that were held each term. These always had some posh kid's nametape stitched in them. But worse had been those dresses bought from the market. Looking back, Donna realized what a pain she must have been. Nowadays, she haunted tat shops in search of bargains and cast-offs and even had an aversion to new furniture – yet still she had this fear of being destitute.

In the corner of the Lion, Wes had a drink waiting for her and had taken possession of a table.

'Hiya, Donna,' he said. 'At last – thought we'd never make it. Thing about the blessed job is you lose touch with your social life.'

'What have you been getting up to then, Wes? Cheers. Ta for the lager.'

'Think nowt on't. Lots of aggro. Been to the gym – got to keep fit, makes you feel like that in there, there's that much disease about.'

'I suppose so – Aids and hep C and everything?'

'Oh, yer. You ought to have a hep C jab – you had one?'

'No,' she said, beginning to sweat in case this was a starting point for insinuating that he knew about Shane.

'Well, you should – you can easily catch it, you know.'

'Only through the exchange of bodily fluids,' she dared, staring at him and grinning. This felt like striding across a frozen pond, fathoms deep; if the ice were to splinter, she'd plunge to the bottom – water in her nostrils, heart clamouring.

He didn't respond but quaffed his pint and shook the bag of peanuts into her palm. 'Get stuck in,' he said, pushing the bag towards her.

'Seems like you're feeling down in the dumps?'

'You could say that. Don't seem to be getting anywhere – no openings in the job. Everything you think you might do, no cash. I don't want to be penned up in that shithole until I'm sixty-five.'

She encouraged him to talk and he ran on for a while, moving onto his ex-partner. 'Bumped into her in Boots the other day – I could hardly believe I'd been with her all that time. We can't speak to each other, you know.'

'Difficult,' Donna said.

'You get straight back on the arguments after ten minutes.'

'Good job you're out of it then.'

'Yer, you could say that.'

He glanced over at the *Hull Daily Mail*, which someone at the next table had left as he went to the bar. It was open at an article about the four prostitutes who had recently been found murdered in the city.

'Well,' he said, 'they had it coming.'

'What do you mean?' Donna said, feeling her cheeks flame.

'Women like that know what they're in for.'

'Wes, how can you say that? Don't you understand, whatever they might be doing, have done, they're still human beings and they don't deserve that? I think it's just horrendous. The ones you ought to be blaming are the brutes who battered them to death.'

'OK, OK, Donna. Take it easy, don't go off on one. What is it with you and prostitutes?'

'My best friend from school just happens to have been one of those four.'

She could see he didn't know what to do with that information.

'Look, Wes, this is going to have to be a quick drink because I'll have to get off – I'm absolutely knackered and it's work tomorrow. Got to keep on the ball.'

'I want to get to know you better, Donna,' he broke in. 'But I kind of have the feeling you're holding me at a distance.'

'Go on,' she said and laughed.

'I wasn't born yesterday.'

Alarm bells shrilled. 'Before you get yourself launched, Wes, I honestly have to go. We're friends and it's nice to meet up now and again for a bevvy, isn't it?'

'That's what I mean. Still, next time – if you want there to be a next time – or are you trying to give me the hint?'

'Oh, Wes, I like you and I'm not.' She grinned at him and he grasped her hand. She knew she was playing a crafty game. Her hope was to disentangle herself from him without alienating him – that way he wouldn't get vindictive. No, he couldn't have seen her and Shane. She was safe for the moment – but then again, why else would they have got to talking about the hep C jab?

19

When Ruby first heard the news, she didn't take it in properly and dismissed it as just a bit of corporation blether. But then Jessie from floor fifteen came winging down and tinkled her door chimes. Ruby let her in and she squatted on Ruby's settee and fumed.

'Look, Rube, I've lived here for thirty year and they're not movin' me now.'

Ruby was shocked to realize that she too had been in her flat for that long.

'We moved in when they was brand new. There was nowt but fields down yonder – remember?'

'Aye, that's a fact.' Ruby nodded and gazed out at the barrack-type houses way below. You could see for miles across the whole estate, across roads and the snaking rail track, to where the estuary stretched, a pale smudge on the horizon. She could just make out the shadowy swoop of the Humber Bridge. That bridge wasn't there then, of course, you crossed on the ferry – the ferry, which was her honeymoon journey, a voyage to Lincolnshire with Billy sipping his pint and she her tea and savouring her sausage roll. The day dithered before her in a haze of heat, bleached by memory, and she saw Billy's forearms propped on the bar, arms solid with muscle, the wrists thick, his white shirt-sleeves rolled up to the elbow. He wasn't used to wearing a shirt. His Waistell's jacket was slung over a chair back.

'We can't sit here and let 'em do it,' Jessie stormed. 'There's nowt wrong with this place.'

'That's right,' Ruby said.

Only now was she registering what the corporation edict would mean – pull down the tower blocks, demolish the lot, end of their little community . . . just like when they pulled down the old houses. An amputation. The tower blocks could be seen for miles around, looming up out of the estate, huge white spindles like skyscrapers. Like the skyscrapers that Leroy would see, a part of his landscape. I'm in New York, she used to tell herself, New York, the city of dreams. Thinking that had eased the pain of finding herself beached out there on the estate, far from the bustle of the world where she had grown up with the estuary on the doorstep and the smell of fish in her nostrils.

The first sight of the tower block had chilled her. When they crammed into the lift and she saw the curious cubby-hole in one corner of it and wondered what it might be, a man beside her said, That's for the coffins, love.

In the whole of that great spindle only seven tenants were left now. All the rest had moved out: couldn't stand it, or dead. The place ran riot with drugged-up lads, needles and number two all over, before the corporation took matters in hand. They had a door now in the entrance that locked out the riffraff, the roaming druggies and the vandals. The tower blocks were secured against them, impregnable, whereas the houses had boards at the windows and nobody wanted to live in them because they were raided constantly. There was talk of transplanting refugees and asylum seekers from the wars that Ruby glimpsed on her telly screen. The corporation suggested it, but had to withdraw their plan. The estate-dwellers had made it clear they'd finish the newcomers, if they were dumped on their territory.

When you stood at the window gazing over the blocks of houses, they looked innocent enough, an emerald sheen to the open-plan lawns. You'd have no idea that beneath this bland exterior so much mayhem moiled away.

At ground level the picture changed – druggie lads slinking by, glue sniffers bombed out of their minds, scabby dogs running in packs, young lasses yelling abuse at bairns, young lasses who might end up murdered like Joanne.

'Yer,' Jessie chuntered, 'we was here at the start. They shoved us in here – said it was slum clearance – and now they want to do it again. What do they think we are, eh?'

'Aye, it was going to be a better life . . . fields, country. This corporation feller came round to my nana before she died. You'll have a better life out there, Missus, he said, these houses have had it. She looked him straight in the eye. The only time you'll move me from here is in me box, she said, and she meant it. And that's what happened.'

Ruby didn't mention to Jessie that other strange things had conspired to make her leave the area.

After Ernie died of his heart attack and she was running the Mermaid by herself, she'd sometimes feel a presence near her. It was as though strong hands touched her shoulders, an arm came round her waist – not unpleasant, not at all. In fact, truth be told, this had started before Ernie's death. Ernie complained that the pub didn't suit him – ever since they'd gone there things didn't seem to go right. First he slipped and broke his arm lugging barrels in the cellar, then he said he couldn't breathe, felt breathless all the time. There were other incidents too – but for her it was different. Ruby knew Ernie cuddled Cindy, one of the barmaids, in the cellar, and always had to have his hands on some young girl, but she didn't care, because she felt protected, safe in the pub.

Following Ernie's death she became involved with a chap who always eyed her up when she was working behind the bar. Well, he fell, as though he'd been pushed, down the cellar steps one night and nearly broke his neck, and even though Ruby couldn't care less about him, she started to feel jumpy, and decided that all in all she must move on.

'We'll have to get together and protest,' Ruby said. 'Tell 'em we're too old to move now – been here too long.'

Squawker trilled, honked harshly, and switched to comments in a prissy female voice in an attempt to divert Ruby's attention.

'All right, Squawks, we've heard you,' Ruby said finally.

Jessie peered at him in consternation. 'That's some beak he's got.'

'Aye, I've always liked boys with big beaks.'

Jessie gave a burst of delighted, horrified laughter.

After her friend had gone, Ruby tried to figure out what to do. She couldn't imagine them bringing the great ball and chain and whopping away at the sides of the building. It'd be a disgrace. For a long time now she knew most of the flats were empty and that didn't bother her. She felt secure up there, suspended above the battleground, cocooned in the world of her living room, white fitted kitchen, bathroom, bedroom and corridor with its built-in cupboards. Everything was handy. Heating rose from the floor – no mess, no trouble; a waste chute for her rubbish. No repairs to trouble over, lavs icing up in winter, leaks, slates off roofs.

She'd grown a feeling of kinship with this thirty-year-old megalith. It contained all the ghosts of people who had lived in it for brief spells; the ones who didn't have the stamina to stay on, daunted in the times of shitting in lifts and stairwells and abandoned syringes.

The stalwarts, the famous seven, must have a combined age of several hundreds. She met them in the community charity shop on the estate, when they dropped by to rummage along the clothes rails or just natter to the staff. These of course were all quite recent developments. The old days were shopless, drop-in-centreless. For a long time it was hope-for-the-best, make-your-own-way on that waste of grass and half-built maisonettes, right away from the city centre and the heart of things you'd known all your life. But once transplanted you could adjust. These wild, mad, drugged kids had grown up anchorless, without a history. All they'd ever known were the lines of estate houses with metal clothes poles and boarded-up windows and cig packets and crisp bags bowling along in the wind, people dropping rubbish at random, and dads, if there were any, drawing benefit, turning violent and braying them and their mams.

Ruby realized, and not for the first time, that in her youth lads like the estate vandals and druggies would have been on trawlers – young men, men of Billy's ilk, bursting with go, who needed to test themselves, pit their energies against a world greater than themselves and their muscles, a sea that could kill them. Now, though, there was nothing for these lads, no challenge – they didn't fit. They'd forfeited that valour, the valour that trawler life demanded. Billy hated the sea but it was his life – he couldn't have been anything other than a trawlerman. That kid, the 23-year-old who'd overdosed, he didn't know who he was – never found out, just dodged the issue and died.

Whenever Maggie told her that she should leave the estate, which she did frequently, Ruby's reply was always the same: I'm staying put. Been here too long to uproot – it's what I know.

Later that day Ruby's telephone trilled. There was going to be a meeting in one of the seven's flats on the tenth floor, was she up for it?

'I s'll be there,' she said, already perking with an adrenaline rush. She wouldn't let this place be knocked down with the great iron ball . . . or would they fetch it down with explosives?

Ruby doodled her pink lipstick over her mouth, had a quick squirt of Donna's fruity Christmas spray and then she was ready for the ride up to floor ten.

Jessie's permed grey head bobbed vigorously. She was in conversation with Lydia, whose flat this was. Then there was Ray, who used to work as a bobber on the fish dock years ago. He was one of those very neat types, never been married, minded his mam until she went and had lived on his own ever since. You'd never suspect he'd had anything to do with the sea. Winnie was a stick-thin, wittery woman, another widow.

After Ruby had been in the flat five minutes the last two arrived: Bella, a widowed housewife, and George, who'd worked on the buses for years.

'Right,' Jessie started, 'who wants coffee and who's for tea?'

Hands shot up. 'Which is it, then?' Ray wanted to know.

'Coffee first,' Jessie laid down. Hands dallied, half raised, while people gossiped. Jessie grew a bit tetchy.

After another twenty minutes they settled down with mugs in their hands and a plate of biscuits before them.

'It'll have to be a petition to the council,' Jessie said.

'Think they'll take notice of that?' Ray growled.

'Yes, they'll have to,' Jessie said. She used to manage a shoe shop and her attitude had certainly never taken retirement. Ruby noticed her surveying their footwear with a critical eye. They'd had some fascinating talks about shoes – it seemed they both had a shoe fetish – though Jessie's was more restrained and utilitarian than Ruby's. When Ruby showed her some of her more improbable purchases,

Jessie's response was a sniff. Jessie wore stout, baskety shoes for the wider foot, always in fawn or black, no colours, shoes that had bunion pockets and no drama or music in them.

'What we ought to do,' George said, 'when we've done the petition, is go together to the Guildhall when they're having a council meeting and hand it in.'

'They won't take no notice of us,' Ray said at once.

'Well, what do you suggest instead, Ray?' Jessie said, growing tetchier by the second.

Two hours or so later Jessie fetched out a sherry bottle. Some people had to drink from tumblers. Decisions were made. Residents in the other high rises would be approached to sign the petition – after all, their turn would no doubt come, so they'd better help. Ruby agreed to be part of the signature-collecting group.

'It'll be all right, lad, we s'll see to it, Ray,' George said. 'No need for you to get excited.'

'No, I'm not sayin' –'

'Well, shurrup then!' George finished and Ray subsided.

Ruby couldn't wait to start. The last time they all got moved nobody raised a protest . . . well, they were meant to be going to a better life. That was what the corporation would say this time – but Ruby intended to tell them it was too late for that, they were all too long in the tooth to be fobbed off.

In the lift down to floor six, Ruby reflected on Nana's refusal to move from her house; why she wouldn't come to live in the Mermaid, preferring to be alone there in her terrace. Even when all the other families had been bought off, she stayed on, every day watching from the window the removal vans trundling up like hearses, and she'd say to Ruby: They've gone now from number six . . . that's Snowdens gone . . .

Ruby knew she could go to live with Maggie, but she wouldn't. She couldn't be doing with that kind of life: the sort of food they ate and the mess, Lee's music enough to burst your eardrums. Anyway they were different from her; she wondered so often how she could have produced a daughter like Maggie, someone who inhabited such an alien world. She'd listen to Maggie talking and half the time she didn't know what she was on about. And the things she said – no wonder Donna never had a steady lad and Lee was such an oddment. Still, that was something you couldn't change.

No sooner was she back in her flat than the phone rang: Frank Prentice. What about it, was she up for the dogs in a few days' time, then?

The next afternoon Ruby decided to take a bus round to Maggie's. There were a number of things she wanted to investigate. She reckoned that Maggie would have to be back from work because that lad had to be fed – and a great lanky lad like that needed some filling. She'd often said to Maggie that the lad looked as though he'd got horse muck in his shoes. Only Billy had been near enough as tall – but of course Billy was no blood relation to Lee.

After the usual repeated pressings on the doorbell, Maggie appeared looking like washday. 'Oh, Mum,' she said, 'how nice to see you.'

'You've no need to put it on,' Ruby said. 'I expect that boy's got his music going.'

'It wasn't that. I couldn't hear because I'd got the radio on.'

Ruby snorted. 'How are you then?'

'I've had the car nicked. First everybody had their tyres slashed – that was four weeks ago – and now I go out into the street this morning and it's gone.'

Ruby laid her mac on the sofa and sat down by the table. 'Can you turn that off, Margaret?' she said. 'Music like that gives me the pip, makes me think of the crem.' She supposed it was what Maggie would call 'classical'. 'Police never do anything,' she pronounced.

'Are you having some tea, Mum?'

'Well, I've come but I'm not stopping.'

Maggie was at the cooker stirring the thing she called a wok. Ruby hoped whatever it was wouldn't be so undercooked it got under her palate. Before any sort of conversation could get underway they heard thunder from overhead, and Lee hoofed into the room. 'Oh, Mum, is there any food?'

'Hello, Lee.'

'Oh, hiya, Gran.'

'I'm dishing up now,' Maggie said. 'Noodles and stir fry.'

Ruby waited for him to groan, but he didn't.

'Got to be quick,' he said. 'Doing fly-posting tonight.'

Ruby knew about these forays. The lads went out with paste pots and stuck fliers in the streets announcing their latest gig. She noticed them stuck on sides of buildings, post boxes, electric installations, fences, hoardings. Before Maggie had explained it to her, she hadn't understood that these were underground messages, which Lee's age group could pick up. For such as Ruby, Maggie as well she supposed, they were just mindless pieces of rubbish, defacing public places. Now though, she took care to read about Big This and Fatty That or Ear-Blasting Detonations, Pressure Pumps, etc. Returning from a visit to Ivy one evening, Ruby had run into a group of lads. At first she had felt a twinge of panic. They all wore caps or Burglar Bill woollen pull-down hats, flapping trousers and boots that thwacked the pavements. They toted plastic bags crammed with an unknown cargo. She thought of muggings, then noticed that Lee was one of their number. He'd nodded at her and blushed. Hi, Gran, he'd muttered and then they were gone.

Ruby's ears pricked up when Lee raised his head from his gufflings and said, 'Eh, I saw Don in town the other night with a chap.'

'How do you mean?' Maggie said.

'What you on about? She was with a chap, like, holding hands.'

'Right. Who was it, then?'

'Is this an interrogation or something, Mum?'

'I just wondered if we knew him.'

'It was that feller who was working on our wall.'

'Oh.'

Ruby noticed how Maggie went quiet. Now she couldn't wait to know the significance of this news. Not long afterwards Lee blundered out. Blasts of music thundered from above and then the front door crashed to and the house quivered. Ruby heard Maggie sigh.

'I always wonder what he'll be getting into,' Maggie said, 'and I dread the phone ringing.'

'Who's this one who was doing the wall then, Maggie?'

'Er . . . it was a chap Donna said she knew from the prison.'

'You mean a warder?'

'No, I mean a prisoner.'

'What!'

'Yes, Mum, but we can't assume that just because he's been to prison he's beyond the pale. I mean if we do that we're perpetuating the . . .'

Ruby had already shut off. Maggie was doing her usual: lads mugged old women because they were poor and their dads were cruel to them or they hadn't got any dads – always some excuse. Nobody was ever responsible for his own badness. And then there'd be that tripe about lads not menacing old women – they went for other young lads, apparently, 'according to the statistics'. Maggie thought everything could be proved with a few numbers. Ruby snorted.

'Well, mark my words, Donna'll be heading for trouble with him. She's playing with fire and she'll get burnt.'

'Yes, yes, Mum, but God help us if we're going to write everybody off who ever transgresses.'

There she was, off again. Ruby didn't want to listen. 'Maggie, do you want your daughter to end up with a jailbird? And what about that lass, that Joanne, she got murdered, didn't she? They've not got anybody for that yet, have they?'

'Mum, for God's sake.'

When Maggie offered to call a taxi for her a while later, Ruby declined. She was in a huff but she was also agitated and upset about Donna. What was it that was opening up? Her grand-daughter and a convict . . . Ruby decided that she'd need a stiff port and lemon when she got back. She'd tell Squawker all about it.

20

Donna woke in the night. Shane's reassuring body wasn't there. She lay alone in the darkness except for the furry splodge of Rups near her feet. She tried to disentangle herself from a dream where she was out with Joanne. It might have been somewhere in town – perhaps a café in the Quay. Joanne's white leather jacket made her look anaemic but she was so delighted with her outfit that Donna hadn't the heart to say anything.

She tried to slide back into sleep but she was unsettled. She remembered the wretched bungee jump – she ought never to have volunteered for it.

By eight o'clock she was up and dressed and still struggling to throw off the feeling of having been with Joanne – perhaps Joanne was trying to tell her something. Gran always said dreams were significant. She said when her nana had dreamed of having teeth out, it meant a death. The night before her first husband drowned at sea, she dreamed she was washing clothes and that meant he'd not come back.

Spring bank holiday, a fête in the park to raise money for charity. Today was the big day. Donna had volunteered to do a bungee jump to raise money for Aids Action. Still the same humid weather: thick rods of rain came in bursts, followed by dry spells where the sun hung like a ripe grapefruit beneath the clouds.

She'd roped in Gran, Mum and Lee to attend. Both Mum and Gran issued dire warnings but Lee remained fairly detached, only showing any interest at the mention of bands and beer tents.

Donna had stomach ache. Why did she deliberately put herself in these positions, where she was scared out of her mind? She'd only had a mug of coffee and a piece of toast and raspberry jam before she drove down to the park, because they told you once you were in the air and somersaulting you could throw up or have a diarrhoea attack. The indignity of your breakfast slopping down your chin or a stinking brown patch spreading on the leg of your jeans was too humiliating to be contemplated. But now she was ravenous. Adrenaline pumped; her pulse raced; the day, people round her, all wafted a way off and increased her spaced-out feeling.

Crowds milled over the wide grassy circle of the park. The crane with the bungee equipment was over towards the children's play area. Donna glanced across at the yellow giraffe neck and shivered, though it was a day to make you sweat.

Another ghastly thing, perhaps the worst, was that your eyes could drop out and dangle down your cheeks with the pressure.

She tried to shut out her panic by looking at the stalls. Tie-dye shirts and cotton trousers, velvet trousers with drawstring waists – but they always made her backside look vast – trailing skirts reminiscent of the sixties. She'd investigate those afterwards, if she survived. She promised herself that she'd never do anything like this again.

Stalls offered Tarot card readings, aromatherapy, Indian head massage and all manner of New Age body therapies, as well as home-made jam and cakes, and geraniums and herbs growing in their pots. An Amnesty International stall exhorted people to fight injustice and support those imprisoned by brutal regimes. The Buddhist table was attended by shaven-headed monks in saffron robes. They protected their pamphlets with plastic sheeting; hapless flies scrabbled about trapped underneath.

The band in the marquee-cum-beer tent thundered and screeched and groups of lads in Lee's uniform of wafters and hooded tops strode out towards it, heads down, impervious to anything else.

Little kids queued by hot-dog and ice-cream vans, expectant faces raised.

What if she couldn't jump when she stood at the top looking down? Or the line holding her broke and sent her crashing to earth, snapping her bones?

Gran and Mum were shambling towards her, Lee trailing behind them and pretending he didn't belong. She caught sight of Jade with some kids in tow. Donna flapped her hand in her family's direction and went up to Jade.

'You aren't up for that, are you?' Jade said, laughing nervously.

'Yer, can't imagine why – must be mad.'

Jade puffed on her fag and coughed. She lurched along in her white stilettos.

'Mam, can we have some goodies?' a little blond girl pestered.

'I've told you, Sheralee, in a minute.'

'Wanna lolly,' the boy whinged.

'Yer, yer, in a minute. Wait on.'

Donna felt Mum and Gran earwigging and imagined them judging. Mum would want to help because she could see Jade was struggling. Gran was a different matter. She'd be thinking how badly behaved the kids were.

Jade was making for the bouncy castle in the children's play area. In an instant the three had shot off and soon flung themselves to and fro on the heaving structure. Donna sat down beside Jade on the plastic chairs intended for those supervising the kids; her whole body strung taut like a guitar string.

'How are things?' Donna said.

Jade inhaled deeply and gazed straight ahead, blinking. 'All right. You jumping in a minute, like?'

'I expect so.'

'Shane's not here, then?'

'No.'

Jade appeared to consider this for a while, then, distracted, she lit another fag from the butt of the last. Donna watched her trembling fingers.

'It's none of my business, right, like . . .'

What on earth was she going to say? The awful prospect of the bungee jump receded as she waited for Jade to speak.

'You can tell me to shut up, right, only you and him . . . well, it seems, like, funny . . . I mean, he's my brother an' all, but . . .'

'Yes?' Donna said.

'Well . . . he's . . . I mean, he's not like you.'

'Things are never what they seem,' Donna said and grinned, because Jade couldn't know how in tune she felt with Shane, how they had become part of each other.

'Yer, sure. But like . . . with you telling me about your friend, about Joanne.'

The skin on Donna's arms and back began to prickle with iciness.

'How do you mean?'

'Well, I wouldn't like anything to happen.'

In the silence between them kids shouted on the bouncy castle and music thumped from the marquee and the pit of her stomach burned, while her shoulders froze. Jade knew something deadly important, something she wasn't telling.

'I don't know what you're saying.' Donna heard her own voice sounding casual, as if unaware of Jade's agitation and the warning she wanted to give.

The children came pelting up. 'Lolly, lolly. You said. Mam, you said.'

'There's things you don't want to know. I've said all I can, see. OK, you kids, but you'll have to come now. Got to move, Donna,' she said, and Donna realized that Jade wanted to get away from her because she didn't trust herself any longer.

In a daze, Donna headed back to where Mum, Gran and Lee were waiting.

'All set, are you, love?' Mum said. 'Who was that you were nattering with?'

'Oh, just a friend of a friend.' Donna felt her mother's searching look – she didn't miss a trick and something about Jade had made her curious.

'I shan't look when you jump,' Gran wittered. 'I can't. I s'll have to turn my back.'

'Hi,' Lee mumbled. 'When is it then?' He was straining at the leash to get to the beer tent.

'Like soon.'

Being with her family diverted her a while from Jade's odd warning and from her inner terrors. She was frightened of heights, always had been. She used to wake up at night sweating with fear after dreaming of a ladder from whose broken treads she'd glimpsed a dizzying drop, then missed her footing and began to tumble down, screaming silently. And so she jerked awake. This jump could be that nightmare come true. Only what Jade had just hinted at was the real nightmare – leaving her hanging over a precipice. Dear God, what was this? What did it all mean? She wished now that Shane had been there and not her family – she'd been so careful not to mention the fête because she didn't want him to run into them. But if he had been there, Jade wouldn't have dropped those hints. Perhaps they didn't like each other. He never wanted to talk about her, didn't ever mention her. That could be why Jade was so negative about him.

'I'd best be getting on, seems they're ready,' she told Mum and Gran. Lee's eyes were already straying towards the marquee. He hated waiting for anything. She was amazed he'd even managed to get out of bed at this hour. The back of his T-shirt was emblazoned with the words FUCK UP. He was obviously off his head with dope or he wouldn't have worn it. Since he'd bought it, he'd been dodging about behind Gran, never in front of her. It was like when he'd pestered her till she took him to have his nipple pierced – Mum probably still didn't know about that.

Off she strode towards the tent and the crane. A chap sat at a table with a list. She gave her name and he ticked his list. She couldn't stop hearing Jade's voice: Well, I wouldn't like anything to happen. What could happen? She was slipping back into that world of battered bodies and severed limbs floating like weeds in the drain.

'Identification?'

She showed her driving licence and then zipped it into a pocket in her jeans. She could hardly focus on what the man was saying.

'Sign here, please.' He had to ask her twice and she stared at the paper, not taking in the print.

'You any false teeth?'

'No,' Donna said. Supposing you had, it would be too embarrassing, taking out your dentures and emerging toothless with fallen cheeks for all to see. Where would the teeth be put? The chap could hardly stack them up in piles on the table.

'Heart condition?'

'No.' But she had got a heart condition, a bad one . . .

'Don't have owt in the pockets, no jewellery or watches. Got your pockets empty? OK, wagons roll!'

Another chap outside the tent asked her to jump on the weighing scales. She liked this second chap better but he too had a dodginess about him – he didn't meet her eyes. His bony, handsome face reminded her of Shane's, but coarser. He ran through the questions again, then shook her hand. His firm handclasp reassured her and helped banish the horrors for a while.

'You're sure you've nothing in your pockets?'

'That's right.'

'OK, you're on.' He helped her into the harness. 'Right, now get in the cage,' he told her.

Once she was in, she had a moment of sheer panic. Gran's Squawker in his cage – like him, after her flutter round, she'd be locked in. She couldn't face not going through with this, but could she confront it and go on? The man got in the cage with her and fastened the gate.

'You'll not have time to look round. Do exactly what I say and you'll be fine.'

Up they zoomed by the side of the crane. Her T-shirt stuck to her. Why couldn't Jade tell her whatever she had to say? But she did trust Shane, she had to, she'd passed beyond the point where she could hold him at a distance. She kept her eyes on the metal struts of the cage.

'When we get up, I'll secure the cage and count three, then blow my whistle three times – on blast three you dive down towards the blue tent. Wave your arms on the way down but cross them on your chest when you start the ascent.'

Love can conquer anything, she thought.

As the man hitched the cage to the crane Donna looked down. The city spread out beneath her: the park, the bunchy green tree tops; the network of parallel roads; the green onion domes of the museum and art gallery; grey roofs and staked-out gardens; high-rise blocks; even the orange towers of the prison; crane arms by the dock; a gleam of water. She concentrated now on the park, desperate for the sight of someone she knew because the height diminished her, as though she wasn't there any more – she'd lost her sense of identity. She couldn't see Mum and Gran, Lee or Lisa, who was meant to be there somewhere; only ant-small strangers scurrying round stalls. At the fair on the loop-the-loop or the big wheel you could always wave at your friends down below, but not here – up here you were on your own. At the end you had to trust in whatever was out there, because there was nothing else . . .

Astronauts orbiting the earth must surely know this sensation, this feeling of being detached from all the familiar little things that made up an individual's life.

No, she couldn't possibly do it. She must ask the man to take her down again in the cage. She couldn't jump. If she did, she'd die; her eyes would drop out; she'd have a heart attack. But this was nothing, nothing compared with the nagging doubts that Jade had sowed in her. If only I could soar free of them, she thought, just take off into the blue out yonder.

The man said, 'I'll give you a hand if you get into difficulties,' which must mean 'a push'. Could she bear to be pushed over the precipice? She lived the moment of hurtling through the air, knowing that she'd strike the earth and that her bones would splinter on impact.

She must tell the man it was impossible and not to shove her out.

'Right, I'm blowing the whistle,' he said.

I'm twenty-eight and I don't want to die, she thought, wrestling with anguish . . . but Joanne didn't want to be murdered, did she? She dived. As she tumbled through the air, time ceased to exist. There was just the fall and then the bungee halted her with a jerk. Hysteria bubbled in her throat and she laughed and screamed and cried out in a mad release. Nothing mattered, just the soaring and plunging. She was buoyed up by a great sweep of energy. Laughing and screaming, she swooped and then passed into the descent.

As she was lowered upside down, two men moved forward to catch her.

Her mother's eyes streamed with tears as she hugged her. Even Lee looked more alert than usual. Gran hadn't dared to watch and it was only now that she turned round.

'You're a brave girl,' Mum said.

'What did it feel like?' Lee asked.

'Fantastic,' Donna said, not mentioning the terror.

'Are you all right, love?' Mum asked, her face creased with concern.

'Yes, fine. I'll just have a quick look round.' Donna wanted to get away by herself to think. After the clarity of the jump her head was suddenly a jumble, full of confused fragments and Jade's words repeated over and over.

Donna dawdled off through the park, meandering by the stalls. A *Big Issue* seller she knew from the prison flashed her a toothless grin. Music boomed and zizzied. She felt a hand on her arm and came face to face with Shane.

'Don, you're here.' He smiled into her eyes and his irises looked like grey satin flecked with greenish lemon. Pleasure rushed up in her at the sight of him. He took her hand and laced his fingers through hers. His touch sent spirals of electricity up her arm. 'You've made my day,' he said.

'I wondered where you'd got to, Donna.'

Donna stiffened. She found Maggie giving Shane a long look and Gran peering in her suspicious way. Both women waited. Donna knew there was no escape; she would have to do the introductions.

'Shane, this is my mother, Maggie, and my gran.'

He shook hands with them and grinned.

'I think we've met before,' Donna heard her mother say to Shane. 'You were helping resurrect our wall, weren't you?'

'Yes, that's right.'

'We're heading back home now. You coming for some tea, Donna?'

'Yes, in a bit. See you then.'

Donna turned to Shane. Now they knew, so maybe there was no point in hiding. 'Shall you come back with me for tea, lover boy?'

'Your mother asked me if I'd been working on her wall. Did you tell her you knew me from the nick?'

'Yes, because she asked how I knew you. But that was ages ago –'

'No, I can't come with you. I'll see you later.'

Donna looked up at his face and it was as though a shutter had come down. The colour of his eyes had turned to slate.

'All right,' she said. 'Later, then.' It hurt to walk away from him. She wanted to fling her arms round him and squeeze up against him, bury her nose in his armpits, smell his body.

'See you later,' he'd said – when would 'later' be? He was behaving as though she'd betrayed a trust when all she'd done was tell her own mother the truth.

She drove up the avenue of lime trees; the sound of the bands in the park growing fainter. The day felt out of kilter, distorted, and she could trace the tension in her shoulders. Shane had gone off in a cold rage; Jade had told her not to trust him; and now Mum and Gran were getting ready to chew the fat about him. When she'd stood high up gazing over the city earlier, she'd been scared, but for a different reason. Up there you were isolated, a tiny living spark. Down here the threat was worse because you didn't know what it was. Or if it really existed.

She didn't want to go into her mother's house and have a conversation about Shane, though she'd brought it on herself – she ought to have lied to Mum in the first place and then she wouldn't have hesitated about asking him back home. But they were expecting her, so she had to present herself.

Mum and Gran were in the kitchen and the big brown teapot squatted on the table under its stripy, knitted tea cosy. Three mugs waited. Mum was burning the teacakes, as usual, and of course she and Gran were busy gossiping. Donna could guess the subject.

'Oh, hello, love, tea's made. How many teacakes?'

'One unburned, please.' Donna decided that she would try to joke her way out of it, try to carry on as though the encounter with Shane hadn't happened.

'You never brought that young man back with you?' Gran said.

Donna felt her heart race, her cheeks flame. This was it then, quicker than she'd expected.

'Well, nobody asked him, did they?' She wanted to unleash all her frustration and despair that her family couldn't accept what diabolical lives people had to endure through no fault of their own. Why were they so condemning? Couldn't they see, feel?

'Your mam says he's somebody you met in prison,' Gran said, steadily appraising Donna.

'So?'

'He's a criminal, lass. And a leopard never changes –'

'If you say so.'

'Why can't you find a decent young man with a proper job? Why does it have to be a jailbird?'

'You can't condemn him, Gran, just because he's been to prison. I mean, it could happen to anybody.'

'You're just like your mother, always finding excuses – and it does you no good. I'm having to say this because your mam won't tell you straight out. Donna, we love you, we don't want to see you get hurt. Just leave off with that feller.'

Donna sat fuming with the mug of tea in front of her and the charred teacake untouched on her plate. 'Gran, I'm surprised at you. I thought you were a free spirit. What about that Leroy you went dancing with? You said people wanted to spit on you because you were going with him.'

'That was quite different. Leroy was no criminal – he was a serving soldier.'

'Don, I don't think it's a good idea to bring up your gran's past,' Mum said in the tired, pacifying voice she used with Lee. 'You're making assumptions about things you don't really know about.'

'As a matter of fact I do know – she's told me. Your attitude makes me sick. You only ever have time for me when you want to stick your oar in and meddle in my life. I'm fed up with being force-fed advice.' Donna jumped to her feet, pushed back the kitchen chair and left the house, taking care to slam the front door as she'd heard Lee do so many times.

In the same fury she unlocked her car, plonked herself down in the driving seat and gunned the accelerator back to her own road, where she forced herself to slow down to avoid cats and kids.

In the late afternoon she gouged the blade of her spade into the clay and couch grass in her neglected garden, while tears slid down her cheeks. Gran should have understood, Gran of all people. But then what could you expect? Gran belonged to another generation – she liked to listen to the Queen blethering away at Christmas and thought capital punishment should be brought back. For God's sake!

Gran might condemn Shane but she wasn't going to let her opinions affect her relationship with him.

Donna wanted to ring Lisa. Normally she'd have spent aeons on the phone with Lisa working through any family spat, but this was different. She couldn't tell Lisa about this row with Gran, because Lisa didn't know about Shane's past and she mustn't tell her. How could Gran dismiss Shane like that when she didn't even know him? *Jailbird* – that really rankled. What chance had Shane ever had – what had any of those men in prison ever had for that matter? She couldn't bear it. She didn't think she could ever trust Gran again. She hated her for being so rigid – well, she always had been, no change there. *She* was the leopard who'd never change *her* spots.

Oh, yes, there'd always be good solid honest citizens like Gran who never broke the law, and the rest – the outcasts, people like Shane – who were doomed. She didn't want him to be doomed; she wanted to give him a better life, and it seemed possible . . . almost. She wouldn't think of the doubts, of Jade's warnings. Why did people have to be so pessimistic? Did they enjoy preventing others' happiness?

21

Ruby spent so long experimenting with some eye make-up Donna had bought her and blending the thing now known as blusher, formerly rouge, into her tropical pancake cheeks and then deciding which outfit to wear, that she missed the bus. This was nothing new for Ruby and she didn't allow it to agitate her in any way. She'd arrive when she would. Meanwhile she stared out at the high rises and mused.

As predicted, the corporation wasn't taking the petitions seriously. They'd their own agenda. Ruby found herself growing increasingly angry at the way the tenants were disregarded. She was zipped back in time to the compulsory purchase order all those years ago, and Nana's despair. During that period she'd realized that corporations had minds of their own and, like huge lorries with failed brakes, they belted on regardless, crushing and pulverizing anything in their track. Yes, after thirty-odd years in this estate, she and the others were now to be shifted again willy-nilly because somebody in an office somewhere had got the idea that it would be neater and cheaper to be rid of them. Well, what were they anyway, except a group of old buggers, no use to anyone?

Young 'uns didn't understand the simplest things. Look at Donna, going with that jailbird. Of course, Maggie never said anything. She wouldn't. So as usual it was left to her to tell the lass. And the girl went red in the face and stormed out, said she didn't care what they thought. And a lot more stuff that might've come out of Maggie's mouth. She told Maggie as well, when the girl had gone, that she'd been nowhere near firm enough with those children.

By the time the bus reached town and the terminus, Ruby was in a fair old lather. Stepping down onto the pavement, she saw Frank Prentice giving her a good hard stare.

'Oh, Frank, there you are,' she said, her face easing out.

'Thought as you was standing me up,' Frank said, 'you're that late.'

Ruby looked surprised. 'Am I? Oh, yes. Buses. You know what it's like on the estate . . . well, you don't, do you? Aye, well, coming into town's like a journey to the end of the world.'

Frank seemed to be mollified. Ruby imagined he was perhaps not such a good timekeeper himself. Ernie would have exploded – for him you had to be there dead on the dot (which she never was) or there were fireworks. They ambled along to the bus stop and fifteen minutes later reached the stadium.

'I thought as we'd have a meal, like, first, at the Stadium club . . . food's all right, like.'

Ruby considered Frank looked particularly dashing and chancer-like, belted into his dark mac and with his trilby jammed down on his pate.

'You wouldn't think it was summer, would you?' he remarked.

'No, it's that hole thing in the ozone, isn't it?'

''Spect so. Never stopped rainin'.'

Ruby lingered over the golden crispness of her chips and bit into the soft white centres of the breaded scampi with relish. She paused now and then to sip her lager.

Frank ate fast. She'd almost forgotten why they were here but he clearly hadn't.

'I s'll be puttin' me bets on the Tote,' he said and she realized he wanted her to choke the rest of her food down pronto.

'Right,' she said, wondering what on earth this Tote thing was. She listened to him drumming his fingers on the table-top. 'No racing at Sandown,' she said, spearing up a chip.

'Be finished soon, will you?'

Frank hummed under his breath and narrowed his eyes once they were outside in the stadium. The arc lights splashed the great oval with an orange wash. People shuffled about the stands, chewing, gesticulating, guzzling from drinks cans, consulting racing pages and smoking.

'They'll be off in a minute,' Frank said, digging his hands down into the pockets of his mac. He was a man on tenterhooks. He rumbled on about having an 'each way double' – some betting strategy, which mystified Ruby. He went to great lengths to explain it, but Ruby operated her off-switch.

All of a sudden six skinny dogs in coloured jackets shot out of a line of traps. A roaring went up. Men bit their programmes, waved their arms, yelled their heads off and craned to see. The women, very much in the minority, were lost in the straining, rubbernecking mob around them. Ruby drank in the excitement rippling in the air. She couldn't see very much but didn't mind about that.

A hoarse voice bellowed out the winner over the tannoy.

'Fuckin' hell.' A man beside her tore up his betting slip and flung it to the ground. 'Pisses you fuckin' off. Don't mind me, Missus,' he said, aware that Ruby had heard him. Ruby gave him a sympathetic smile. Years of bar work and Ernie had taught her that when a man was angry you didn't make a jocular comment, or any comment at all come to that, because you were bound to be misconstrued.

Frank didn't say very much. Ruby got the idea that he'd come up, and he trundled off to collect his winnings.

'A nice little earner, that one,' he told her in his silky, hospital voice. Oh yes, she could see him pushing trolleys along and having a peek at the forms beneath, being so tender . . . comforting as toasted pikelets and tea when the wind lashed the sides of the high rises. She was lulled by the sound of his voice; it didn't really matter what he said.

Ten minutes or so passed while people shambled about placing bets, having a smoke and scrambling to and fro.

'They'll be off in a minute,' Frank informed her.

Ruby couldn't stop mulling over the problem of the high rises. As she listened to the yells of the crowd and saw another line of dogs shooting along the track, a resolve began to form in her. That first time she'd let herself be shifted – well, if she were honest, a number of considerations came into it – but let her not forget, Nana died rather than be moved. This time, like Nana, she'd not be shuffled off. Jessie seemed to be of like mind but the others fell short of declaring themselves properly. Ray needed a shove, which George might provide. George wasn't one to let people walk over him. In a business like this what you needed was determination.

Several more races followed and the shouting and cursing and urging on formed a pleasant backdrop to Ruby's musings. Frank was shut off in his own world, racing paper folded, pencil behind his ear, eyes narrowed and focused on the creatures sleeking ahead. Greyhound man, Ruby thought. Yes, that was what he resembled, with his head straining forward to see and his lean shanks and the swanky gangle of his walk. Definitely a long-shanked, keen-nosed, smooth-haired type. He'd catch the hare with a nip to the back of its neck from his pincer teeth.

'A good night!' Frank declared when they were out in the road once more. Ruby deduced from this that he'd won something, enough to give him a lift.

'I hope I haven't missed me last bus,' Ruby said, worried.

'Oh, don't get excited, love,' Frank said. 'I'll get you a taxi.'

'It'll cost,' Ruby said.

'No matter.' He gestured the expense aside as a mere trifle. Frank was gifted at the waving of an arm as though to open a great narration. Ruby decided to accept the offer, but he'd better put down the driver's cash at the start of the journey or she'd end up paying.

'Madam,' he said, 'this has been a great pleasure.' He kissed her cheek, catching the brim of his trilby on her face and pressed a tenner into her hand. 'Until next time, toodle-oo.'

Ruby gave a regal wave and luxuriated in the pleasing warmth as the taxi sped onwards through streets spilling over with white-shirted lads and bare-armed, salon-tanned lasses. Lights winked over take-away shops and the pubs. On, on they bowled into the estate, where life was just about to get underway. Shadowy groups of youths slunk between the houses.

'Don't like comin' up here,' the driver announced.

'Is that right?' Ruby said. 'I've lived here thirty year – it's not so bad.'

'You could fool me.'

22

Maggie had cooked his favourite, macaroni cheese, and had made a crisp salad sprinkled with French dressing because Lee wouldn't eat lettuce unless it was well disguised. She went to the bottom of the stairs and shouted up. Silence. No sounds of mixing or lads' raucous laughter, just silence. She called again and then began to feel spooked by the unusual lack of movement. Normally Lee would be bursting into the kitchen clamouring for food and complaining at what she'd cooked. She mounted the stairs. 'Lee, I do wish you'd answer me,' she said to the silence. Why the hell must he be so annoying? Why couldn't he have been one of those steady, hardworking boys like Mark, who did well at school and moved on to university without a hitch?

Pausing outside his room, she looked back down the stairs – the house seemed so quiet, too quiet. A shadow passed behind the front door. She shivered. Ever since she'd heard the news of Joanne's death she'd grown more introspective, nervous, aware of pitfalls – and now there was Donna having a relationship with an ex-prisoner. Mum shouldn't have called him a jailbird; that was bound to get Donna's back up and so it had. If Donna drifted away from them all and got into difficulties, they'd not know, so they wouldn't be able to help. Joanne had been isolated like that and she was murdered. But Maggie dared not dwell on what problems Donna might stir up, because she wasn't sure she could take any more at the moment.

She pushed open the door. The room lay submerged under the usual confusion of dirty clothes, take-away cartons and crammed ashtrays and over it all hung that unmistakably sweet smell of cannabis. She wouldn't let herself imagine what other substances he'd been taking. Lee himself wasn't there. It occurred to her then as she stood in his bedroom, a room normally out of bounds to her, that he'd not answered that morning when she'd called him – nothing new there – but it meant that she hadn't actually seen him since he'd gone out after dinner last night.

Maggie unbuttoned the neck of her shirt as she walked down the stairs. She was suffocatingly hot and her palms sweated. Anything could have happened to Lee and she wouldn't have known. He could be lying dead somewhere. What had she been thinking about Joanne's mother? How she hadn't taken enough care, hadn't been aware of how her daughter was going under. She saw it every day at school with those raw-faced kids – the ones who never received enough attention and were left to roam. They went wild, became hyperactive, always looking for something they'd never had. She hadn't been watchful enough. She reckoned that Lee was going through a self-destructive phase, but so were a lot of the other lads round about and she hoped it would pass if she could just keep him in school and not alienate him entirely. As long as they were communicating with each other, there was hope. She'd been through all this before a million times and nothing changed.

I must talk to someone, she thought. I can't ring Mum – she'll just go on about my not clamping down on him enough. It would be all right; he'd most likely have stayed over at the Billingtons' or the Waters', their lads were his two best friends. She rang both families. After parental prompting, the lads were hauled to the phone and she got their usual monosyllabic replies. No, no clue, they hadn't seen Lee. Now she was panicking.

She dialled Donna's number and Donna answered in a guarded, off-hand way, as though she didn't want to talk. Maggie pressed on, unable to hold back.

'Donna, I'm worried out of my mind.'

'What's up?'

'I went to call Lee for his dinner and he didn't answer – as per usual. Anyway, in the end I went upstairs and he isn't there.' She told Donna how she hadn't heard him come in last night and hadn't really registered the fact. 'He always says I'm interrogating him if I ask what he's been doing. I'm so nervous, constantly trying to avoid getting his back up.'

Donna didn't answer immediately and Maggie wondered if she was trying to decide how serious it was. 'I'll come round,' she said at last. 'See you in about fifteen minutes.'

Maggie was in the kitchen washing up a stack of dirty pots when Donna arrived. 'Hiya, Mumsie,' she said and gave her a hug. Maggie struggled to prevent herself crying. 'So that nerky Norman isn't back yet?' Donna said.

'No, love, no sign.'

'What a geek!'

'I just wish he'd let me know what he's doing. All this cloak and dagger stuff – half the time I've no idea where he is or what he's up to. I've cooked the blessed dinner and now he's not here.'

'You should have yours – no point in waiting for that div. He annoys me so much. He is so inconsiderate.'

'Maybe I'd better. Have some macaroni cheese with me, Donna?'

'Ta, but I've had mine. I'll make a coffee. Lee is such a prat,' Donna continued, 'he doesn't think about others at all.'

Maggie half listened to Donna berating Lee, but she couldn't get the spectre of Joanne out of her head – Joanne dead because none of them had cared enough. The rubbery macaroni wedged itself in her gullet and after a couple of mouthfuls she gave up. What if Lee went the same way as Joanne? She was going to go mad if she didn't stop dwelling on the worst that might happen.

'I get to feel it's my fault he's like he is. Maybe I didn't give him enough attention. I was always so preoccupied with work and –'

'Oh, Mum, for God's sake. He has to be responsible for himself. If anything, it's that he's spoilt, used to everybody waiting on him hand and foot.'

'Do you think I should phone the police?' Maggie said, staring out at the new wall. Did this fear exist only in her head, or was it all around? Ever since the girl was found battered to death the terror had grown. Violence was everywhere – like that car abandoned on the school field, destroyed by the end of the school day because the police didn't arrive in time to move it. Suppose Lee was lying dead in the park – her son, and she'd have caused his death, she'd have failed as a mother. She hadn't even known where he was and who he was with. But how could she cross that gulf of incomprehension? Her attempts to connect with him he'd brushed off as attempts to 'control' him. She'd tried not to keep on saying 'don't do' this or that and praise any signs that he'd thought of somebody else beside himself – but nothing seemed to have worked. She hardly dared to glance across at Donna because in her face she saw her own dread reflected.

Just as Maggie was about to go to the phone it began to ring. Donna met her eyes. 'I'll take it,' Maggie said, as she wilted under a surge of heat and palpitations. She thought she might faint. A pleasant male voice on the other end asked her name and whether she had a son called Lee. Now he was going to tell her they'd found Lee dead. That time he'd come home with a black eye and a swollen cheek after his bike was stolen, she'd thought then: Yes, it hasn't happened this time, but it could. She wanted the man to hurry up and say it. He took his time, trying to shield her from shock, but making it worse. Lee had been beaten unconscious the night before. He was lying in the infirmary. Until he'd regained consciousness nobody had known who he was or where he lived because he wasn't carrying any form of identification.

'Oh, Christ,' Maggie said, when she put the receiver down. 'I've always dreaded something like this.' At the news Donna turned pale and her eyes filled with tears. 'We must get to the hospital,' Maggie said. 'It's times like this when I need the bloody car.'

'It's all right, Mum, I've got mine.'

The journey to the hospital seemed to take ten years. Maggie wanted to be with Lee instantly but they must go through all the palaver of driving there, paying £2.50 for a ticket from a machine, displaying it on the windscreen and then hurrying across the wide stretch of uneven ground between the rows of parked cars. Maggie braced herself. She mustn't break down in front of Donna – Donna had been through enough lately.

Now they were in the infirmary heading for the huge spooky lifts. Eighth floor. 'Why can't they use apostrophes?' Maggie said, pointing to the sign that said NURSES STATION. She was concentrating on holding back her tears. Just the late-night feel of the building sent a chill into your heart. It was a place of long vigils by the beds of chronically ill patients – only this time it was a lad of seventeen, who ought to have been able to move about his home area carefree and unafraid, but who'd been battered half to death.

'You OK, Mum?' Donna said, and grinned at her. Maggie nodded.

The staff nurse gave them a keen look and motioned them into a side ward. Lee, his head swathed in bandages, lay propped up in bed against white pillows, gazing towards the door.

'Hello, love,' Maggie said, making a big effort not to weep. Donna's face shone with tears and she couldn't speak. Maggie wanted to take her son in her arms and hug him to her but she was frightened of hurting him.

'Hiya, Mum. Hiya, Don.' His voice sounded weak.

'So what's been happening, love?'

'I was, like, on the way back from the Welly and this gang of kids came up to me and they started putting the boot in – and then it all went black. First thing I knew, I was in here. Was real weird.'

'How do you feel now?' Maggie said, though she had a fair idea, as she looked at his bandaged head and the dark puffy flesh about his left eye. Lee wasn't the sort to bear pain stoically.

'Shit,' he said. 'Every bit of me hurts. I thought they were going to kill me.'

Maggie shuddered. They could so easily have murdered him – he could have died alone there on the pavement in the early hours. Those pitiful details were the worst – they could unhinge you.

'We'd no idea you were in here,' Donna said, trying to smudge her tears away.

'No. Well, first I knew, they kept asking me my name and that was pissing me off, because my head hurt too much to talk. The cops have been here most of the time.'

'Do you know who the lads were?'

'Estate lads. They kept saying *student*: "You're a fuckin' student. Eh, there's a right clever fucker here" – and they tried to push me off the pavement.'

'Prats!' Donna said and her tone spat.

Lee, exhausted, lay back and listened as Donna talked about some young prisoners she'd seen who'd beaten up a university student in the town centre. 'I think they did it out of envy, or just because he looked different from them.'

After a while the nurse reappeared and said that, in view of the time, she thought they should leave. Lee needed to sleep and she was going to give him his medication.

Once the hospital doors had slid to behind them, Maggie said, 'Phew, didn't he look awful?'

'Ghastly. Diabolical geeks to do that to him!'

'And to think we'd no clue. There we were expecting he was at some mate's . . .'

Maggie looked at her watch and seemed surprised to find it was ten thirty. 'The light's only just gone. Come in and have a nightcap, Donna, can you manage it?'

'I bloody need it.'

The house didn't seem itself without Lee and his cronies barging about upstairs. They sat at the pine table and Maggie poured them both a glass of chilled Piesporter. 'You could have something a lot stronger, Donna – but best not as you're driving.'

'Ta, that's fine, Mum. You know you still haven't got a blind sorted for this window – anybody could look in.'

'I know, love, I will. It's just that lately I've been so busy. And that's just it – I've been so busy bellyaching about school that I've not done enough about Lee. It all fits so neatly into the stereotype, doesn't it? Children of single mothers going to the dogs.'

'Don't think I don't feel bad about him as well. I know I'm always banging on about how he annoys me, but it doesn't mean I don't love him. Oh, God, when I saw him in there it was awful. I just couldn't hack it. And what kind of makes it worse is I've worked with kids in the nick –

miserable little geeks, basically off their heads – the types who'll have done him over. They're pathetic but, Mum, they're bloody dangerous.'

'I can't bear to think about it. We've escaped a tragedy by the skin of our teeth.'

'Let's just hope they get somebody for it, Mum. Stop those bastards roaming the streets.'

'Yes, I know, love. That phone call – it was horrific. I was convinced the man was trying to tell me Lee was dead. I'd better stop going on about it . . . sorry, it just takes time to take it all in.'

After another glass of wine, Donna looked at her watch. 'I'd better get back, Mum, or I'll never be up in time in the morning.' She rose and went to kiss her mother. 'Love you,' she said. 'You're the best mum in the world.' Maggie's eyes filled with tears. 'Oh, Mum.' Donna flung her arms round her. 'Everything's going to be all right. I think you need a good night's kip – go to bed once I've gone.'

Maggie stood on the doorstep watching Donna get into her car and drive off into the night. How precious they were to her, those children, Donna and Lee, and how easily this evening might have slipped into tragedy. An owl hooted and Maggie shivered at its hollow call. Somewhere Joanne's mother would be sorrowing, wishing she could turn time back, reverse what had happened, escape from the nightmare. You couldn't know what pressures she'd endured. She'd have been struggling against poverty for sure – and lovelessness, hoping to find affection from those awful men. Maggie was back in the time when Tom left – the space in the wardrobe where his clothes had hung; meals for one after she'd fed Donna . . . the awful loneliness and the desperation, the craving for love, for a man to tell her she was attractive. She'd got stretch marks and those blue thread veins in her legs – she was only twenty-two but felt forty and done for, used.

As she climbed the stairs to bed, Maggie returned once more to Donna's new boyfriend, the ex-prisoner, and she had to admit that she felt fearful for the girl. She might be heading into something that could hurt her. Joanne's murder had opened up a new vulnerability. Whereas before, you read about traumas like that in the papers, they happened to people you didn't know; now it was different, it was personal. As she entered her bedroom Maggie smudged the tears away from her eyes.

23

Driving home from Maggie's that night, Donna burned with rage. She thought of the druggie lads on D wing, kids Lee's age: they were the sort who'd have battered him, battered him because he didn't look like them, because he wore wafters and hoodies, not their bastard Nike and Adidas sportswear.

She sailed down her road, the one-way street lined with parked cars, on the look out for the dark shapes of darting cats. Youths sauntered by, eyes sharp on the cars and houses. She glared at them and drove on. It took several minutes to manoeuvre into a gap, yank out her steering wheel lock and fasten it on, then she was off down the narrow paved way, watching out for the potholes. Her heart galloped at the thought that Shane might be there waiting for her. If only he were.

A light shone in the hall but she'd left it on when she dashed to her mother's. She put her key in the lock. Let him be there, she prayed.

Rups padded to her feet and miaowed. 'Rups, hello, love.' She picked him up and nosed his fur.

'Hi, where have you been?' Shane appeared from the back room, seeming very tall in the narrow hallway.

'At the hospital. My brother's been beaten unconscious by some yobs.' His voice had sounded cool and strange, but once she spoke he seemed back to normal.

'Couldn't understand where you were.'

'Mum phoned me.'

'Right.'

'I'll make a drink.' She wondered that he made no comment about Lee – not, Oh dear, or How dreadful, just let the information pass unacknowledged.

'Don't bother,' he said and, putting his hands on her shoulders, drew her to him. 'You've been drinking.' It sounded like an accusation.

'Just some wine with Mum. We needed something – Lee looked so awful.'

He didn't answer but his hands were urgent on her body. This fierceness unnerved her, like his questions. She hadn't questioned him about his whereabouts in the last two days, so why should he react like this simply because he'd not seen her for a couple of hours?

He turned her round, wrenched down her jeans and knickers and bent her over the sofa arm. With his hands on her upper back, he thrust into her. Saliva formed a damp patch on the sofa where her open mouth pressed. His unfamiliar roughness shocked but intoxicated her. He gave a final thrust, groaned, and she felt as though a firework had exploded, shedding molten particles that leapt from between her legs into her belly and burned in her head.

Zipping himself up, he sat back on the sofa, while she disappeared upstairs to the bathroom.

This whole day, she reflected, as she ran hot water into the sink, had been unnerving, with Joanne's ghost moving in and out of her head. The same violence that had battered Joanne had struck at Lee. Even as the evening unfolded, she'd recognized its rawness, felt terror lurking just below the surface. And yet there were moments of extraordinary calm, like when she and Mum had sat at the kitchen table and she'd felt how much she loved her – not since early childhood could she remember having felt so close to her and anxious for her.

As they fell asleep there was a curious tenderness between her and Shane. He didn't seem to want to talk and she couldn't bring herself to ask questions. She woke in the early hours to find his erection pushing against her thigh and she turned into his arms. His body felt very hot and she smelled the spiciness of his armpits, and sighed with a feverish pleasure.

Next morning she woke late and left him still sleeping as she rushed to get to work. Rupert had spent the night downstairs, as he tended to do if Shane stayed. Now he cocked a pale lemon eye at her and yawned. She muttered a greeting to him, made herself a quick mug of coffee and jammed a piece of bread in the toaster. She peered at her face in the kitchen mirror and grimaced. When was she going to ask him why Jade felt they weren't suited? She couldn't say: Shane, your sister's warning me off. But what if she did? At least then she might get a definite answer out of him. If he could bring himself to talk frankly to her about his life, she felt sure they'd be able to go forward together.

24

After another day in the prison interviewing clients, Donna drove into town, sensing that it was about the time she'd previously run into Jade near the Drug Advisory Centre. Shane's strangeness last night made her determined to ask Jade about him. With any luck she might catch her again.

When she'd parked her car, she sauntered out into the road. No sign of Jade. Perhaps she'd have a coffee in the library snack bar and keep an eye open for her. She'd have to walk past on her way to the bus station, more than likely. She sat down at a table with a cappuccino and became engrossed in the latest *Screen* cinema brochure. She jumped when she looked up and saw Jade standing in front of her. For a moment she searched for something to say but her head was empty.

'Thought as you might be in here.'

'Having a coffee?'

'Yer, ta. Two sugars please.'

'How've you been?' Donna asked, trying to organize her thoughts, and watching Jade's trembling hand holding her cigarette.

'All right, near enough. Been talking to my social worker. You know when we had a talk last time in the park?'

'Yes,' Donna said, keeping her voice neutral, but she was tensed against what might come next.

'You didn't tell Shane what I said, did you?'

'No . . . there was no reason to,' she said. Then: 'You've never really told me about Joanne.'

'Well, I knew her a long while, didn't I? Like I said, sometimes we worked together.'

'How do you mean?'

'We'd get dressed up as schoolgirls – use her flat. We'd cane the punters – they'd pay fifty quid a go. We was safer there than on the streets, of course.' She paused. 'To tell you the truth, I hate it, always did, always have . . . but I've needed the money. Was the same for Joanne – once you're hooked, a user, you have to.'

'But why would somebody murder her?'

'Could have been a crazy punter. Mind you, sometimes there's trouble with the women, like, if somebody thinks someone else is muscling in on her patch – getting all the bonuses, right. Or there's . . .' She stopped to stab out her fag. 'Nah, I can't be doin' with it all – you never have a life. It's out nights no matter the weather – and you never know. I don't get to talk to ordinary people – know what I mean? Folk near where I live, I can see in their faces when I go out: Oh, look at that slag. They're peekin' through their nets. They want to make sure their men never get near me. They don't know the half of it.'

'Horrendous . . . I feel so awful when I think that I'd no idea what happened to Joanne. Just didn't think – I mean, I went one way and she went another.'

'You couldn't have done anything.'

'No . . . But don't you feel nervous with all these women murdered? Particularly about Joanne – I mean, you worked together.' Donna looked at the other woman's strained white face.

'You're dead right – believe me, I just want out of it all. I've got to get on a rehab but it's real difficult, and there's the kiddies . . .'

'But then what next?'

'I'd like to do a college course, if I could – if I was bright enough, like – and bring up my kids properly. You're a different class of person from us, been to uni and all that, and it's no good you getting mixed up with people like us. That's why I said to you, don't get in deep with Shane.'

'But why not, Jade?'

Out it came then, in a rush. 'Because there's things he done, like, and you don't want to be with somebody like that – I'm saying it and he's my brother. I can't say it no clearer.'

Donna sat back in her chair, feeling sick. She didn't want to hear this. The words galloped forward, careering out of control, and the sensation terrified her. But she must know.

'Jade,' she said at last, 'I wish you could tell me the truth.'

'I can't tell you.'

'Why not?'

Jade popped her lighter and cigs into her little purse. 'No reason. Can't.'

Donna knew then that she'd have to ask Shane herself. The two coffees she'd drunk increased the feeling of nausea and she felt desperate to get out into the open air.

Jade left fast, puffing on her cigarette. 'See you around,' she said. 'You better not tell him what I said now, will you?'

'No,' Donna said, 'course not.'

She was glad to be outside, the wind blowing in her face and a stormy sky turning overhead. She was going round to her mother's and together they would visit Lee in hospital. Donna tried to centre on Lee and what she could take to cheer him up – perhaps chocolate bars, chocolate peanuts. She'd go to Thornton's and buy a special selection of milk chocs with hard centres – he couldn't bear soft ones, particularly strawberry. The struggle against the buffeting wind on her way to and from the shop prevented her from dwelling on her conversation with Jade. And then she was driving to fetch her mother and take her to the hospital.

As they sat beside Lee's bed, Donna kept noticing the bruising on his skin and stifled a shudder. She could imagine how those blows felt . . . Then her thoughts shifted to Shane and she wondered whether he'd be round that night – and whether she'd manage to break through his secretiveness, that way he had of dismissing any questions about his past life. This time she couldn't hide her shudder and Lee, showing a spark of his old self, bellowed, 'Hey, Don, pack it in!'

'You all right?' her mother asked.

'Yes, Mum, fine. Not bad at all.' She received a keen glance from Maggie but grinned and put on an exaggerated shudder.

'What did you think of him?' her mother said, once they were heading for the car park. The wind had risen and slammed them as they crossed the road.

'Fairish – but his bruises look gruesome,' Donna said. 'When is he coming out?'

'I think it'll be a few days yet. I'm just worried that he'll crack up after an attack like that and hibernate even more in his room.'

'Mm, freaks you out, doesn't it? But I think he's going to be OK. I'll try to get him to open up – he'll sometimes talk to me when he's in the mood. We'll sort him, don't worry, Mum.'

She refused a drink at her mother's and drove on home, suspense churning in her stomach. Of course, he might not be there – but what if he was? Whatever happened, she decided that tonight she must find out.

As she came through the door, he rose from the sofa to embrace her. 'You're late,' he said.

'Been at the hospital – I did tell you.'

'Oh, yes. How is he?'

'Not bad, but he's got a lot of very ugly bruises and he looks quite fragile.'

'Yer.'

She headed for the kitchen and turned on the kettle. 'Tea before anything,' she said. 'Need reviving.'

She battled with the urge to let the moment pass and say nothing but Jade's words hammered in her head: There's things he done . . . you don't want to be with someone like that.

A way into the conversation seemed impossible – her promise to Jade was like a gag. They sat drinking mugs of tea and eating doughnuts just like any other couple, then Donna plunged in. 'I get to despair of some of these guys in the nick, you know.'

He looked hard at her for a moment. 'How do you mean?'

'Well, they're always going to give up. They tell you they'll never touch the stuff again – but give them a couple of months, sometimes not even that, and they're back in the nick again.'

'Yer, yer, that's how it goes.'

'How can anyone ever expect to give up an addiction?' She shot him a direct glance.

'It depends on the person.'

'Yes, but most can't.'

'Then they don't really want to.'

He sounded so positive, so certain – how could she believe he was still addicted? Perhaps she'd been worrying for nothing. But what did Jade mean? There's things he done – what things? She'd heard countless tales of that life of shooting up, gouching and rattling before the next desperate search started – the daily robbings and moves to raise cash to fund a shot to paradise, the sensation that proved stronger than any human attachment. How desperate would he have been? The idea of his unbounded cravings chilled her.

'You know, when people conquer this addiction, well, how does it all look, all that time of robbing and everything? I mean, do they feel regret? Regret for the waste?'

'Donna, you're asking me something.'

Donna stroked Rupert's head and tried to take comfort from the slinkiness of the fur under her fingertips. She almost forgot to breathe. 'You could say that.'

'Who's been talking?'

'Why should anybody have been talking?'

'Come on.'

'Look, Shane, I just don't see –'

'You've never asked before.'

'Maybe not, but that doesn't mean I haven't wondered. It's just that I can ask now because I know you better.'

He rolled himself a cig and sat glaring into space, sucking the smoke deep into himself. She wondered what she had unleashed, wished she hadn't asked – but the fact that he didn't answer only made the undertow worse, more murky, more treacherous.

'You don't trust me, Donna, and you never have. There's always this drawing away. You want to ferret about, pin something on me. It's been the same all my life – there's always been some fucker after me.'

Donna looked at him and all she could see was a mask of anger and dislike.

'It's not like that,' she said, but it was no good, the connection between them had shattered. She didn't know this person who faced her.

'What is it fucking like then? Explain to me. What is it you want to pin on me, what do you want me to say?'

'Shane, take it easy, please. I never meant to upset you, but we've never really talked, have we?'

'Talked? Talked? What the fuck do you want to talk about?'

She shrivelled up; she couldn't press on. She had always hated emotional rows and confrontations, preferring to sidestep them if she could. Everything seemed to be sliding out of control. Why did she have to listen to Jade's warnings and Gran going on about leopards and spots? Why couldn't she simply trust her feelings? Shane was exciting, intriguing, unlike anybody she'd ever met before – what more did she want? Perhaps working in the prison made her suspicious of everyone who wasn't like her.

'Well?'

'You've never said how you came to give up smack,' she said, engulfed now by a wave of clamminess. 'You've never told me about that part of your life.'

'Oh, I can't be doing with this sort of interrogation. I get enough from the cops. I don't need a cop as a girl-friend.' With that he leapt up, seized his denim jacket and banged out. His footsteps echoed on the flags outside as he strode away.

Donna remained sitting on the sofa, Rups on her lap. Tears rained down her cheeks and plopped onto Rups, who twitched and looked up at her. The end: it was over, just like that. Never had she felt so involved with a man before Shane. All the others had drifted out of her life and she'd felt bruised at the time, but it had been nothing like this. What did she find so mesmerizing about him? It was as though he had another life beyond the one that charged at things and wanted to absorb them and press further – even as that wildness intoxicated her, she saw a stillness inside him. At Whitby, standing on the pier, watching the mother-of-pearl sea stretching into infinity, she'd sensed it. He'd seemed to relax into the long spread of water. All the splintered years of his past hadn't crushed him. She traced areas of deep sadness in him that lay behind the silences. Now she'd never fathom them – it was finished.

Right, so he's gone. It's his loss, she told herself. I've got to pull myself together. I've never cracked up and I shan't now. I'll never get over Joanne, though – that's impossible. A wound that won't heal, her being battered. Unrecognizable, they said in the paper. So much anger, so much fucking anger – she knew why there was so much, but on a personal level she couldn't cope with it. She couldn't reason it away. Kids' homes brutalized, turned out men like tinder, and one day they could become incandescent, flare up. But what about their charred victims? Gone to grey ash. Oh, God, the victims. Suddenly she couldn't stop crying. Losing Shane and losing Joanne and the thought of all those other murdered women ran together in one awful, desolate loss.

25

Evening again. Somehow she had existed during the day, occupied with work, but there was always the shadow of loss hovering over everything. She tried to pretend it didn't matter. No more ecstatic evenings entwined on the sofa, or coming together on the floor, or lying cuddled up in bed. No walks on Saturday afternoons out in the country down where the old railway track used to run and cows now grazed grassy slopes. Once they made love in a grove of saplings and she looked up and saw a tracery of tree branches beyond his shoulders. Blackbirds trilled and the ground was hard under her body and his beautiful chiselled face moved to fill her range of vision. She was in that moment, held there consciously, never wanting it to end.

Approaching her house, she stood for a moment with the latchkey in her hand and looked up. The wild geese were flying over as they did every day: in the early mornings they flew to the pond in the park and in the evenings they returned. Seeing them always sent prickles of wonder down her spine. She loved their craking voices and the sound of their beating wings. Soon they had passed beyond the far line of chimney pots.

Here was a place of constant surprises. A brisk twenty-minute walk could bring you into the city centre and yet at night foxes prowled along the backs; one morning Donna had been traumatized to find the dismembered body of a pet rabbit in her garden. Its fluffy white tail lay some yards away, the dead eyes stared out like sucked sweets covered by a film of saliva. At first she couldn't imagine how the rabbit had died and supposed that a dog must have savaged it, but several days later she caught sight of the fox slinking by at dusk. He was a handsome, copper-coloured creature whose presence astounded her. Shane saw him too and they stood spellbound watching him. Donna had asked Shane to bury the rabbit for her because she couldn't bear to touch it. She'd petted it, knew it belonged to two little girls who lived near by. It was an angora with oval, pink-rimmed eyes and fur that made the pads of her fingers tingle. His floppy ears and twitching whiskers had made her laugh.

So Shane wouldn't come back any more. No need to strain her ears listening for his footfall along the pavers. But should she accept all this as though she were at fault merely for asking questions? Was she so passive? Surely he was being unreasonable and paranoid – maybe Gran had a point. Perhaps if you'd been so badly damaged by your childhood that you could never recover from it, the trauma would affect your lover as well. And she still didn't really know what Jade had been hinting at.

She fed Rups and made herself a coffee and tried to imagine what she wanted to eat, but it was as though a weight had lodged itself in her gut and killed her hunger. At the very thought of food she felt queasy.

Lisa rang and they chatted for a while. 'Shane and me have finished,' she told her. Lisa had run into them together again one evening in town and Donna had been forced to say that they were seeing each other.

'Oh, you'll get going again, I'm sure. Bound to.'

'I don't think so.'

The evening stretched before her and she wondered how

on earth she'd get through it. It was only eight o'clock but she toyed with the idea of going to bed. If she could sleep, she wouldn't have to think. Then she heard the footsteps. Her heart thumped.

He came in smiling and bearing a huge bouquet of white lilies and a bottle of wine. The house was transformed by the heavy musky scent. 'I've come to say I'm sorry,' he said. 'I shouldn't have behaved like that, shouldn't have stormed out.'

She couldn't stop herself smiling at him. To have him back seemed the most wonderful thing in the world.

He put the flowers down on the table and they stood a few feet apart looking at each other. 'Have you eaten?' she said.

'No, I haven't. Haven't been feeling very hungry.'

'Nor me. I'll make some spaghetti and a sauce, then we can have the wine with it.' Her heart soared, and she pirouetted as she cooked. He opened the wine and set the table. It would be all right: they'd win through. She'd make Gran see – well, once Gran got to know Shane, she'd change her mind.

He came to stand behind her as she fried onions and garlic. He put his arms round her waist and nuzzled her neck. 'I've missed you so much,' he said.

'Do you think I've not missed you?' Donna said, unable to turn and look at him.

'Not as much as I've missed you.'

'Shall we have a competition?' They both laughed, were still laughing as she carried the tureens to the table. She lit two white candles and an orange glow spilled across the pine surface.

'To us,' he said, raising his glass.

When they'd finished the first bottle of wine Donna fetched another. They sat gazing at each other across the table and eating peaches.

'Donna,' he said, 'I couldn't bear to lose you. Perhaps that's why I blew up last night because I thought . . .'

'Yes?' she said, expecting him to explain.

'I can hardly sit opposite you without touching you.'

They were on their feet, bodies straining together. His mouth pressed and sucked. She heard her own breath panting and felt the dampness of her briefs and armpits. They fell in a tangle of clothes and shoes on the sofa and the tense desperation in him thrilled and scared her. There were no preliminaries. His fierceness seemed to drain the blood from her heart and she found tears spilling down her cheeks. It was like when she'd arrived from visiting Lee in hospital and found him waiting for her, as though he wanted to absorb her, or cancel himself out. The violence of it had made her feel that she was entering unknown territory and she was afraid.

'Why are you crying, love?' he asked a while later as they lay wedged together on the sofa.

'Lots of reasons – sometimes I don't know where we're heading.'

'I didn't mean to upset you,' he said, nuzzling his nose against her cheek. 'Trouble is, I get to feel you don't trust me because you're so edgy all the time – and then I think if you knew what I done, what I'm really like, you'd pack me in.'

It was all happening again. A chill slid over her shoulders and her skin prickled, but she lay quite still, waiting. Her head whirled – she supposed they were both fairly drunk, anaesthetized, but with their emotions flowing more freely. The hidden threat punched you in the gut, and your reaction was immediate.

'You know I'm not like that,' she said. 'I'm not a judge.'

'But,' he said, unable to let it rest, 'what if somebody said I done something real bad – what then?'

Her heart thundered, drumming in her chest and shortening her breath. Into her head came the Robbie Burns poem: they'd sung it, she and Joanne, before they were chucked out of the school choir. She recited it now:

'O my Luve's like a red red rose,
That's newly sprung in June:
O my luve's like the melodie,
That's sweetly play'd in tune . . .'

On, on she went to:

'And I will luve thee still, my dear,
Till a' the seas gang dry.
Till a' the seas gang dry, my dear,
And the rocks melt wi' the sun;
And I will luve thee still, my dear,
While the sands o' life shall run.'

'What's that?' he said, clearly moved.

The moment seemed to gather about them, straining with sweetness and the strange tension of something darker. Through the back door, which was ajar, Donna heard a blackbird singing in the twilight and the bird's song deepened the pathos. Those were such big words – 'and the rocks melt wi' the sun'. Could you love a person that much? Yes, of course you could, love could outlast everything. Love was strong enough to draw a line under the record of thieving and dishonesty – that list he couldn't enumerate.

'Robert Burns,' she said. 'A love poem we used to sing at school, that's how I know the words.'

They sat facing each other on the sofa, most of their clothes scattered on the carpet. 'Why are you so worried about telling me stuff?' Donna said. 'You needn't be.'

'Well,' he said, 'people badmouth you, say all sorts of crap about you.'

Donna could see it was costing him something to speak. 'Like?'

'They said I done this girl.'

Donna's back and shoulders went rigid. 'What girl, what was she called?'

'Joanne – she was somebody Jade knew.'

'How did you meet her, then?'

'At Jade's. They – they worked together. Why you asking?'

This was a rerun of the past. Donna thought the banging of her heart would sound in the room. She was forgetting to breathe.

'Because I can't understand.'

He didn't answer. The blackbird sang on and somewhere along the backs a dog barked.

'So this girl got murdered, then? Why are they saying you'd anything to do with it? Who's saying that anyway?'

Another silence.

He stared about the room and avoided her eyes.

'Stop quizzing me,' he said eventually. 'I can't stand it – had too much of it in my life.'

They'd come up to the same point again. Last time he'd stormed out.

'Shane, I don't want to upset you, but if I'm going to trust you I've got to understand this stuff. It's major, isn't it?' Her voice sounded strange to her, broken up and breathless.

The silence gathered. She thought he'd never speak and when he did finally address her, she jumped with shock.

'She got killed, right, and some lads have tried to pin it on me.'

'Why you?'

'They're like that.'

'But, Shane, you can't let them get away with making such dreadful allegations.'

'It's life . . .'

'Not really, it isn't.'

'Look, leave it now. I've told you and that's it.'

'I still don't understand. I mean, people don't go round accusing others of murder just like that. How well did you know Joanne, then?'

'I've told you, she worked with Jade – known her a long while, like, before I got sent down last time.'

'Shane, you have to tell me this. Were you . . . were you Joanne's pimp?' Christ, now she'd said it, pronounced the unthinkable. 'Is that why they thought you'd done it?'

'For fuck's sake, leave it. Are you interrogating me or what?'

'No, but I need to know – I can't stand these hints and half-truths, they destroy me.'

Silence. Donna gripped her hands between her knees to hide their trembling.

'All right, you've asked for it,' he said at last. 'I was off my head with crack and then I'd wanted to start on smack to bring me down and she lied about the smack . . . and so I hit her. Oh, God, don't ask me.'

Donna gasped. Now that he had said it, she wanted to vomit. All the objects in the room seemed to be a long way away. Her head felt light, like a dried seedpod rattling on a stalk.

She had to escape from that moment with him. She rose and blundered to the kitchen. Hanging onto the sink, her skin hot and clammy, she vomited. After drinking some water, she waited, shivering, until she could make herself return to the room and face him.

'There's something I've got to tell *you*,' she said, now staring straight into his face. 'Joanne was my best friend from school days. We twagged off together – she was my best mate. She was kind of brave – nothing seemed to faze her. I can't believe that you killed her.' Tears ran down the sides of her face and hit her hands. Whatever was this, what had he said? Had she really heard him properly? She felt a giant fist had struck her and her flesh quailed. It was too monstrous to grasp. This must be what Jade had hinted at. This was the unspeakable.

'I never meant to . . . it wasn't my fault.'

'How can you say that? You killed her. How could you? She was a young woman – she may have had problems but she'd got her life in front of her. Joanne was special – and now she'll never know so many things. I can't stand it . . . oh, how could you? I can't believe you did this – you thought smack was more important than her life. She must have trusted you and then you killed her. And I thought some bastard who'd picked her up had killed her. But no, it was you, her pimp.'

'It was the drugs. I was off my head. Oh, Christ, don't ask me, don't ask. I wish I'd never met her – if only I never had. I was clean in nick – knew I'd finished with it. She started me again. I wish to Christ I'd not run into her . . . and then after it happened, after I'd . . . I knew I'd never use again. I believed you'd pull me through. Oh, all this shit . . .'

He was crying now too.

'This is the worst thing you could ever have done. You used her and then you killed her. She was somebody you could bat about, a non-person whose life had no value. Traded for smack. I can't bear to hear any more,' she said. 'Don't tell me. It's too much for me to take in.'

He sat with his head in his hands. Donna's sobs hiccupped out of her. 'Do you understand what you've done? You have treated her as though she were nothing. This is the most godawful thing I have ever heard.' And in that moment she emerged from the wildness of her grief and realized that she herself could be in danger: he'd killed Joanne, why not her too? What would another death matter – just another woman battered to death because he couldn't control his temper? She sat quite still, praying for him to leave, and her flesh crawled at the sight of him.

There must be some core of ice in him that would never melt, for him to have committed such an act and walk away from it, disclaiming responsibility.

As though he sensed the intensity of her revulsion, he rose and left.

For a long time she sat on the sofa, tears flowing. She thought she would never stop crying. At last she went to the back door and stood there, gazing into the June night. Stars spangled the luminous sky and the grass was silvered. A big dark bird rustled past. She had to get out. Without bothering to lock the door, she set off striding along the backs until she reached the road. Soon she was heading for the park. Anybody could be in there but she didn't care enough to worry about it. The sycamores were dense black shapes. Nothing stirred. Ahead of her the pond glistened, its scummy water transformed by the moonlight. Ducks roosted under the trees in the centre – she and Joanne had called it Thorn Island. Remembering those days made her cry again. The park spread out before her. Way over near Prince Albert's statue figures moved. She kept going, head down. Fuck everybody, fuck the world. On past the bowling green she blundered. He was Joanne's pimp and he murdered her. Murdered her and wouldn't admit it – wouldn't accept his guilt. It wasn't me, I didn't do it. Murderers never said, Yes, I did it. I'm to blame. Oh, the vileness of it – now those pictures were in her head, they wouldn't fade.

She passed under the archway at the Beverley Road end of the park. Druggies shot by her like alley cats; some huddled by a phone box. A group of drunks lurched up, calling out, 'Eh, look, there's a lass. Come on, love – he wants to tell yer sommat. Come over here.' She blanked them out. 'Be like that, then – dun't want ter say nowt,' they cackled. For some blocks she saw nobody and she listened to the silence. From time to time a taxi drove past and one or two private cars. In the town centre the last clubbers waited for taxis or started their walk home. She didn't know where she was going but somehow she ended up down by the Minerva, staring out at the estuary. A long time passed while she leaned on the wall gazing out at the black water. Moonlight ran silver squiggles over the waves as they slapped on concrete and wood. She didn't know what to do with the horrors in her head. She was still sitting in the room with him, listening to the silences between his words, what he wanted to hide. She kept on crying. She wanted to moan, to scream, but forced herself to keep quiet – once she began to rave aloud she didn't know where it would end. Watch the water, she told herself, just watch the waves: they've been here for ever and they'll still be here in a hundred years' time when none of this will matter.

She was surprised to feel a hand on her arm, shook it off and swung round.

'How much?' a thickset fellow with greasy hair said.

Taking one look at him she spat, 'Fuck off!' He backed away and left her.

Only the changing light made her realize that now it was morning. As she returned along Princes Avenue she heard the birds setting up a twitter in the trees. Her feet ached but her head seemed quiet. Back home, she paused on her doorstep realizing she hadn't got the key, but then discovered that she'd left the door unlocked. Wearily, she climbed the stairs to bed and Rups raised his head from the duvet to stare at her. Stretched out on her back, she never expected to sleep – but she did, a strange, dull sleep filled with distorted images of faces and empty rooms.

Waking several hours later, she phoned work, apologized for not ringing in sooner and explained she'd been up half the night ill, got some sort of stomach bug, hoped to feel better tomorrow. Then she went back to bed and lay under the covers. Sometimes she slept; then she'd wake to find tears running down her chin and onto her chest. Last night she'd been unable to think anything through; now she decided she ought to phone the police, but even as she picked up her mobile, she knew she'd not phone – that would be the easy way out. It was up to Shane to go to the police, only then would he have accepted his guilt. But had he the guts to do it? She continued to lie there, with whole sequences of those last moments between them churning through her head. She burned with rage that he should have taken Joanne's life – and for smack. Joanne's life, the price of a fix. She dropped again into the pit of the previous night and couldn't climb out of it, couldn't motivate herself to do anything. If Shane were to walk into the room, she felt sure she'd kill him, stab him to death, make him pay . . . She willed him to, imagined she heard his key turning in the lock. She planned how she'd leap up on him. He wouldn't expect it. The little knife she used for slicing vegetables would do and she made herself get up and fetch it, put it under her pillow. Now she was ready for him. More tears, more rage, exhaustion. Her world was grey, suety, hateful.

She slept until late afternoon and when she woke, she listened, expecting his footsteps on the flags outside. How could he have done such a senseless thing? What a monster – and what a fool she was to be so seduced by him. Her insides whirled and echoed. There was nobody she could tell about it. She was totally alone.

26

The next day, back at work, Donna functioned in a desiccated way. She drifted along at a distance from everything around her, disturbed by a sharp sense of unreality. She was grateful it was a Friday. At the hospital, Lee was sitting in a chair; one more test and they'd be letting him go home. That night, Donna lay alert into the early hours. Sure she heard someone creeping about, she'd fumble under the pillow for her knife. Nobody came; it was just the wind creaking a gate, flapping some washing left on a line.

Arriving at Maggie's on Saturday afternoon, she found her mother mucking out Lee's room. She'd heaved the sash window open to get rid of the stench of fag smoke and cannabis which impregnated everything.

'What a pong, it makes me gag,' Donna said, watching her mother dumping empty pizza boxes, lager tins and cigarette packets into bin bags. Grey ash showered, dust rose and Donna sneezed. 'Mum, this is gross.'

'I know. Look at these!' Maggie held up bundles of cheesy, sweat-stiffened socks, retrieved from under the bed. Boxer shorts and T-shirts draped the floor or were stuffed under chairs. 'I kept asking him to put his dirty clothes in the washing machine and he always complained he hadn't got any clean ones – and of course I was forbidden to come in here.'

'Here, I'll get the vacuum on.' Donna hauled out the cleaner and scrubbed away at the floor. She dragged the furniture aside, and flew at the cleaning in a frenzy.

'Don't hurt yourself, Don, that chest of drawers is heavy.'

'Not really.' She delved after ash and dust and reached the most inaccessible corners with the vacuum-cleaner nozzle. Such furious cleaning seemed to help – she'd also taken to showering as though there were something she must expunge from her skin. And the more she tired herself out, the less energy she'd have for thinking.

'Leave it now, Donna, look at the time – we'll be late for the hospital,' Maggie said.

Lee looked pale and thin and a bit wobbly but he grinned and gave them both a hug. Donna fetched the car round to the front of the hospital to save him from having to walk far. On the way back he sat staring out of the window and didn't say anything.

When they got home, he stood in the hall, gazing at the picture of two figures staring out over a stretch of water, and then he sighed. 'Good to be back,' he said, and wandered through into the kitchen. He moved to the sink and leaned there, gazing through the window at the back garden.

Donna looked at his stubble-covered head – strange to see Lee with hair after all this time. She'd grown used to his billiard-ball pate. Her mother had let drop once that it made her think of fascist bullyboys but then she came to regard it merely as a sign of Lee's rebellion. Of course Gran never let up about how dreadful it was.

'I'll make some tea,' Donna said. She needed to be doing something.

'Yer, great.' He sat down at the table, staring about him. 'God,' he said, 'I never thought I'd ever be back.'

Donna wiped her hand across her eyes to smudge away the tears. 'Well, you are. Now then, do you want your old favourite?'

'Cheese on toast and tomatoes?'

'That's the one.'

Once Lee was eating and Mum had returned after a lengthy phone conversation with Gran, Donna announced that the mucking out of Lee's room had put her in the mood for giving her old room the same treatment. She lugged the vacuum cleaner, dusters and polish upstairs, and stood in her bedroom at the back of the house, staring down the wild garden to the allotments beyond. They'd always felt like a magical place where anything could happen. She was back with Joanne, out there playing hidey with a gang of kids from round about. They hid in an allotment hut scarcely daring to breathe as Rick, the kid who was 'on', searched for them. The dust made Donna sneeze and Rick pushed open the door and captured them. From time to time old men in trilbies would rear up from among the raspberry canes, making the kids run for their lives. Joanne always wanted to play there late on when it was dark. She'd jump out on Donna and leer at her, wailing so that Donna collapsed with hysteria. The smell of the past was in her nostrils. She remained at the window, her vision blurred with tears. Loss was a hollow inside her.

It was late before Donna and Maggie were alone together. 'Come and have a nightcap,' Maggie said, and they went into the front room. 'You know, Don, Lee getting beaten up has made me think a lot about how it must be for Joanne's mother – I mean, her knowing that there's nothing on earth she can do to wind time back. She's just stuck with her daughter battered to death, and the awful feeling of grief.'

All the time she was listening to her mum, she felt herself braced for something to happen. She couldn't tell anybody but the crushing weight of it never lifted. Finishing that glass of wine, she drank another. Behind the moment wormed the fear of what she might encounter when she went back home – but she had to go. To stay at Maggie's would mean she'd given way to her night terrors . . .

Lee slid into the room. 'Hi,' he said. 'Just wanted to tell you how great my room looks – thanks, Mum.'

'Don helped as well, love – in fact she did loads.'

Donna and Maggie exchanged glances.

'Ta muchly,' he said and vanished upstairs.

'What a difference,' Donna said. 'He's actually saying thank you.'

'Yes, I think the attack has really affected him. It must have been such a hideous shock, it's made him think.'

After the third glass of wine, although Maggie said she shouldn't drive, Donna forced herself to go home. She felt sick with fear and her head pounded. She couldn't stop thinking about Shane battering Joanne to death – she could picture it so vividly. He'd have panicked, perhaps lugged Joanne's dead body to the ten foot. How could he, with that crime on his hands, then get involved with her, say he loved her? The day they'd spent in Whitby he'd seemed so loving, so sincere that she'd believed in the dream they'd created. But how could he? How was it possible to put aside the murder of another person as though it had never happened? It meant that the whole of their relationship was a lie. It was nothing – just another way of making sure that he didn't have to face up to what he'd done. It was beyond comprehension.

27

Maggie stood for a moment in the late-night street after she'd seen Donna drive away. Nowadays she always felt the need to watch the girl leave, to stand on the doorstep and wave until she'd disappeared from view. It had become a magic ritual, something she must do to ensure her daughter's safe return. Owls hoohooed behind the houses. She glimpsed wide wings scything past. Donna troubled her. She'd always been a restless girl, moody, one minute buoyed up by enthusiasm and the next cast down. At the moment she seemed too hectic, too bouncy, as though she were trying to hide a new disaster. Whenever she'd suffered a setback, she'd not come out with it, just let the hurt fester and pretend it hadn't happened.

The house felt different now that Lee was back. She relived the moment in the hospital walking down the corridor towards the ward, her body tight with suspense, dreading what she'd see when she turned the corner – and then he was there gazing directly at her with his face lit up. Mum, he said, and she knew that moment would stay with her for the rest of her life.

She stood in the hall, listening, but could hear nothing. He'd be asleep now most likely but she'd still check on him – something she hadn't done since he was a child. For years his room had been his lair and out of bounds to her. She went upstairs and tapped on his door. He didn't answer so she eased it open a fraction. In the twilight of the room, she could make out his sleeping form, head turned to the window, his breathing a slight rustle. She tiptoed nearer the bed and looked down at him. In sleep his face was again that of the young boy – she could trace the fuller curves beneath the sharpening of the cheekbones. For some time she watched him, then kissed his forehead and crept out.

The day they heard of Joanne's murder, it seemed to her, marked the end of innocence. Before that, they'd bumbled along in a slightly haphazard way, but with their own kind of certainty. She hadn't questioned anything much beyond the immediate parameters of her daily existence: straining to get ready for the Ofsted inspection, annoyance and worry about Lee, Donna and Ruby. Abruptly, everything changed. You understood that you could take nothing for granted; that one shift could change irrevocably the lives of those you loved most in the world.

Two hours later Maggie was still awake. She went to check on Lee once again and found him still sleeping peacefully. The birds had begun to sing in the plane trees lining the avenue.

28

'Well, you roped me in at finish, didn't you? I had doors slammed in me face. That stray dog bit us, didn't it?'

'Yes, yes, you've said all that.' Jessie pushed aside his moanings.

'And it didn't do no good, did it?' Ray started again. 'I told you they'd take no notice of them signatures.'

'Give it a rest, Ray,' George intervened. 'If we don't give it a whirl, we've only ourselves to blame. We didn't do owt earlier when they was leafleting about it and had them forum things so now it's last chance saloon.'

Ruby listened in. She'd decided that no matter what happened, she'd not be leaving her flat, nor the block, behind. 'You can quit if you like, Ray,' she said finally, 'but they're not getting me out of here. This is where I stay.'

Ray looked a bit sulky, but said no more.

'Wherever you look,' Ruby went on, 'nobody ever takes any notice until you get the papers involved. We need some publicity on this.' Ruby saw the headlines:

OAP REBELS SAVE THEIR TOWER BLOCK

OAPS DEFEAT BULLDOZERS

VALIANT OAPS LOCKED IN LIFE AND DEATH STRUGGLE

The more she thought of it, the more she warmed to the idea. She'd ring up Frank and ask him to drop by the *Hull Daily Mail* offices in town.

'Well, they've give us final notice – out by the end of the week, they said, so we s'll have to be ready for 'em,' Ruby said. She felt sizzling with energy, focused, all ready to act. She was able to throw off her worries about Donna and that poor dead lass and Lee getting beaten up like that and Maggie's inability to take a strong line with both her grandchildren.

'Right, kiddos,' George said, 'we need a plan of action.'

Ray, blinking furiously, said, 'What'll happen if we don't shift?' His facial twitch was so disconcerting that, when he'd recounted the dog-biting episode, Ruby had been forced to look away. Now, faced with this new threat, it gathered momentum and Ruby kept her eyes fixed on Jessie's bunion-pocket shoes.

'They'll drag us out if they can,' Jessie said with relish.

'Yes, if we let 'em,' Ruby added. 'When the bulldozers or the dynamite or the ball thing come, we'll just chain ourselves to the block. But first we have to tell the papers so they'll send up a photographer and a reporter.'

'Eh, I can't be involved in a carry on like that,' Ray wailed.

'Go on,' George said. 'You're just like a daft lass, Ray.'

'I'm frigging not.'

'Oh no, big boy!'

'Eh up, you two, you're makin' a right pig's ear of it. That'll do,' Jessie said. Ruby could imagine how she ran the shoe shop all those years. She wouldn't have tolerated insubordination: you could see iron in her back, straight as a ruler, and the way her quarter-to-three feet went clonk-clunk-clonk. With a prow like hers you'd expect her to break out into a great warble. She breathed properly and didn't sit round-shouldered, pecking at the air.

The seven of them resolved to stick it out to the bitter end and to face down the buggers from the council, who were bound to pester them before the final confrontation.

George started quoting that famous Churchill speech about beaches and got quite carried away. Ray looked on impressed.

Ruby decided she wouldn't say anything to Maggie or Donna. There was no point in them knowing about any of this in advance, they'd be bound to try to stop her.

They all stood up, drank a sweet sherry toast to 'The Campaign', and the pact was sealed.

During the week they had five more group meetings to keep their spirits up and confirm their plan of action, reinforced with more glasses of Jessie's sherry. The first person to receive a visit from the council was to phone the rest.

Ruby got several phone calls from Frank Prentice. Did she want to go to the dogs? What about having their dinner in the Punch Bowl? Ivy rang up, too, with bingo invitations. Ruby told them both that things had hotted up and she'd got to stay put because she couldn't afford to have the evictors snooping round in her absence.

'You can go to the *Mail*, Frank, and Radio Humberside and the TV,' she said. 'Tell 'em something very important's to happen on Friday.'

It occurred to Ruby that nobody would know what it was all about if they didn't display some notices: when you saw demonstrations and things on telly, the agitators always brandished placards. She phoned Jessie, who became very excited at the idea.

'All right,' Ruby said, 'I'll just pop round to the charity shop – bet they've got a bit of card or something we can use.'

She went round to Jessie's, bearing five big pieces of white card and some batons. A young chap with a ring through his nose and six in each ear had showed her how to impale the card on the poles and even lent her some board-markers for writing.

'Yes, he said we want 'em real bold – got to make 'em sit up, like.'

Ruby reflected that this young chap, in his big boots and baggy cotton trousers with everything wafting about him, was very similar in appearance to her grandson – except this one had hair, long hair in a pony-tail, only a wide bald patch yawned on his pate. Privately, Ruby decided it would have been less noticeable if he'd cut his hair close to his head all over. At least he had an excuse to go in for Lee's awful convict-cut.

She spent a tense afternoon with Jessie and Ray writing out their protest messages.

PENSIONERS AGAINST EVICTION

SAVE OUR FLATS

30 YEARS IN FLATS: PENSIONERS PROTEST AGAINST COUNCIL BULLYBOYS

FLATLANDERS FIGHT FOR HOMES

Ray, who turned out to be quite artistic, decorated the placards with a few curlicues and got quite carried away, drawing miniature pictures of the tower blocks, gulls flapping over them.

By now they'd all received eviction notices. Phone calls from the council had threatened that, come what may, if they were still in occupation of the premises on 2 July action would be taken against them. What this 'action' might be wasn't specified.

They'd agreed that when they spotted the officials approaching, they'd stand before the door of the tower block with their placards and refuse to move. George had got hold of some big locks and chains from an old mate of his who'd once had a tat shop, and they were to lash themselves to the door handles.

*

All Friday morning they waited in a state of suspense, but nothing happened. Nobody appeared. The usual dogs skittered, tails curled up, across the open-plan lawns. Fag packets jumped in gusts of wind and women pushed buggies to the precinct. Traffic hurtled by on the road, ignoring the speed camera signs. Buses choked and panted, bearing small children to school.

'Perhaps it'll be this aft,' Ruby said, as she and Jessie peered from Ruby's window.

'Perhaps they'll try to catch us napping – when they think we won't be ready for 'em,' Jessie said.

'That'll be a nuisance – this feller I know has got the journalists coming and a photographer.'

Then, as though by magic, the cars bearing the officials and the press and photographer arrived together. The press proved to be two young women who couldn't spell (Ruby soon got the measure of them), and the photographer was a dark, smouldering type.

'Would you like to tell me what's happening here?' a little brown-haired lass in a suit asked Ruby.

Ruby was put off her stroke a bit by George and Ray struggling to get the locks snapped shut round the door handles. Every time they moved, her own chains tugged and clanked, and she realized that her best white blouse was going to get marked. She'd put it on because it was what she'd decided, long ago, she wanted to wear in her coffin. This after all was a coffin event . . . or could end up as one.

The diversion of the chains gave Ruby a moment's breathing space and now she looked at the girl and launched into how she was first moved from her home over thirty years ago; after all that, she must be shifted again.

'Like some bundle of laundry,' she said, 'and I'm too old for that.'

'So, Ruby.' Ruby bridled with resentment at this young lass, whom she had never met before, calling her by her Christian name. 'What exactly are you saying?'

'That I won't move. They'll have to take me in my box first.' Nana's words echoing down the years made Ruby draw herself up straight and glare ahead of her. She was gratified at the way the lass looked shocked and the photographer got snapping for dear life.

'But you don't seem to have any option.'

'We're not movin',' Jessie backed Ruby up.

'Too right,' George said. 'Us Flatlanders are here till we snuff it.'

Ruby nodded her head and beaconed at the girl to indicate she meant business.

The smouldering photographer now positioned himself to the side to capture a clear view of the chains and placards. Ruby gave a haughty smile. He took four or five pictures in rapid succession, lurching to secure odd angles. The officials seemed to be at a loss, not sure what to do next, particularly in view of the press interview, which continued in spite of the council presence.

By this time a radio journalist had appeared with a box slung over his shoulder and an object like a black ice-cream cone in his hand, which he thrust in Ruby's face.

'Madam, may I ask your name?'

'Mrs Smith,' Ruby said.

'And can you tell me why you're here, Mrs Smith?'

'Yes, I can . . .' Ruby gave her do-or-die oration, which the officials interrupted by saying that they were moving in and would have to remove the protesters forcibly from the entrance to the flats.

A TV van shot up and, from nowhere, a posse of policemen marched onto the scene. Overhead the police helicopter swooped and whined, the noise growing menacingly louder as it hovered, propellers scything the air. Several black cars with lights flashing and, worst of all, a big white van had parked close by. That, Ruby realized, was the Black Maria – these days it was white, evidently. She recollected dramatic scenes in the far past when the Wilmot lads, Billy's brothers, fought in the front gardens after a boozy do. Neighbours had phoned the police and the Black Maria lumbered up like some primeval monster from the slime and scooped them all up. At that time she'd never imagined the wheel would come full circle and one day she too would end up in one. For a few seconds her resolve faltered, and then she thought, To hell with it. I've been through too much in my life . . . the War, all that bombing and desolation; the chaos when they killed the fishing industry off and pulled the houses down. No, she hadn't lived through all this to be steamrollered by the corporation now.

She gave another chap holding a microphone an earful. He kept nodding his head and then moved the cone away and talked direct to camera.

'Yes, the atmosphere on the estate is growing very heated. The police have moved forward, but are being met by seven protesters, all senior citizens . . .'

'Come along now, Sir, Madam, shall we call it a day?' a policeman wheedled.

Ruby could see Ray's lips quivering and hoped he wouldn't succumb to the softening-up treatment.

A crowd had gathered. Young women with bairns and buggies and toddlers hanging on to their legs; druggies just out of bed and not yet on the nick; all the young 'uns on benefit who never got up until dinner or later. Ruby surveyed them and smiled. Then she spotted Frank with his trilby pulled down at a dangerous angle – he'd be missing the racing to come and watch.

What should she do if the police came and forced them away from the doors? She'd seen demos on telly where people ended up on the ground and were borne away kicking and struggling. She couldn't imagine doing that. Anyway, they were all Lee's age, not OAPs. You didn't get OAPs being wrestled about like that, though she remembered how roughly they'd treated the elderly protester who tried to stop them taking live animals for slaughter in France.

When the police officer put his hand on her arm, the shock went right through her body and she winced. The crowd started to jeer at the police. Ruby felt a sense of kinship with the young mothers and the dodgy lads and all the other oddballs out there. And it came on her in a rush of pride that this was an important moment in her life . . .

George put up a bit of a struggle and got arm-wrestled to the ground. He went down puffy and red-faced and the crowd yelled, 'Shame on yer, shame!'

'Listen, young man,' Ruby said. 'This is our home. How would you feel if it was yours?'

'Come along, Ma'am.'

'Don't touch her,' Ray started up, surprisingly protective.

Ruby felt the policeman's grasp tighten on her shoulder. Someone else cut and disentangled the chains. The crowd bellowed and stamped, dogs yapped and streaked about, babies screamed.

George was carted off to the white van with mesh-covered windows. The TV crew were busy filming. Ray went down in such a vigorous tussle with two police officers that Ruby thought he must have reconnected with his old fish-dock bobber days.

The police seemed to be leaving her and Jessie till last, perhaps because dislodging old women was more problematic. They'd be scared of breaking their bones.

'Over my dead body!' Ruby spat again, staring the police officer dead in the eye.

'Come on, love,' he said. 'You know as well as I do that this is all a bit of theatre. We're just doing our job. They'll pull these blocks down no matter what you do.'

'Don't be too sure. And I'm not your "love", I'm old enough to be your nana.'

Ruby prolonged the dialogue as long as she could before she and Jessie were bundled into the van. At this point the crowd's shouting and stamping crescendoed. One lad pulled down his jeans and presented his naked backside to the police in a reverberating fart. The police trundled on, visors down, and the van swayed and lurched out of the estate.

29

Interviewing prisoners, filling out forms, writing letters all prevented Donna from having to think too much about her personal life. During working hours she made herself bounce along as usual and sometimes she almost came to believe that she was this airhead, this loony extrovert. But beneath it all she felt broken up – inside her was a raw wound, which she dared not touch.

You're always happy, Wes said to her, that's one of the things I like about you.

You don't know the half of it, she thought, but simply grinned back at him.

Most evenings she called at the video rental place and picked up two or three videos. She'd spend the hours until bedtime with Rups on her knee, staring at the screen in an attempt to block out free-floating fear – the memory of a recurrent dream, where a man came upon her from behind, began to strangle her, and when she tried to scream, nothing came out.

She'd just started watching some cheesy American film about a family with flawless teeth and unlined pretty faces, when the phone rang. Her mother kept asking her to come round, but she'd made excuses and often hadn't answered the phone. This time, her conscience got the better of her.

'Oh, Don, I'm glad I've got you. You never seem to be in. I just wanted to tell you what's been happening.'

There were none of Maggie's usual questions about the prison and how she was. She seemed unstoppable.

Her mother ran on and on, about school and the inspection. 'I don't know where we go from here. By the way, Lee's doing fine. He actually gets up in the morning and goes to school, believe it or not.'

When her mother turned her attention to her – 'How are you, are you all right, really all right?' – Donna fended her off with a suitable vagueness and some bright, silly chatter. She felt incapable of telling anyone what had happened. She'd been living with a strong sense of suspension, as though she was waiting for something. The nights were interminable: she'd lie awake for long stretches, always listening for his key grating in the lock.

Her mother rang off, and Donna decided she couldn't bear to watch any more of the video. Instead she turned to *Look North*. What she saw made her gasp. There was Gran being hustled into a police riot van. Crowds booed and stamped. A helicopter circled overhead. The camera took in the high rises of the estate and the reporter stood before one of them, explaining how the remaining residents had lived there for more than thirty years, from when the flats were first erected, transferred there from their homes in the fishing community off Hessle Road.

Stunned, Donna gawped at the screen. She hadn't been in touch with Gran since the row over Shane and recently she'd felt even more reluctant to resume contact – everything was too raw. Anyway, she still smarted at how Gran could lump all ex-offenders together as 'jailbirds'. But now she knew that Shane had murdered Joanne, maybe Gran would say she was right. His behaviour numbed her; she couldn't think straight any more, it had robbed her of her own sense of reality. Shane was not as she'd imagined. No, it was all too complicated. But you couldn't just dismiss things the way Gran did; although that too seemed trivial in the face of this new development. She felt a livid fury at the sight of her gran being bundled into a police van – this was her gran. Gran, who when the chips were down, behaved weirdly like herself. After all, Donna supposed, they both had very definite ideas about life and always thought they were right. Looking back, a lot of things – even Gran blowing up about her tattoos – indicated Gran's certainties. Donna realized that she could be equally dogmatic in her responses too. Somehow, recognizing this likeness comforted her.

Donna dialled her mother's number. 'Mum, Mum, they've pushed Gran into a police van. I've just seen it all on telly. We must do something.'

'I know, I've been watching it too. I bet she's in the police cells by now,' Maggie said, sounding apprehensive. 'We'll have to get down there.'

'I'll come and pick you up.'

They had to wait on a row of chairs, facing a counter. From this vantage point, they could see men in suits strutting to and fro with files. From time to time a police officer strode in from the street. Sometimes his radio crackled and voices burbled. Donna stared at all the paraphernalia strapped about him – handcuffs, baton, and other menacing objects that she didn't recognize.

'You're looking a bit pale,' her mother said.

'Am I? Haven't been sleeping too well.' She thought her mother looked washed out too, but didn't say anything.

Just then a police officer appeared and said they could see Mrs Smith. He led them down a series of corridors flanked by white doors, some bearing nameplates, then branched off to the left and into a stark room.

'Mum,' Donna said, agitated, 'you can't credit this – it's a closed visit.'

'A what?'

'Look.' They were shown to a booth behind which two chairs were positioned, facing a window of wire-mesh-reinforced glass. 'Gran will have to sit on the other side of the glass.'

'I don't believe it,' her mother said. 'An elderly woman protester and they go to these lengths!'

They sat down then and the police officer brought Ruby into the room on the other side of the screen.

'Mum!' Donna heard her mother gasp. 'What on earth is going on?'

'You'd better ask him.' Ruby nodded in the direction of the policeman.

Maggie took no notice of the policeman. 'Are you all right, Mum? What happened?' She had to raise her voice because Ruby was struggling to hear through the glass.

'The demonstration. I did hit the copper with the pole a bit, but it wasn't much. It was self-defence and anyway he deserved it. They say we caused an affray – but I told 'em straight: I'm not movin'.'

'OK, Mum, you've made your point, but this is too much. They'll have to pull them down – it's too expensive to keep practically empty tower blocks going.'

'They should have thought of that first.'

Donna was amazed at Gran's determination. Her eyes flashed and she looked remarkably high-spirited – she was clearly enjoying it.

The officer told them time was up and Ruby was led away.

'This is madness,' Donna said, ready to explode again.

'Look, Donna, it's no use raging at them.'

'Oh, yes, I can see that. But think of it – they're all pensioners, there's no need for it.'

'I've said to her time and time again that she should move.'

'Yes, Mum, but she's lived there for ages,' Donna said. 'All my lifetime, anyway.'

'I know. The main thing is we must get her out of here – I'll have to try and raise a solicitor. I mean, for heaven's sake – she can't stay all night in the police cells. It's just not on.'

Donna saw her mother's habitual cool deserting her – she didn't remember ever having seen Maggie so incensed. Of course she was pretty wound up about Lee before this, but generally, since Nick, Lee's dad, got the push, she'd been very laid back.

'Here, Mum,' Donna said, trying to distract her from her anger, 'if you want to phone.' She handed over her mobile.

After they'd waited for what seemed like ages, Maggie's solicitor finally mounted the steps outside the police station. Donna watched her mother as she stood outside in conversation with him, gesticulating and vehement. The solicitor, a fuddy individual with wide hips and a speckled suit, nodded and frowned and made notes on a pad. Then he approached the reception window in a confident, honking manner, was allowed behind the counter and disappeared.

Maggie resumed her place and Donna tried to find out from her what had been happening but didn't take much in. After another lengthy wait, the solicitor strode up, document case wedged under his arm, with Ruby beside him.

'Gran!' Donna rushed to give her a hug. Tears smudged her mascara as she held Ruby against her – here was Gran, back safe and sound, Gran, battered and huggable.

'I can't leave all them others,' Ruby said. 'There's Jessie and everybody in there.'

Maggie gave some more instructions to the solicitor and he went off again behind the scenes while they waited some more.

A long time afterwards they all left the police station together. Donna was amazed and oddly impressed by the way her grandmother and the other protesters fell into one another's arms, chattering away in garrulous, high-pitched voices. These monumentally ancient people had been transformed – lit up by a passion that made them vigorous and alive.

Once in the car, Ruby declared that she was going back to the estate.

'No, Mum, you can't,' Maggie said, 'you've been evicted. You'd better come back and stay until we get things sorted out.'

'I'll have to ring a friend about Squawker,' Ruby said. 'I've had to get him looked after. It'll have upset him being moved – well, it's his home too.'

'So where is he?' Donna asked, intrigued.

'There's a man I know and he's fetched him – had to get a taxi, a black cab, so Squawker's cage could go in.'

'Do you want to ring him on my mobile?' Donna said.

'No, love, can't be doin' with them gadgets – they're not big enough. I like something I can get hold of. I'll wait till we get your mam's.'

Lee met them at the front door, grinning. 'Wow, so you didn't get sent to prison, Gran?'

'Police cells,' Maggie announced with pride.

'Cool. You're going some, Gran!' Ruby rewarded him with a modest smile.

'We'd better have peasant omelette,' Maggie said, and Donna took this as a sign to start slicing onions and tomatoes, and putting potatoes on to boil. She hunted around for mushrooms and capsicums, glad of having something to do, and half listened to Gran describing the affray with the police. She found it difficult to believe that this was her grandmother, the person who always laid down the law, declared that National Service should be brought back, that women getting tattooed was a disgrace – and piercings, well, they were barbaric. Leave them for savage tribes, she always said. That Gran should have ended up in the police cells for tangling with a police officer seemed totally out of character. But then how did you ever know how someone else would behave? She was back with Shane: if she'd been so wrong about Gran, perhaps she'd missed some sign in him – though how could she have known he was capable of murder? She'd realized from her prison work that murderers were no different from other people, but she'd never assimilated that knowledge on a personal level.

The past wheedled its way into the fresh smell of the capsicum as she shredded it. And then the realization hit her: yes, she herself could kill too, she was quite capable of it. Hadn't she got that knife under her pillow at home and didn't she know that she could have used it on Shane if he'd come to the house? For a few moments she halted; transfixed, understanding. And then the moment expanded and she was with him again . . .

They stood together in the graveyard amongst the toppling stones, high up on the cliff top at Whitby. Below them the sea was full of galloping white horses. I shan't ever forget today, he said. I've never known anything like this before.

Other days, running down sand dunes together, holding hands and feeling the wind on their faces, and knowing that later they'd lie naked holding each other.

But he'd also killed Joanne.

'Watch it, love, you'll be burning the onions,' Donna heard her mother say.

'Sorry.' She kept going, slicing and then turning the frying onions in the pan. The potatoes needed draining, slicing and throwing in too. She'd already added garlic although Gran usually moaned about it. But she wouldn't complain tonight, Donna decided. This evening was so extraordinary that she'd never notice what she was eating.

Anyway, Mum was plying her with the port that she kept in especially.

Gran's protest, Donna thought, was really about what had happened with Hessle Road before she, Donna, was even born – and yet Hessle Road linked her and Shane magically. Vistas of childhood: his leaping on barges and exploring; her visits to Boyes and Gran showing her the area where Nana had lived – they'd stood at the Bull Nose watching the flurrying of the water and all that knotty, brown swirling had made Donna afraid.

Oh, aye, I used to come and stand there looking out to sea after Billy drowned, Gran had said. And the words seemed doubly tragic now, echoing down the years.

Gran trundled off into the hall to make her phone call. Mum had bought the evening paper and she stood at the table reading it.

She let the newspaper drop on the table and Donna, turning, saw the headline on the front page: 'I KILLED HER OVER SMACK': JOANNE'S KILLER GIVES HIMSELF UP. Beside it was a photograph of Shane. Her mother had obviously seen it too and Donna couldn't avoid her direct glance. They didn't speak. Gran came back into the room then and Maggie pushed the newspaper into a shopping bag. Donna caught her mother's eye and quickly turned to the cooker.

Soon they all sat round the table with the omelette on a wide brown plate in the centre. Salad filled a wooden bowl and there was a long stick of French bread.

Donna kept her head down and made herself hold back her tears. Her mother poured out glasses of red wine.

'Maggie,' Ruby said, 'I've got this feller coming round with Squawker – he'll be landing here in a taxi in a minute. I couldn't leave the bird with him overnight, it wouldn't be right. He'll stay with me. But I'm not going to be here long, Maggie.'

'Mum, there's absolutely no problem with your being here, and of course Squawker's welcome as well.'

'It's not our home.'

'You can't go back to the high rise.'

'No, I'm going back where I belong. I'll be able to put up with Ivy for a bit until I find me own place round there.'

Donna jumped when the doorbell pinged. Gran went to the door, returning with an unlikely betrilbied person who looked like a character from an old American film, the sort shown on late-night TV. He wore gauntlet gloves and in one hand gripped the handle on Squawker's cage. 'He's a heavy bugger,' he remarked.

'You mean his cage is,' Ruby said. 'There you are, Squawks, you've missed all the fun.' She peered in at him and the bird perked up and let out a series of high-pitched trills and watery sounds. 'He knows who his mam is, don't you, lad?' Squawker swung on his perch, pausing to let fly a poison-green splat on the bottom of his cage.

'Good job it's in there,' the man remarked.

Gran had to do the introductions all round. The man was called Frank and allowed himself to be pressed into having a whisky.

'It was very good of you to look after Squawks,' Gran said. 'It was a bit difficult seeing as I should never have had him in the high rise – they don't allow pets.'

Donna listened in amazement to a long and involved story about how Squawker had to be hidden every time the council snooper came round and breathtaking moments when Squawker whistled and trilled in the cupboard.

'You were lucky nobody spragged on you,' Frank said.

'No, they never would have. The young lads, the druggies, they didn't know their arses from their elbows and anyway, they were up to that many scams they'd never have said owt about my bird. I mean, I could have spragged on them, couldn't I?'

Lee was looking at Gran with new interest. 'Did you live up there as well?' he asked Frank, who shook his head.

'No, up there's too far off me stomping ground.'

'So where's that, then?' Lee asked.

Ruby helped herself to another glass of port and Frank started on one of his sea stories.

'I'm just going upstairs to sort things,' Maggie said, looking pointedly at Donna.

'Oh, right,' Donna said, following her out of the room. 'I'll give you a hand.'

'We'd better get the bed stripped and made up. It needs a clean duvet cover,' Maggie said.

Donna fetched fresh sheets and pillow cases and was about to make a start, when her mother said, 'I saw what it said in the paper, Don. I'm dreadfully sorry. It must have been one hell of a shock for you.'

Donna let the sheets drop on the bed and burst into tears. Once she'd started to cry, she couldn't stop. Her mother's arms came round her, holding her tight.

'Love, I am so sorry . . .'

'Mum,' she gasped, 'he really is a good person – but he did this terrible thing. I can't seem to make these two things come together. It just breaks me up. When I think of Joanne and how she was and that her life's over because of him . . . and that I was involved with them both. And in the end, at last, he's had to face what he did. Oh, Mum, when I think of their lives . . .' Her voice cracked in a new onrush of tears.

She felt her mother's hand stroking her forehead like she used to do when Donna was ill in bed with a high temperature. 'Mum, why can't people be good all the way through? Why do they have to be bad as well? I can't handle the bad bits – I thought at first he's evil, just evil, a monster . . . but he isn't.'

'Don, a lot of things happen because of circumstances –

it's just where people happen to be at a certain time. If Joanne hadn't had her sort of background I don't suppose she'd ever have ended up becoming a heroin addict, and maybe if Shane's history had been different this wouldn't have happened. And you know, it's possible to hate what someone has done but still love the person. When this comes down to a personal level it's hard to take – part of me feels fury that you've been hurt so deeply, that Joanne died so horribly – but at the same time I can see Shane must have had a lot that's good about him or you wouldn't have loved him so much.'

They were sitting on the bed, Donna leaning against her mother's shoulder. 'Mum, it's such a relief to be able to talk about it. I've felt so alone, alone like I'd go mad because I couldn't tell anybody. I've felt guilty as well – guilty because I've loved someone who killed my friend. It made me feel savage, too: I wanted to kill him, I was that angry. And I knew that if he didn't give himself up, he'd not have accepted his own guilt and there'd be nothing I could do about it.' She was crying again. Her tears formed a wet patch on Maggie's shoulder. She was conscious of the warmth of her mother's arm around her; it helped the tension drain away from her. 'Sorry, Mum,' she said, 'I'm wetting you through.'

'Maybe I needed a wash – begun to feel a bit grubby.'

From downstairs they could hear Ruby's laughter and Squawker's trills mingled with Frank's guffaw and Lee's lighter laugh.

'Come on, love, we'd best get this bed sorted,' Maggie said. 'You know what your gran's like.'

'It won't take long,' Donna said, leaping up and dragging off the old sheets.

'Your gran'll be on the look out for something to complain about. Tuck it in well, she's very particular about her feet.'

When they'd finished, Donna went to the bathroom to wash her face and try to camouflage any signs of her tears. She stood a moment in front of the mirror, thinking how amazing her mother had been: she hadn't said I told you so, or ranted on about Shane's awfulness and Donna's own foolhardiness – which she could have called stupidity. No, she'd been thoughtful, loving . . . the realization made tears prickle again at the back of Donna's throat. She'd seen the situation as it was, muddled and full of awfulness and beauty. Donna recognized this as a very strange moment in her life, because she was standing back, gazing at tragedy and yet glimpsing goodness, a wholeness beyond it.

A long time later, when Frank had whistled his way out of the door, and Ruby had debated whether Squawker should roost in her bedroom or remain downstairs, Lee finally lugged the cage upstairs for her and they both went off to bed.

'Let's have a cuppa,' Maggie said.

'I'll have to go home after this,' Donna said. 'Rups will wonder what's happened to me.'

'Toast?'

'Two please, Mum.'

'This is just what I need.'

They munched their toast in peaceful silence and from time to time exchanged smiling glances. Not long afterwards Donna hugged Maggie to her. 'Thank you, Mum, I couldn't have got through this without you.'

'Bless you, love.' Maggie kissed her cheek and brushed back the tendrils of hair from her forehead. Then Donna headed for home.

As she parked her car, she looked up at the disc of the moon hanging over the rooftops. She'd seen it like that on many nights with Shane. The night he gave her the necklace, she had looked up and glimpsed it through the window as she lay on the floor with him. Even now she was still wearing it – at first, when he confessed he'd murdered Joanne, she'd thought, I'll donate this to a charity shop – but not now. No, she'd wear it, wear it because it was given in love, an expression of his good side, of how he was at his best, how he might always have been. If only he'd shown Joanne that side too. Joanne was out there, her laughter and energy in the wind, her fearlessness part of the shifting clouds, the air, the scabby grass in the strips of garden.

She walked down the path in front of the terrace of little houses, and words came into her head – Joanne's part of me now, and of Shane and Jade, and Lisa, part of everybody who ever knew her. Tears filled her eyes but not of rage, or grief – she'd gone beyond that. The pathos of Shane's dreadful deed and Joanne's death had opened up an area of darkness that thrust her outside the world she knew; forced her to stare down into an abyss at such monstrousness it could drive you mad. But the horror had been forced back, because she'd felt her mother's arm round her shoulders and she was comforted by Gran's chuntering and Lee's puckish grin . . . somehow they held her steady, those dear, annoying people.

She unlocked her front door and Rups met her in the hallway miaowing. She scooped him up and nuzzled his furry head. His body vibrated with a deep, rumbling purr.

Acknowledgements

My warmest thanks to Emma and Alan at Tindal Street for their imaginative advice and enthusiasm, also Helen C; Chris K for re-creating the past with local history walks; Imo, Helen and Eloina for help with factual information; Jean and Margo for their interest and valuable comments; Angus Y for putting me in touch with sources of vital information.

PIGGY MONK SQUARE
Grace Jolliffe

'A stunningly well-written novel. I didn't want it to end. Tense, joyous, terrifying, comic, tender, magic and tragic – just like childhood itself'   *Willy Russell*

1970s Toxteth, and nine-year-old Sparra is running out of places to play. It's no fun at home, what with her Mam and Dad snapping at each other and Auntie Mo dishing the dirt. Along her street prowl mortal enemies Uffo and Lippo, mad Harold and his skinny wife, psycho-killer Stabber and old ladies going 'tut tut tut'.

So Sparra and her best mate Debbie make a bombed-out house on Piggy Monk Square their own special hide-away. When a policeman disturbs their games, he warns them to keep out the Bommy. Two Scouse girls, they know better than to trust a Sniffer-Cop. But suddenly he's at their mercy and they're pitched into trouble deeper than they could ever imagine.

'Streetwise but innocent, suffused with Catholic guilt, Rebecca and Debbie are scallywags whose favourite game is playing in a derelict house – which is how life comes to take a terrible turn. Within a very few pages this novel draws you in with its vivid Scouse vernacular . . . it deserves success and would cer-tainly make a good film'   *Publishing News*

ISBN: 0 9547913 4 7

www.tindalstreet.co.uk

ASTONISHING SPLASHES OF COLOUR

Clare Morrall

Shortlisted for the Man Booker Prize 2003

'Kitty, the narrator of this absorbing and sure-footed novel, has been brought up in a large family by her painter father. Surrounded by older brothers, she has no real recollection of either her mother, who was killed in a car crash, or her sister, who ran away from home.

'At her very first attempt, Morrall has written a genuinely satisfying work of fiction, skilfully plotted and fielding a cast of fully realised and individualised characters. More please'   *Sunday Times*

'This is an extremely good first novel: deceptively simple, subtly observed, with a plot that drags you forward like a strong current'   *Daily Mail*

'The title comes from Peter Pan's description of Neverland – a magical leitmotif in what emerges as a moving novel about loss, and particularly lost children'
Guardian

'Morrall reveals [Kitty's] mystery artfully and convincingly, telling a story that is shocking, heart-stopping and completely absorbing'   *Observer*

ISBN: 0 9541303 2 4

www.tindalstreet.co.uk